Stories of family and romance beneath the Big Sky!

"Don't forget to come by my place tomorrow,"
Tag told her at the front door.

"Uh, right. What time would you like me?"

I'd like you in the morning, in the afternoon and all night long. "If you come in the afternoon you could stay for dinner and experience one of my famous barbecued burgers."

"Stay for dinner?" Linda nervously bit down on her lower lip.

"I think you'll like Samantha," Tag said in a casual tone.

Linda relaxed considerably. When he'd said dinner, she had immediately envisioned a cozy dinner for two. But his little girl would be there, and he certainly wasn't going to try anything in front of her.

"Yes, all right," she said. "Want me to bring anything? A salad, maybe?"

"Just bring yourself." Tag reached out and gently moved a straying tendril of her long hair from her cheek. "See you tomorrow," he said quietly.

Then he was gone. Almost starry-eyed, Linda closed the door and made sure it was locked. Tag Kingsley was pure dynamite.

But maybe it was time she walked through a minefield.

Montana ★ MAVERICKS™

JACKIE MERRITT

Moon Over Montana

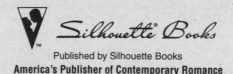

Silhouette Books

Published by Silhouette Books

America's Publisher of Contemporary Romance

Special thanks and acknowledgment to Jackie Merritt
for her contribution to the Montana Mavericks series.

 SILHOUETTE BOOKS

ISBN-13: 978-0-373-36240-0

MOON OVER MONTANA

Recycling programs
for this product may
not exist in your area.

Visit Silhouette Books at www.Harlequin.com

Printed in U.S.A.

JACKIE MERRITT

is still writing, just not with the speed and constancy of years past. She and her husband are living in southern Nevada again, falling back on old habits of loving the long, warm or slightly cool winters and trying almost desperately to head north for the months of July and August, when the fiery sun bakes people and cacti alike.

Chapter One

The students and teachers at the Rumor High School were looking forward to the end of the school year, some more than others. Art teacher Linda Fioretti was more inclined to look ahead to the new school year rather than rejoice in the completion of this year's curriculum.

But then, Linda had only been a teacher for a short time—living in Rumor that same duration and loving her new job. Having been born and raised in the Los Angeles area, this was Linda's first experience with the slower pace of a small town and she was amazed by how quickly she had adapted. Of course, liking the pretty little town and the people she had met created a sound foundation for contentment.

She had established a comfortable routine, Linda decided while feeding her dog one sunny Saturday morning. Did she really want almost three months of total freedom from routine? Driving around the country and setting up her easel in places that took her fancy held much appeal, granted. But recently—Rumor's influence, undoubtedly—she'd been discovering things about herself that she hadn't known before. Maybe she was even less like her oddball parents than she'd always believed. Considering her unusual upbringing, it was a simple matter for Linda to assume that Vandyne and Hilly Vareck, her mother and father, had absolutely no conception of the word *routine,* if they even knew it was part of the English language. Certainly routines weren't something they had put into practice in her presence.

"There you are, Tippy," Linda said as she set his bowl of dry food on the old newspaper on the floor of the tiny laundry room in her apartment. She returned to the two-stool counter in her small kitchen, sat on one and picked up her cup of coffee. She still had three weeks to prepare for the end of the school year, as well as the science fair she'd organized with the science teacher and local inventor Guy Cantrell. Plenty of time to decide how she would spend the summer.

She was just beginning to relax and read the front page of the *Rumor Mill,* the town's newspaper, when someone rapped on her front door.

Tippy came tearing out of the laundry room, food forgotten, barking and sliding around corners in his haste to reach the front door and save Linda from whatever monster was daring to make noise just beyond the door.

"Tippy, calm down," Linda said. "Sit," she told the little white dog, which he did, but with a watchful, suspicious eye on the door.

Linda peered through the peephole and saw a man she hadn't yet met. He looked innocent enough, not at all like the characters that had recently called on her and then practically run for the street, mumbling something about having the wrong address when she opened the door. She'd been amused the first time it happened because the man had been wearing a perfectly ghastly-looking toupee. The second time it occurred she wondered if she should alert the law about the man dressed as an overweight woman who had just knocked on her door.

But hadn't she laughed herself silly at the way he had hastily limped away in huge high heels? Where on earth did a man find shoes like that? Anyhow, she'd decided the guy was probably the town's one eccentric and that she really shouldn't cause trouble for someone so obviously a cookie or two short of a full box. She certainly hadn't felt threatened by him or his penchant for knocking on strangers' doors, after all. At any rate, she hadn't alerted anyone. The sheriff would probably have laughed it off anyway.

When the normal-looking man on her doorstep knocked again, Linda opened the door and said "Yes?" in a polite but questioning manner.

"I'm here."

Another eccentric? Good grief! Linda suddenly wasn't so polite. "So you are," she said dryly. "Would it be too much trouble for you to explain *why* you're here?"

"No trouble at all. You're next on my list."

How many nutcases lived in Rumor? Linda asked herself with an inner sigh. This one was awfully cute with his longish dark hair and twinkling hazel eyes. Very tall—over six feet, Linda was sure—and lanky. And he had the most incredible mouth—sensual lips—and an adorable grin. But precisely what *list* had he placed her on? Should she be worried?

No, she wasn't afraid. This good-looking guy had to be a salesman. She started to shut the door. "Thanks, but I'm not interested."

"Whoa, wait a minute. Didn't Heck tell you I was going to be here today to get started on the renovations to your apartment?"

Heck Sommers managed the building, the man from whom she'd rented her cozy and rather unusual two-story apartment. The two bedrooms were on the second floor. One had a tiny wood balcony, just big enough for a couple of chairs, and the other had a skylight. Linda had signed the lease immediately, envisioning warm summer evenings on that little balcony. Plus, the bedroom with the skylight made a perfect studio.

Heck had mentioned some building renovations when she'd

first rented, but she'd put the whole thing from her mind. Besides, she liked her apartment just fine, and she had turned it into a cozy little home for her and Tippy.

"I don't need you to do anything in here, but thanks," she said, and again tried to shut the door.

"Look, my name is Tag. Call Heck for confirmation if you wish, but I have a contract to do some work in this apartment and I'm supposed to start today."

"Good idea," Linda snapped, getting impatient with this guy, cute or not. "And I *am* going to shut the door while I make that call, so let go of it!"

"Fine." Grinning, Tag stepped back.

Linda slammed the door shut and made sure it was locked. She went to the phone and dialed Heck's number. When he answered she got right to the point.

"This is Linda Fioretti. There's some guy named Tag at my front door who says he has a contract to destroy all the improvements I've made in my apartment. Does he? Do I have to let him in?"

"Now, Linda," Heck said in a voice that Linda found annoyingly obsequious; Heck Sommers wasn't even slightly servile in person, and he was putting on a big act to soothe her ruffled feathers. After all, teacher or not, she was still just a woman. Sexist attitudes really fried Linda, but she let Heck finish without interruption. "Tag has a contract to do renovations to the whole building. He's a darn good carpenter and painter, and I'm sure he isn't going to destroy any of your improvements." Heck was suddenly his normal gruff-speaking self. "Which, by the way, consist of what? Your lease clearly states no painting or wallpapering without owner approval."

Oh, for crying out loud! "Believe me, I haven't challenged or compromised the terms of the lease in any way. All I've done is hang a few pictures and…oh, forget it. I'll let him in. Goodbye."

Linda returned to the front door and jerked it open. "Come

on in," she drawled. "Make yourself at home, which for some reason I'm certain you fully intended to do."

Tag had been told that a single lady lived in this apartment, and now that he'd seen her he deemed that information to be good news because she was just about the prettiest woman he'd ever met face-to-face. He was especially taken with her long blond hair and gorgeous green eyes, although the rest of her was just as noteworthy.

He held out his hand. "Tag Kingsley."

Linda didn't want to shake his hand. She touched it tentatively and said, "Linda Fioretti." Drawing back quickly, she asked, "So what are your marching orders? How much mess am I going to have to contend with?"

Tippy yapped, which Linda knew was a bid for attention. Obviously, the little dog didn't sense danger from Tag, and if the nice man wasn't dangerous he was a friend.

"Tippy, Tippy," she said with a sigh that labeled her best buddy a traitor.

Chuckling, Tag bent down and petted the dog's head. "So you're Tippy," he said. "Well, maybe your mistress will let me bring you doggy treats next time I come by."

"No, she won't," Linda said, getting more put out by the minute. "I would appreciate knowing what you intend doing to my apartment."

Tag stood again. "I'm going to check the woodwork and paint in each room, for starters." He took out a small spiral notebook and pen. "Where would you like me to begin?"

"How about Siberia?"

"Very funny." With a crooked grin curling his lips, Tag walked away from her and went into the kitchen.

Linda stewed for a moment then followed. He had the nerve to look into her cupboards! Every one of them, even the one under the sink.

"You're a good housekeeper," Tag remarked, making some

notes in the spiral. He went on to the adjoining laundry room, checked it out and made more notes.

Linda followed him into the living room, stood in the hall while he inspected the first-floor powder room and then up the stairs into the bedroom she used as a bedroom. Then there was the main bathroom and finally her studio.

"Hey, you're an artist," Tag said, visibly impressed by the canvases he could see around the room.

"Big deal," Linda muttered.

"It *is* a big deal." Tag squatted to better see the detail in a painting leaning against a wall. It depicted a crowded-street scene. "This is terrific. You didn't use Rumor as a model for this one," he said with a laugh.

"Of course not."

"Is this oil or acrylic?"

"You actually know there's a difference?" she asked with a raised eyebrow.

Tag stood and, eyes twinkling, looked at her. "Imagine that," he drawled good-naturedly. "So, what's on the easel? May I take a look?"

"I'd rather you didn't. I never know if I'll finish anything until it's actually…finished. Some pieces start out good and then inspiration sort of dribbles away to nothing."

"I know exactly what you mean. I've started dozens of projects in my shop through the years that ended up on the scrap heap. Of course, being good wood to begin with, I keep every piece. Never know when something I'm working on will require one more length of mahogany, or redwood or teak, or…well, you get my drift."

"I'm not sure I do. What kind of projects do you work on in your shop?"

"Oh, tables and things. I'm a carpenter."

The light dawned. "Oh, you have a *carpentry* shop. Then home renovation isn't your only job."

Tag grinned. "It's not even my second job. I don't consider anything I do a job."

"But it's how you make your living, isn't it? What is carpentry to you if not a job?"

"A passion. After my daughter, carpentry is the most important part of my life."

Surprisingly, Linda's stomach sank; he was married. "You have a daughter. How old is she?"

"Five. My wife died when Samantha was still a baby."

"Oh! I'm...very sorry."

"Thanks." He looked around the room. "These walls could use a coat of paint. Could you spare the room for one day? Actually, it's a small area and I could probably do it in half a day." He swung around to see Linda again. "What do you think?"

She shrugged. "You're the one with the contract. What do *you* think?"

"I really hate the thought of me causing a blip in the progress of great art."

"Oh, come on. This is hardly great art."

"Looks pretty great to me."

"Oh, sure, like it should be hanging in the National Gallery."

"Maybe it should. Maybe it will. Someday." Damn, she was pretty. How long had it been since he'd been instantly attracted to a woman? Had he *ever* been instantly attracted to a woman? Wasn't this some kind of first for him? "Do you sell your paintings?"

"I've sold some, yes, but not since I moved to Rumor."

"Where, then?"

"In Los Angeles. My parents are both artists, quite well-known in the L.A. area." Linda felt her face color. Why on earth was she running off at the mouth with a man she'd just met? She never volunteered information about her past, her life-before-Rumor, so to speak. Was her divorce anyone's business? Her unusual childhood?

"When did you move here?" Tag asked. "I don't remember seeing you around town, and I'm sure I would have noticed."

Linda's pulse quickened. He was flirting with her! He'd *been* flirting from the moment he stepped through her door. "If you hung around the high school, you would have seen me. I teach there," she said, cursing her inability to put an end to this question-and-answer session. Yes, she'd been as guilty of curiosity about him as he was about her, but this was all extremely foreign territory for her and it might be safer to nip it in the bud.

Tag's face lit up. "You're the new art teacher! I've heard about you."

"Yes, well, I've only lived here a short while, but it didn't take long to discover that very little goes on in Rumor that doesn't spread with the speed of light."

"Rumor's a typical small town, Linda. People gossip, sure, but it's still a great place to live."

She actually felt a thrill go up her spine when he said her name. It occurred to her to ask him to call her Ms. Fioretti, just as she had told her students to do.

But how childish would that be? Just because she was feeling giddy over a good-looking guy, experiencing physical sensations she'd only been equipped to imagine before this, didn't mean she should turn prim and proper and forbid him to use her given name.

"I take it you've never lived anywhere else?" she said, definitely not speaking her mind.

"Rumor's always been home and probably always will be. You know, I live on this same street, other side of Main. You should drop in sometime and see what I've got to offer."

"Wha—what?"

Tag chuckled. "Sorry, that didn't come out the way I meant

it to. I was referring to the finished pieces of furniture in my shop."

Linda's face was flaming. "Oh...I see. Well, are you through in here?" She began sidling toward the door.

Tag wrote something in his notebook and shoved it into his shirt pocket. "My inspection is over. Now all I need to do is discuss what needs to be done and set up a work schedule convenient to yours."

"You need a discussion. I see. All right, let's take care of that in the kitchen."

"Anyplace is fine." Tag followed her down the stairs and to the kitchen. He'd spotted the almost full pot of coffee his first time in there, and it smelled awfully good. He could ask for some, but he would rather that Linda offer it.

The newspaper and a single cup were on the counter in front of one stool, so he went to the other and waited for her to sit first.

She did, then he did. He took out his spiral again and began flipping through it. Automatically, so it seemed, Linda reached for her cup and realized the coffee in it was cold. She sighed inwardly. She couldn't get coffee for herself without offering some to Tag.

Oh, what the hay. "Would you like some coffee?" she asked, sliding from the stool. "I'm getting myself some."

Tag smiled. "I would love some. Thanks."

My Lord, this guy's smile could melt solid steel! Feeling clumsy but managing to fill two cups without knocking anything over or spilling coffee, she brought them to the counter.

"There you are," she said. "Do you need milk? I don't have any cream. Or sugar?"

"Nope. Black is perfect. Thanks." Tag picked up his cup and sipped. "You make good coffee." He had the strongest feeling that Linda did everything well. It was a thought that went straight to his groin, and he instantly sent his brain in another direction.

"Um, the whole apartment could use a coat of paint," he said. "And some of the woodwork needs refinishing. But I shouldn't be in your hair for more than four, five days."

"Beginning when?"

"I'd like to start today, if you can put up with me."

"And you'd start in which room?"

Tag looked around the kitchen. "This room will take more time than any other. I'd like to get it done first."

"You already have the paint and other materials you would need?"

"Every apartment in this building is painted the same shade of white, so I'm ready to go, yes. Unless you want a different color, which I'm sure you know has to be approved beforehand."

"Heck was kind enough to remind me of that clause in my lease," Linda said dryly. "I do prefer more color on certain walls, but this apartment is very small and decorator colors would have to be carefully planned so it wouldn't appear even smaller. Maybe I'll do something about the walls later on—with approval, of course—but for the time being white is fine."

"You're still not completely settled in, are you?"

"What gave you that idea?"

"The stacks of taped boxes in the closet of the room you're using for your artwork."

"Those boxes contain books. I don't have anywhere to put them. I shopped for bookshelves in Billings, but this apartment doesn't have a lot of available wall space and everything I found was too wide. Tall is fine. I can use tall, but I need some very unusual widths. Anyhow, I can't unpack my books until I figure out what to do with them."

"I can build bookshelves in any width," Tag stated.

Linda slowly turned her head to look at him. He was looking

at her, as well, and the warmth in his eyes was unmistakable. He liked her. She knew that as surely as she knew anything. What's more, she liked him. It surprised her that she actually *knew* she liked him. Never before had she formed an opinion that seemed so ironclad about a man this fast. Of course, there'd only been one man in her life, the one she had married...and divorced.

The word *divorced* went around and around in her head, and she was struck by an impulse to tell Tag about it. And about her screwball childhood, as well, her peculiar parents and the untraditional way they'd brought her up. *Dragged* her up was more like it, for they had unquestionably lived the typical bohemian artist's life. They hadn't believed in babysitters, so wherever they'd gone, so had she. She had fallen asleep on many a strange sofa back then, a tiny little girl dressed like a doll and treated as one, as well. Treated as a plaything rather than as a living, breathing child that needed regular meals and bedtimes.

But maybe another time, she told herself. Liking a man at first sight didn't—or probably shouldn't—include an immediate baring of one's soul.

"If you came by the shop and saw my work for yourself, you might feel good about ordering some custom-made bookshelves from me," Tag said quietly, though his blood had started running hot and fast in his veins. Her eyes were stunningly beautiful, the most unusual shade of green he'd ever seen. A man could get lost in Linda's eyes, he thought, and wouldn't he just love to twine his fingers into her glorious mane of hair.

"I...I suppose I could do that," she stammered huskily. "One day when you're there instead of here. You'd have to let me know."

"I never work away from home on Sunday. Come by tomorrow."

So soon? Just so she could stop looking into his eyes

without making her retreat blatantly obvious, she glanced at her cup before raising it to her lips. "I might be able to do that," she murmured.

"Are Sundays busy days for you?"

"Well, there's church…and next week's classes to plan… and student work to look over."

"Yes," Tag said solemnly. "I can see how those things could take up an entire day. But maybe you could squeeze out fifteen or twenty minutes to see me? I should say to check out my work. You wouldn't be stopping in just to see me, after all."

Linda cleared her throat. He was the biggest flirt she'd ever met. But he was also the *nicest* flirt she'd ever met. And he was *so* cute. For some reason, telling herself that Tag's brand of good looks meant zilch in real-life situations wasn't doing a bit of good—she still felt breathless sitting this close to him and listening to his line of hooey.

But that was the bottom-line problem. She *liked* his line of hooey.

"Will you try to make it?" Tag asked quietly, boring a hole in her with his penetrating gaze.

She flicked a glance at him and immediately looked away. "Yes, I'll try."

"Great!" Tag picked up his coffee and took a swallow. "So is it all right if I start working in here today?"

"How can I say no?"

"You can always say no, Linda," Tag said softly.

A frisson of sensual awareness traveled down Linda's spine, giving her a tiny shiver. His voice did that to her, she realized, and when he combined it with sexual innuendo, the result was even more intense. Not that she couldn't stop this… this thing building between them from growing too huge to control. At least she was pretty certain that she could. But did she really want to stop it? She had never felt so womanly before, so warm and fuzzy and tingly because of a man. And being a voracious reader, she knew that women should feel something during lovemaking. Although she'd never told a soul, she never had.

"All right," she said without looking directly at Tag. "You can start today."

"You're a sweetheart." Getting off his stool, Tag bent over and planted a brief kiss to her right cheek.

Shocked to speechlessness—no one had *ever* kissed her without provocation before, and she would swear that she had not invited any such familiarity—she sat there all the while he hauled in cans of paint, brushes, rollers, a tool chest and so many other items that she stared in amazement. Her kitchen floor was practically covered with the tools of his trade.

Shaking her head over the tornado called Tag—Tag who?— that had suddenly infiltrated her comfortable little world, she got off the stool and departed the kitchen. Tippy stayed. He had to sniff everything the nice man brought into his home, after all.

Chapter Two

Linda restlessly roamed her apartment. Every few minutes she heard Tag whistle a few bars of a song. Her Saturday was ruined, as far as she was concerned. Maybe she should be able to ignore having a man in her kitchen and go about her own business, but she just couldn't seem to relax.

Finally, deciding to get out of there for a while, she ran upstairs, changed from her slacks and blouse to fleecy gray shorts and a comfy old top, put on her walking shoes and returned to the first floor. Wishing she kept Tippy's leash anywhere but where it was, she took a big breath and headed for the kitchen with what she hoped was a look of irrevocable indifference on her face. Every time she'd thought of Tag's brash kiss to her cheek, she'd suffered a hot flash. She didn't like the confusion she felt over the incident, mostly caused by the fact that she hadn't *dis*liked the kiss. It had been rather sweet, actually.

"Pardon the interruption," she said as she forced herself to enter her own kitchen. "But I need to get Tippy's leash from the laundry room."

Tag turned and looked at her, and her determined expression completely deserted her. He had such marvelous eyes, she thought, suddenly feeling a bit weak in the knees.

"You're not an interruption." Tag's features softened into what Linda perceived as just about the nicest smile she'd ever seen on a guy's face. "Drop in anytime," he added. "I like the company."

He was flirting again! Linda swallowed hard. "Oh, well, I...I just need the leash...for, uh, now."

Tag nodded. "Sure thing. Help yourself."

"Thanks, I will." Stepping around drop cloths and the other things with which Tag had all but filled her small kitchen, Linda went into the laundry room and came out with the leash. Tippy perked up his ears and began dancing around.

"Looks like he knows what that means," Tag said with a laugh.

"Yes, he always gets excited when he sees his leash."

"That's an associative response. You taught him that without even trying. Did you raise him from a pup?"

Linda bent over to attach the leash to Tippy's collar. "No, I've only had him since my move from California about two months ago."

"Did you get him from the local vet?"

"I guess you could say I found him."

"Or he found you. Well, he's a lucky pooch. Looks to me like he got himself a good home."

"He deserves to be treated well. I don't think he was before I found him. He was begging for scraps of food at a place in Nevada where I stopped for gas. He was filthy, dirty and a pitiful sight, but he won me over the second I saw him. I talked to the only person around, a grouchy old man running the place who said that Tippy had been hanging around for a week, bothering customers and disturbing his thriving business. Believe me, the place wasn't thriving. It was in the middle of nowhere, and I remember thinking that a nice little dog just might do wonders for that old guy's nasty disposition.

In any case, he didn't want him, no one had come looking for him, and he told me to take him."

"So you adopted him on the spot."

"I had to. Look at that adorable little face and those trusting eyes. No way could I have driven away and told myself he would be all right on his own. He was hungry and frightened, and he probably wouldn't have lived very long if I had left him there. I gave him a bath in my motel room when I stopped that night, and…well, you can see how white his coat is."

"All except for that little patch of black on the tip of his tail."

"After seeing that, could I call him anything else?"

"Nope. Tippy fits him to a tee."

Linda was suddenly embarrassed over her unnecessarily detailed story. For one thing, her rambling had kept Tag from his work much longer than an abbreviated version of the story would have. For another, it wasn't like her to make mountains out of molehills when relating a simple incident.

"I'm going now. See you later," she said almost sternly, although any chastisement in her voice was for herself and her ridiculous urge to impress this man.

"I'll be here," Tag said cheerfully.

Tippy ran ahead of her to the front door. Pondering Tag's extraordinary effect on her, Linda took Tippy outside.

At the street she automatically went to the left. In that direction State Street led to Lake Monet. It was only about three miles away, and Linda had been smitten by the pretty little lake on her first visit. The water level was lower than normal for June, people kept telling her, as the area had had very little snow last winter, followed by pathetic little rainfalls instead of the hard, drenching rains that spring usually delivered.

But even if the water was shallow in Lake Monet, Linda saw great beauty in the bulrushes, pussy willows and lily pads along its southern curve. There were also amazing light patterns and colors in the water itself, and she understood very well why some romantic had named the small body of water after the great artist Claude Monet. Still, her thoughts weren't on art today, or the lake, and she only walked about a quarter of a mile when she turned around and went in the opposite direction. When she came to Main Street she crossed it and kept walking. Tippy was happy. He didn't care where they went, as long as they were outside.

Linda had driven every street in Rumor, just to acquaint herself with the town. She knew where the businesses were located, and she could put together most of the people she'd met with their homes. But until today there had been no reason even to notice the striking, lightly varnished wooden house that sat on a large lot with a number of evergreen trees. The name on the mailbox read Taggart Kingsley, and while Linda slowed her steps so she could take a really good look at his home, Tag's last name registered. He was a Kingsley!

But he was a carpenter—such an honest, basic, simple vocation—and why would one of the incredibly wealthy Kingsleys paint and renovate apartments?

Frowning, Linda pondered that puzzle and decided it made no sense. She'd heard about the Kingsleys. They were wealthy from decades of successful cattle ranching even before they'd created MonMart, which was a huge superstore on Kingsley Avenue that sold groceries, clothing, household goods, tools, garden supplies and almost anything else a Montana resident might need. MonMart was, by all accounts, extremely profitable. Gossip had it that many more MonMart stores were planned for Montana, and some predicted that the Kingsleys wouldn't stop until the whole country was peppered with their stores.

But that image didn't coincide with Linda's impression of Tag. Could he be a shirttail relative of the more ambitious Kingsleys? Should she ask around and find out?

No, Linda thought vehemently. She was not going to pry into anyone's affairs, family or otherwise. Everyone deserved some privacy, which, she had already been warned about several times, was difficult to preserve in this small town.

After another thirty minutes of walking, Linda turned around and headed for home. When she passed Tag's place, though, she slowed down again, and this time she spotted the building in the trees that appeared to be his shop.

She admired his yard and from her present viewpoint was able to see the swing set in back, some scattered toys and what appeared to be a sandbox—all evidence of a child. Thinking of Tag's personal life—widowed so young and with a little daughter to raise—Linda walked on.

Past his place, she picked up her pace. Inside her front door she freed Tippy from the leash and the dog ran for the kitchen yapping a "Hi, I'm back" for his new friend's benefit. Linda hung the leash in the foyer closet and then started up the stairs for a quick shower. She hadn't done any running, but she had walked fast and worked up a sweat. The day was warm, bordering on hot. According to longtime residents, it was much too hot and dry for this time of year. Actually, Linda thought the weather was just about perfect, but she knew that a lot of people, including the U.S. Forest Service, were concerned about the tinder-dry conditions throughout the area.

She was halfway up the stairs when she heard Tag say, "Linda, a friend of yours came by. A man."

Linda turned. "A friend? Did he give you his name?"

"No, he didn't."

A frown appeared between Linda's eyebrows. "Well, did you know him? I mean, was it someone from the school?"

"I never set eyes on the guy before today, but he walked in without knocking, so I figured you must know him very well."

Linda's jaw dropped. "He *walked* in? That's impossible. I locked the door when I left and just now unlocked it to get in." She held up her key for him to see.

"You had to unlock the door because I locked it after that guy took off."

"Wait a minute." Linda went back down the stairs and confronted Tag on the same level. "Listen to me. I *locked* the door when I left."

"Then that guy must have a key."

Linda's voice became slightly shrill. "*Nobody* has a key!"

"Well, he got in, and he sure as the devil didn't announce his visit with a knock. Linda, are you saying you don't know this guy?"

Linda was breathing deeply to calm her racing heart. Who in Rumor would just walk into her apartment? Even if the door *had* been left unlocked.

"What did he look like?" she asked, sounding a little breathless.

Tag frowned. Was Linda scared of someone? Scared for a reason? "Like a fish out of water, to be honest," he said slowly, watching her closely as he spoke. "When I heard him come in I thought you were back, but then I didn't hear Tippy and something felt off-kilter. Anyhow, I came in here to see what was going on and the look on that guy's face when he saw me was almost funny. He mumbled something about being in the wrong apartment and took off so fast he practically left skid marks. Kind of strange, don't you think?"

"Yes…strange," Linda murmured thoughtfully. Was she wrong about having locked the door? Could she recall with detailed certainty stepping outside, inserting the key in the lock and turning it? Try as she might, she couldn't. It *was* possible that she hadn't locked the door.

Which didn't explain someone off the street taking a notion to just walk in.

"Maybe you should call the sheriff and file a report," Tag suggested.

Linda mulled that over for a moment. "I don't know. No harm was done."

"Meaning you'd rather not involve the law. Why not, Linda? Is it because that guy could be someone you know?"

Tag's suspicion rubbed her wrong. If she *did* have a male friend with a key to her apartment, it would really be none of Taggart Kingsley's business.

"No, not because he could be someone I know," Linda snapped with biting sarcasm, immediately regretting her feisty comeback. She liked Tag, and she didn't want him thinking that she was morally loose, although to be perfectly honest she wasn't sure what she *would* like him to think about her.

"Look," she said in a more normal voice, "no one has a key to this place but me, and probably Heck. Since I like my doors locked, I assumed I had locked it when I left. Obviously I hadn't."

"Yeah, obviously," Tag said, still frowning.

"Was the man short, tall or somewhere in between?"

"Around five-eight, I'd have to say. Kind of short for a man."

"Considering your own height, five foot eight probably looks short to you. What color was his hair?"

"I think his hair was dark. No, you'd better scratch that. He was wearing a stocking cap and sunglasses. I couldn't say with any certainty what color his hair *or* eyes were."

Oh my God, was that another disguise? Was today's visitor the same guy who came to my door twice before? Did he simply walk in today because I left the apartment unlocked? Is this something I should be concerned about?

For some reason, Linda couldn't quite believe the poor sicko, whoever he was, was someone to fear. Twice she had opened the door for him and twice he'd immediately run away. If he had meant her any harm, it would already have happened. She just had to be more careful about locking the doors and windows, although the more she thought about it, the odder it all seemed. Did he want to rob her? She had some nice things, but a robbery in broad daylight in Rumor would not go unnoticed.

"Are you positive you've never seen him before?" she asked.

"I know everyone in town, Linda."

"You didn't know me. He could have recently moved here."

"I suppose that could be true." He could have reminded Linda that while he hadn't actually met her until today, he'd heard about the great new art teacher from a number of sources. Strangers normally did not go unnoticed in Rumor.

Linda squared her shoulders. "He merely walked into the wrong apartment," she told Tag. "When he saw you he realized his error and left. Let's both forget it."

Tag felt uneasy about the incident, particularly Linda's cavalier attitude toward it. "Are you sure it should be forgotten?" This time he couldn't resist warning her. "The guy's a stranger, Linda."

"So am I, Tag."

"Not the same thing. You're new to the area, but you immediately went to work as a high-school teacher. You're a respectable member of the community."

"Maybe he is, too. He might be from somewhere else and is in Rumor now to visit someone."

"Or to walk into other people's homes just because the front door isn't locked. Hell, Linda, I leave my doors unlocked most of the time. So do a lot of other folks around here."

"Well, they shouldn't. *You* shouldn't! Who can tell when some awful person might decide to walk in?" She realized what she'd just said at the same moment it registered with Tag. He grinned, and she grinned. "I think I'm losing it," she said with a shake of her head, and headed up the stairs again.

Tag watched until she reached the second floor and went into her bedroom. He wasn't completely comfortable with her attitude toward a stranger walking into her house, but he had to admire her spunk. She wasn't a coward, that was certain. Of course, a woman living alone didn't dare cringe in fright at every little thing. She'd drive herself batty if every noise and shadow scared her.

He liked Linda Fioretti, he thought again. He liked her more than any woman he'd ever known on such short acquaintance. She was a pleasure to look at, intelligent, independent and talented. Yes, *really* talented. Her paintings were incredible. Samantha might be a good artist someday. She loved to draw and color pictures. If she had a teacher who knew art the way Linda did…?

"That's a darn good idea," Tag said under his breath as, whistling and, pleased with himself, he returned to the kitchen and his bucket of paint.

The sun beating through the panels of glass of the telephone booth was so unbearable that Alfred Wallinski, aka Al Wallinski, aka Al Malone, had to leave the door open while he talked. Alfred's favorite alias was Max Malone, just because it sounded tough and together and perfect for a guy with his natural abilities. He wouldn't waste that great name on this crappy little job, though; he was saving it for the day when he'd finally made the grade and ranked as one of Paul Fioretti's pals. It would happen very soon, Alfred was sure, if he could just finish up in this ungodly wilderness and get back to Los Angeles.

"Paul, I got into her apartment today, but there was a guy there and I had to beat a hasty retreat."

"You're always beating a hasty retreat," Paul said disgustedly. "Alfred, if you can't handle one simple little job, why don't you just say so? I can't believe you've been in that town for weeks and *still* don't have the book. What in hell's wrong with you? Was your mother a jackass? 'Cause you sure are."

"Ma was no jackass," Alfred said huffily, defending his

mother's honor. "And I ain't either. I'll get the book. You got no idea how crappy this town is. I can't just up and leave my motel room whenever I feel like it. Someone's always around, and when I finally do give everyone the slip and get near her apartment, there're people there, too. I know every bush and tree on this damn street, 'cause I've hidden behind every one of 'em. And before you get too mad at me, answer me this. Have you ever come face-to-face with a bull or a bear on a dark night?"

"Oh, for hell's sake. Don't expect me to believe bears are wandering the streets of that town. Bears live in the woods."

"What d'ya think is all around the place? Woods, Paul. Trees by the thousands. And a bull is just as bad as a bear, anyway. I've seen plenty of them."

"You've probably seen milk cows, you dolt."

"Well, what about those other animals, the deer and the moose? And those owls hooting in every tree after dark? I tell you, Paul, it'd scare you, too."

"Don't count on it. Listen to me. You get into my ex-wife's apartment, find that little book with the brown cover and get your butt *and* the journal back here. I know she still has it because she would rather burn in hell than throw out a book. She probably unpacked her zillion books without even noticing that one, so it's on a bookshelf somewhere in that apartment. Stop your damn sniveling about bears and owls and get the job done. I'm tired of your whining. I want results, and I want them now!"

"I'll get the job done, Paul, I swear it."

"See that you do. The next time you call, I had better hear that the journal is in your hands!"

"It will be."

In his office at the back of his restaurant, Fioretti's, Paul slammed down the receiver. He never should have trusted Alfred Wallinski with this job, which was even more crucial to Paul's good health than he'd told the little worm before sending him off to Montana. That journal contained enough information about his illegal bookmaking ring that if it ever fell into the wrong hands and Paul's partners got wind of it, he'd be pushing up daisies faster than he could say "Alfred Wallinski."

Beads of perspiration broke out on his forehead. This was the worst mess he'd ever gotten himself into. What in God's name had made him think he had cleverly figured out the ultimate hiding place for the journal? He'd been positive that Linda had so many books she would never notice the addition of one thin, nondescript volume. And she hadn't. But then everything had gone upside down.

"Stupid, stupid, stupid," Paul mumbled, recalling the day he had rushed to their house to discover strangers living there. She'd sold the house! He'd left in a daze, calling himself names, calling *her* names, cursing the night she'd told him that she could no longer tolerate his dishonesty, his adultery or his disgusting friends. Their marriage was over, Linda had coldly said, and then she'd asked him to move out.

He'd been shocked to near speechlessness. How had she found out those things about him? He'd always been so careful. She had no proof, he'd decided. She was just in a mood. Thinking that she would come to her senses with a little time, he had taken his clothes and left her alone to think things over.

Well, she'd meant everything she'd said, and she had rushed to Nevada for a quickie divorce. He'd been stunned to receive his copy of the divorce decree, and that was when he'd driven like a madman to what he had still considered "their" house. Linda was gone.

And so were her books.

He'd panicked. Hell, who wouldn't have? And he'd racked his brain to come up with some guy he could trust with a life-and-death mission. It had been another blow to realize he had no real friends, no one in whom he could confide something so serious without worrying the story would be bandied about until it reached the wrong ears. And then he'd thought of Alfred Wallinski, not a friend but a guy who hung around the fringes of Paul's crowd with a hopeful look in his eyes. He wanted to be part of the group so badly the poor slob was like a homeless puppy, doing everything he could to be noticed.

Alfred was, sadly, the best that Paul had been able to come up with, and he'd sent Alfred to the old neighborhood to ask around about Linda. To Paul's surprise she hadn't kept her whereabouts a secret, and Alfred had discovered in one day that she had moved to Rumor, Montana. Alfred had been so proud of the good job he'd done that he'd told Paul all about it with tears in his eyes. Paul had been touched by the man's apparent sense of loyalty and decided on the spot that Alfred deserved a real break. "You, my friend, are going to Montana for me," he'd said, and then watched the little guy wilt.

"I ain't never been out of L.A.," Alfred had said in a shaky voice.

"Hell, man, you'll love Montana. I'd love to go there myself, but I couldn't do what you could. Linda's never set eyes on you. You'll be able to get in and out of her place the first time she's not at home." Paul had explained what Alfred would be looking for. "You'll be back in L.A. in a week."

"Yeah, probably," Alfred had said weakly.

But it wasn't going the way it should have, the way Paul had figured it would. Thinking of Alfred's idiotic fear of animals—probably of his own damn shadow, too, the little wimp—he slammed the top of his desk with his fist. *That fool is probably hiding in his motel room instead of watching Linda's place! This should have been over and done with weeks ago.*

Paul was more right than he knew. When Alfred exited that stifling little phone booth, he hurried back to his motel room. Worried because Paul was so angry with him, he began defending himself in front of the mirror above the scarred dresser. "Yeah, Paul, it's real easy for you to be so tough in that cushy office of yours. You have no idea what I'm facing in this burg. Sheriff's cars everywhere, animals everywhere, that yapping little dog in your ex's apartment, people coming and going all the time around her building. Yeah, Paul, you ain't got a clue about what I'm going through here.

"And now there's some guy living with her. What am I supposed to do about him, huh?"

Chapter Three

Shortly after four that afternoon Tag began packing up his tools and supplies. Linda heard what he was doing from where she sat on the living-room sofa, using the coffee table as a desk. Not that she was bogged down with teachers' homework. There was really very little planning needed to finish out the school year; her students were mostly working toward completing projects with an eye on receiving a good grade for their efforts.

Linda, with Tippy on her heels, went to the kitchen door. "You've finished all the walls," she said, amazed that he had accomplished so much.

"And the ceiling," he said with a grin. "These cupboards could use some sanding and fresh stain, but I'll have to check with Heck on that."

"Well, that's between the two of you," Linda murmured. "The cupboards look fine to me. Oh, there are a few places that could use some touching up, but overall they're in pretty good shape."

"We'll see what Heck says about it."

"Fine. You must be very fast. I had no idea you'd do the whole kitchen in less than a full day."

"It's a small kitchen, Linda." Tag smiled at her. "But I am pretty fast, all right. And good. These walls just shine, don't they? I used semigloss in here."

"I see you're very modest, along with being fast and good," she stated dryly. "But yes, the walls look wonderful. At least ten shades lighter than they were. You know, when I moved in, I washed down everything in here. The walls were sort of tacky to the touch. Not horribly dirty, but the former tenant must have done a lot of frying. Anyhow, I thought I had done a good job."

"You did. It's just time to rejuvenate this old building."

"It's not that old, is it?"

"About six, seven years, I'd guess." Tag picked up his toolbox. "Since I won't be here tomorrow, I'm not going to leave anything behind for you to trip over. On Monday, though, I might ask if you'd mind my leaving some of these things in an out-of-the-way place, just so I wouldn't have to haul them back and forth."

"Oh, sure, no problem."

"Thanks." Carrying some of his things, Tag approached the doorway.

Linda watched him coming toward her and felt his presence so acutely that it took her breath. No man had ever affected her in quite this way, not even the man she had married. Maybe *especially* not the man she had married. That had been such a dreadful mistake.

Tag stopped in front of her. This woman intrigued him like no other. He had never believed in love at first sight, and he couldn't say it was happening to him now. But something was. Something was stirring his blood and causing images of lovemaking to overwhelm everything else in his brain.

Linda looked into his eyes for a moment, felt a feverish intensity that seemed like a warning bell, broke eye contact and stepped aside for his passage.

Without a word—or a grin—Tag went on by her and out the front door.

When he was outside, Linda sucked in a huge breath of air. "My Lord," she whispered, wondering how a decent woman dealt with such mind-bending chemistry and kept her reputation intact. It was as though a cloud of unmanageable hormones had descended upon her apartment the second she opened her door for Tag.

Tag made another trip from the kitchen to his truck with his gear, then came back in with a tape measure.

"Show me the places you'd like to have a bookshelf," he said.

Forcing her soaring imagination back to earth, Linda led him to the available wall space in the living room. She pointed, he measured and wrote in his spiral, then he said, "I should probably ask how many books you need to shelve."

"You saw all those boxes in that upstairs closet, and you probably know that each tenant also has a small storage room at the front of an assigned carport parking space. Well, mine is full of books. In boxes, of course." At his cocked eyebrow, she declared with her hands out, "What can I say? I love books."

"In that case you're probably going to need some shelves upstairs. If memory serves, there's wall space in both your bedroom and studio."

"Yes, you're right." She walked to the stairs.

Tag watched the way her body moved as she ascended in front of him. He was only halfway up when he told himself to cool down or the fit of his jeans would embarrass both of them.

They went to the studio first and Linda realized that she was reluctant to put anything in this room but her many art supplies. She had covered the carpet under the easel with a large piece of tightly woven outdoor carpeting, as she disliked working on plastic, canvas tarps were too cumbersome and she didn't want to have to worry about dripping paint while she was concentrating on a creation.

"You're a considerate tenant," Tag said with a nod toward the easel area.

"It's something I would do in my own home if I had to work on carpet, so why wouldn't I do it in a rented place? The perfect floor for an artist is concrete. Someday that's what I'll have."

Tag smiled. "So you can splash paint every which way?"

"Something like that. Tag, I'm going to skip this room for now. If I absolutely have to, I'll put bookshelves in here, but I'd rather not." She smiled. "I wouldn't like my books spattered with paint any more than I would the carpeting."

Tag loved her smile, even though it made his legs feel a bit wobbly. Did she know how beautiful and sexy she was? Or the kind of power a woman like her wielded over a man?

He cleared his throat. "Okay, fine, let's check out your bedroom."

They found two adequate areas of wall space that would nicely accommodate bookcases. After measuring and making notes, Tag shoved his spiral into his shirt pocket.

"I think that does it," he said.

"Yes," Linda murmured huskily, wondering why on earth she would feel giddy, awkward and almost tongue-tied just because there was a bed in the room with them. Had she ever enjoyed sex? *Never!* Then why keep thinking about it now? *I must be losing my mind!*

She hurried from the bedroom and felt Tag behind her every step of the way.

"Don't forget to come by my place tomorrow," Tag told her at the front door. "You won't have any trouble finding it."

"Uh, right. What time would you like me?"

I'd like you in the morning, in the afternoon and all night long. "If you come in the afternoon you could stay for dinner and experience one of my famous barbecued burgers."

"Stay for dinner?" Linda nervously bit down on her lower lip.

"I think you'll like Samantha," Tag said in a casual tone of voice.

Linda relaxed considerably. When he said dinner, she had immediately envisioned a cozy dinner for two. But his little girl would be there, and he certainly wasn't going to try anything in front of her.

"Yes, all right," she said. "Want me to bring anything? A salad maybe?"

"Just bring yourself." Tag reached out and gently moved a straying tendril of her long hair from her cheek. "See you tomorrow," he said quietly.

Then he was gone. Almost starry-eyed, Linda closed the door and made sure it was locked. Tag Kingsley was pure dynamite.

But maybe it was time she walked through a minefield.

Something had changed. The apartment seemed cramped. Linda felt edgy and disconnected, a form of angst that she couldn't recall having endured before, and she'd been so sure that she had suffered it all before her move to Rumor. Apparently not. Apparently liking a guy on such short acquaintance, and then facing and even enjoying fantasylike thoughts of a physical nature—because of him—delivered its own brand of emotional conflict.

Linda tried to elevate her mood by reminding herself how dismal her love life—if one could even call her one experience with an uncaring member of the opposite sex a love life—had always been. It didn't seem to do much good; she was still full of sighs when she was in her nightgown and ready for bed around ten that night.

The downstairs lights were off and only a bedside lamp still burned. Linda pushed back the sliding glass door and stepped out onto her tiny balcony. The night air was fresh and smelled wonderful. She went back inside, switched off the lamp, got out the shawl she often used on nights like this and draped it over her shoulders. She then returned to the balcony to sit in the dark. Tippy lay at her feet, as relaxed as any dog could be, while his mistress looked at the stars.

The Montana sky at night still amazed Linda. There were no clouds blocking the view, and the sky seemed alive with twinkling starlight. Rumor was like another world, she thought, not for the first time. She had always lived with city lights, sirens and the sound of heavy traffic. Here there was barely a sound. A car started somewhere, maybe down the street at another apartment complex, and far off in the distance a dog barked. It was all so serene, so lovely. It was also dark enough that another resident of the building, or anyone else who should happen by, would have a hard time seeing her. She liked the sensation of privacy that the darkness and the position of her balcony gave her.

Feeling her tension give way, Linda put her feet up on the second chair and got really comfortable. Her mind wandered, from Tag to her teaching job, then from the upcoming science fair to the lazy days of summer ahead. She had found peace in this small community, and she wanted to hold on to it. It was too precious a feeling to destroy with careless or shabby behavior.

Linda sucked in a quiet breath. Certainly a normal adult relationship with the man she had met today wouldn't be in the shabby category, would it? Unless Tag had a reputation she shouldn't get near, it wouldn't. But in this small town where everyone knew just about everyone else, and few residents hesitated to pass on gossip, some people were under closer scrutiny than others. Teachers, for example, had to be particularly watchful of their reputations. Linda had never disagreed with that attitude, but then there'd been no reason for her even to think much about it. Certainly, she hadn't come to Rumor with hopes of finding another husband.

"Lord love a duck," she whispered, shocked that she would even think of such a thing. One husband had been more than enough for her. She'd been positive for a very long time— even prior to her divorce—that she could happily live out the remainder of her life as a single woman.

Until today, that is. Until meeting a good-looking guy with laughter lurking in his eyes, a mouth designed for tender, sensual kisses and just enough brashness in his personality to create sexual unrest in a woman who had not been seeking any such thing.

Linda heaved a long sigh, laid her head back, shut out the beauty of the sky by closing her eyes and let life-before-Rumor unfold in her mind.

It wasn't that her parents hadn't cared about her. As a child she'd been given almost anything she'd asked for; anything, that is, but hugs and time and regular meals and the kind of life that the few friends she'd had back then had lived. Their mothers and fathers had scolded and then hugged and kissed their children. No one had ever scolded Linda, because Hilly and Vandyne Vareck had believed that no one had a right to tell anyone else what to do.

Linda had been a lonely child and had discovered the magic hidden in books at an early age. The collection she had to this day included some childhood favorites, and while her parents worked on their incredible art, or attended all-night parties with their artist friends, Linda had exchanged reality for the setting in whichever book she was devouring.

In high school, Linda had kept to herself. She made top grades but her friends lived between the covers of books, and whenever she noticed couples holding hands or stealing a kiss in school, she simply told herself that she had other interests.

Then she met Paul Fioretti and his dark good looks finally broke the back of her indifference to the opposite sex. He was a sharp dresser, drove a new car, always had plenty of money to throw around and he was five years older than she had been. He had told her that his college years had been spent in the East; he had graduated from Yale, an Ivy League school, and he'd brought her to the restaurant he owned, a small but busy place that served delicious Italian food. She'd been impressed by his plans to expand to a second restaurant and then a third, and on and on until Fioretti's became a chain. She'd also been grateful that he was a businessman and knew little or nothing about art. She had not wanted art for her own career, but her talent was inborn, apparently, and wouldn't be ignored. She dated Paul until her college graduation, and when he proposed that same day, she agreed to marry him.

At her wedding she'd realized once again how unusual her parents were, for they hadn't attended the ceremony. Instead, they'd sent her the deed to a very nice house in suburban Culberton as a wedding present. By then the Varecks' eccentricities no longer hurt Linda, and she had written a lovely thank-you letter, which they never acknowledged. Paul had been openly thrilled about having a house without a mortgage, but when Linda had suggested that he, too, contact her folks to thank them, he'd hemmed and hawed and never did get around to it.

One thing about Paul that had truly pleased Linda was that he hadn't pressured her into making love before their wedding, as she'd had some very sweet ideas about being a pure and virginal bride. Then, on their wedding night, Paul had shattered her romantic fantasies by taking her roughly and without any consideration for what she might be feeling.

That had been the first blow to the hopes she had permitted to penetrate her somewhat cynical take on life; obviously, she had been delusional for a while. That very night she had wept quietly while Paul snored beside her. Any hope she'd had for a perfect marriage was utter nonsense. As for children, the ones she would love with all her heart and soul, Paul had refused to discuss the subject. He didn't want children.

But even with such serious flaws, Linda had tried to make her marriage work. Little by little, however, she'd had to face facts. Paul lied about everything, from serious missteps to trivial incidents that weren't worth the effort it took to devise a lie. His lying became unbearable for a woman who valued honesty as much as Linda did. Plus, Paul's friends were disreputable people that Linda suspected lived on the wrong side of the law, which meant that her husband was, more than likely, involved in illegal activities.

The final straw was his infidelity. After far too many years of kowtowing to an immoral, dishonest man who didn't have a tenth of her intelligence, a man who had never given her a moment's pleasure in bed and refused to discuss the problem with her, or even admit that there *was* a problem, Linda had called it quits.

One afternoon while Paul was gone—only God knew where—Linda packed his clothes and personal possessions. She didn't throw his things into boxes, she folded everything neatly and filled every suitcase in the house. And when he got home that night, she was up and waiting for him. She told him their marriage was over and she wanted him to take his things and move out.

He had laughed at her and told her that she would come to her senses. She hadn't cared what he thought, as long as he got out of her life. She breathed freedom again after he'd loaded his car and driven away, and it had felt absolutely wonderful. The very next day she drove to Las Vegas, rented a small apartment, moved in some of her things and saw an attorney to file for a Nevada divorce.

The end of that chapter of her life had arrived in the form of a divorce decree. She had already acquired her present teaching job and sold the house, which had remained in her maiden name because Paul never got around to changing that, either—and within two days, she was on her way to Rumor, Montana.

And here I intend to stay. Linda opened her eyes and felt unusually emotional. The beauty of the vast velvety sky with millions upon millions of sparkling stars touched her soul. Why on earth was she ruining her mellow mood by thinking about Paul?

Of course, her mood wasn't *entirely* mellow. There was Tag now, an intrusion on her peace, to be sure, but was that all bad? He was so darn attractive with his grin and open personality. She would be willing to bet that Tag Kingsley had very few, if any, secrets.

And he was a carpenter. Could any other job suit her better?

Deep into her own thoughts, Linda barely heard the snapping twig. Still, it brought her out of her reverie and back to the small piece of earth she inhabited. The yard around the building was dark. Over by the connected row of carports, one of which contained her SUV, were two lights, one attached to the roof on each end of the structure. A few windows in various apartments threw light. Her place was not one of them; she sat in total darkness.

But there it was again! Someone was stealthily walking near the building. Linda noticed Tippy's head rising from his front paws; he had heard—or smelled—whoever was creeping around out there. The little dog growled low in his throat, and Linda laid her hand on him to keep him from throwing a barking fit and waking up everyone in the building.

She sat without moving, one hand on Tippy's head, the other at her own throat, which seemed to be the place where her heart had leaped and was now pounding a breath-stealing cadence. For moments she sat frozen in that position, then became angry, mostly with herself. She was not and never had been a woman to freeze in fear. Whoever was out there probably had a perfect right to be.

But then she heard a discordant scratchy sound that was absolutely foreign to anything she'd noticed before. Something wasn't right, and whatever was going on seemed to be occurring in the vicinity of her front door!

"What in the world?" she mumbled. At the same moment, Tippy eluded her calming touch, jumped up and began barking at the sliding door. "Hush," she said sharply. Tippy stopped barking, but he whined and scratched at the glass door. "What is it, Tippy?" she whispered. Was someone who *didn't* live in the building attempting a burglary this very moment? Maybe trying to get into *her* apartment?

"You're not getting away with it, buster," she muttered as she hurriedly went inside and, without turning on any lights, made her way through her bedroom and down the stairs. Tippy raced ahead of her and began barking furiously. This time Linda didn't hush him, and when she reached the door herself, she quickly snapped on the outside light and peered through the peephole. She saw nothing. Anger filled her. Just because whoever had been snooping around had been fast enough to elude her light didn't mean he hadn't been out there. Should she phone the sheriff's department and make a report?

Frowning, Linda pondered the situation. Was tonight's intruder connected in some way to the parade of weirdos who had been knocking on her door in broad daylight, one of whom had walked in without knocking while she'd been gone today? She'd been so sure she had locked the door, she always did, but how else could he have gotten in?

Oh my goodness, is he clever enough to pick locks? Had he come back after dark to walk in again?

But at night she secured the dead bolt and the security chain on the door. Was he good enough to get past those additional precautions? If she had been asleep and he'd gotten in…? Linda shuddered a moment, then got hold of herself and thought, *For pity's sake, Tippy would have thrown a fit and woke not only me but the neighbors, as well!*

If a guy was haunting her for some unimaginable reason,

he must be incredibly stupid to keep overlooking a live-in burglar alarm like Tippy.

Incredibly stupid or incredibly desperate.

Desperate to do what? Slowly Linda climbed the stairs. What did she have that a man she'd never met could want so badly that he kept returning and risking his own life, liberty and pursuit of happiness to get hold of? Oddly enough, she sensed no threat to herself. Both times that she had opened the door to the person in those pathetically comical disguises, all he'd done was get out of her face as quickly as was humanly possible. Maybe she should have called the law this afternoon and again tonight, but to tell them what? That someone had walked into the wrong apartment today and then tonight she had heard strange noises?

"Not unless you want it getting around town that the new art teacher is a hysterical female," she drawled disgustedly. She was *not* a hysterical female, not now, not ever and, with everything so quiet, the noises she'd heard—or thought she'd heard—could have come from a block away. "Get a grip, lady," she told herself. After locking the sliding door and pulling the drape, Linda crawled into bed. Tippy settled down on the small rug at the foot of her bed. All was quiet again, and, ordinarily, Linda fell asleep within minutes of retiring. Tonight she stared into the dark for a long time.

Whether she had imagined an intruder or someone had actually been sneaking around the building, the incident had left a mark. Linda hated admitting it, but the marvelous peace she had found in Montana seemed to be slipping away.

But that elusive—and possibly imagined—intruder wasn't the only Montana male chipping away at her peace of mind. Turning to her side, Linda let Tag overwhelm her thoughts. There was a raw sexuality between them that she'd never experienced before. It wasn't just Tag's adorable grin and twinkling eyes drawing her in, there was a feeling in the pit of her stomach that teased and taunted and dared her to be a real woman.

Sighing softly, she admitted that she *wanted* to be a real woman. She wanted to explore her sensual side, which had certainly not been tapped or touched by Paul. It seemed almost impossible that she had stayed in a loveless marriage for so long. She had wasted years on a man who hadn't given a damn that she never derived any pleasure from their lovemaking. And worse than that sin, he had refused to let her have children.

A tear spilled from Linda's eye and dribbled down her temple to her pillow. There was no question about it: the peace she'd found—or *believed* she had found—in Montana was definitely ebbing.

Her last thoughts before sleep were as far from her intruder as they could be. They were about Tag. He was a carpenter with a child. He was handsome and sexy and funny and sweet.

And he just might be her perfect match.

In room six of the State Street Motel, Alfred lay facedown on his bed and wept with his fingers digging into the pillow. He hated the town of Rumor with every fiber of his being. He hated Montana with its wild animals—those horrid cows and horses included. He hated the hootie owls that scared the stuffing out of him every time they let out one of their bone-chilling cries. This place wasn't fit for civilized human beings, and why in hell would Paul's ex-wife move to such a godforsaken speck on the map? It was no damn wonder Paul had broken up with the bitch. She must have a screw loose or something.

When she had turned on that porch light tonight, he'd nearly passed out. He'd gotten away only because self-preservation had taken over and caused his legs to run without a conscious, direct order from his brain.

Alfred pounded the pillow in frustration. Tonight he had failed again, and he'd been so sure, when he'd spotted her dark apartment, that she had gone out. But being the pro that he was, he had cautiously checked each side of her end of the building before trying her door. He hadn't heard even one yap from that crappy mutt of hers, which had reinforced his happy opinion about the apartment being empty. What did she do, sit in the dark and hope some poor unsuspecting stranger tried to get in?

"Eeee," Alfred moaned. His stomach was killing him. Rumor was giving him an ulcer. He longed for the lively streets of his old neighborhood in L.A. He ached for noise, for traffic and lights and people, for favorite hangouts with loud music and even louder patrons. The only place that he dared enter to get a beer was the dive next door, the Beauties and the Beat strip joint, and being Saturday night, there was plenty of noise coming from it. But he was afraid to show his face in there too often for fear that someone would start asking questions, especially when there were so many cars in the parking lot. No telling who was in there tonight.

He wept fresh tears. He couldn't go home without that stupid book. Paul would probably kick his butt clear around the block, and he'd be laughed out of the neighborhood.

But couldn't fate give him just one tiny break and put him near that apartment when that woman and her dog were both gone somewhere? Damn! How much more could he take?

Chapter Four

A car horn tooted. Linda checked the rearview mirror to see who was behind her. Recognizing her colleague, Guy Cantrell, she pulled over. He parked his car behind hers, got out and came up to her window.

"Good morning," she said.

"Morning, Linda. I was heading for the high school when I saw you. Did I call you this morning?"

Linda smiled. Guy was a sweet man, nice-looking with dark hair and blue eyes, and extremely intelligent, but sometimes he reminded her of the proverbial absentminded professor.

"No, were you intending to call me?" she said.

"Oh, I remember now. I *started* to call and something interrupted my good intentions. What was it?" Guy narrowed his eyes for a second, then shook his head. "Couldn't have been very important. Anyhow, I was only going to tell you that I needed to start figuring out where each of the fair's entrants should be placed in the gymnasium. Would you have the time to join me? You have such a good eye for layout, and I really would like some artistic symmetry in this year's event."

"If you want artistic symmetry, then that's what you shall have. I'm on my way home from church, Guy. I need to change clothes, but then I'll go to the school. Shouldn't take me more than twenty minutes. Thirty, at most."

"Thanks, Linda. See you at the gym."

Linda drove off thinking of her promise to Tag. But she hadn't planned to go to his place until midafternoon—probably around three—so she could take her time at the school. There'd been so much talk among students and teachers alike about the science fair, that Linda had become quite excited about her part in it. Actually, the upcoming event had her thinking about something similar for art students. Those with a little talent and a lot of hope would benefit greatly from community recognition.

But that would have to wait until next year, although it certainly was food for thought during the summer months ahead.

Driving west on Main Street, Linda felt the heat of the sun and switched on the air conditioner. It wasn't nearly as hot as it got in inland California, but no one could call it cool in Rumor today. Linda glanced up at the brilliant, blue, cloudless sky. People were worried about the hot, dry conditions, but the area was so lovely to Linda's eyes that she wondered if they weren't worried over nothing.

But what about the low water level in Lake Monet? And the yellow, crisp grass? The people who are worried have lived here much longer than I have.

Linda laughed at her one-sided conversation. She'd talked to herself in California, too, because she had spent almost as much time alone during her marriage as she did now.

"Oh, well," she said under her breath, eluding another trip down memory lane like the one she had taken last night.

But last night had been pretty weird, what with outside noises causing her imagination to run wild. And then there were those thoughts about wanting to be a real woman. Good grief, if she wasn't real now, what was she? Funny how different things looked under a bright sun.

Linda parked in her assigned space and walked from the carport to the apartment building. This complex was especially attractive because of the huge pine trees on the property. Also, Heck kept the lawn watered and neatly trimmed, which created a pleasing sense of being surrounded by cool greenery.

Halfway between the carport and the building, Linda caught a movement out of the corner of her eye. She turned her head in that direction and saw only large pines. Either her eyes were playing tricks on her or one of the neighborhood kids was. She smiled and continued on to her front door.

Lurking behind one of those pines, Alfred was close to hyperventilating. Making sure that he stayed concealed by the girth of the tree, he raised his arm and wiped the sweat from his forehead with the sleeve of his shirt. He hadn't been able to get near her apartment because that miserable dog inside had barked louder than a foghorn without stopping for air until Alfred had sidled away. His hope now was that she would take that little yapper for a long walk.

Linda went in and greeted Tippy with a smile and a pat on the head. He ran around in circles for a minute to show how happy he was to see her, then followed her up the stairs and settled down on his rug.

She took off her dress and pulled on pale green slacks and a blouse. She was ready to go in minutes and Tippy followed her back to the first floor, where she took time to check his water dish. She had walked and fed him before church and he didn't act as if he needed to go outside again, so she refreshed his water, patted his head and said, "So long, slugger. I have to leave again for a while. Keep the bad guys at bay, all right?"

That was what she usually said to her adorable pooch before leaving him alone in the apartment, and she had always considered her request to be rather funny. Tippy wasn't much bigger than a large cat and she couldn't imagine his keeping anything at bay. Actually, his ferocity, although he did have a loud bark, would probably earn nothing more than a dirty look from a cat.

Alfred spotted Linda leaving again—*without* Tippy—and muttered some choice curses under his breath. The trouble with apartment buildings—especially this one—was that the units were too close together. If that woman didn't have a dog, he would have gotten into her unit on his first try, found the stupid book that Paul wanted so badly and already be back in Los Angeles. Oh, how he wished he were back in Los Angeles!

A groan accompanied Alfred's burst of self-pity. He was not a violent man. He might despise Linda Fioretti and her dog—and blame them for his misery in this awful place—but he could barely make himself step on spiders. And Paul had made it clear that his ex-wife was not to be harmed in any way. Alfred recalled feeling very hurt that Paul would think it necessary to say such a thing to him.

But he really should not have let it injure his feelings, because Paul and his circle of friends—the exact group that Alfred wanted so much to be an important part of—only knew Al Wallinski as a tough guy. Alfred's chest expanded a bit at that thought. He liked Paul thinking of him as tough, and when this job in Montana was finally accomplished and Alfred returned to California, Paul would probably praise him to high heaven and invite him to Fioretti's for a meal with his closest pals.

Daydreaming about future glory was Alfred's favorite pastime. But it occurred to him that he had better stop wasting time and make a move.

But what move would that be? People were coming and going around the apartment building. Five or six kids in bathing suits had started running through a sprinkler not far from Linda's front door. And if he dared get near her door, that rotten dog of hers would make so much noise someone would probably call the cops.

Discouraged and hot, Alfred made his way from tree to tree until he reached the huge bank of bushes and shrubs at the back of the lot. Cautiously he crawled in among the leaves and scratchy limbs. When he came to the piece of bare ground that he'd been using off and on to conceal himself and still keep an eye on Linda's apartment, he lay down and made sure he could see through the dense foliage.

He didn't mean to fall asleep, but lying in that cool place, with the laughter of children at play and the soothing, repetitious sound of the sprinkler spraying water on grass and small people alike, Alfred's eyes got heavy. He was snoring in five minutes.

There were three cars and two bicycles parked near the entrance to the high school's gymnasium. Linda parked her SUV at the end of the line, got out and went into the gym. Spotting Guy at the far end of the room, she started toward him. A youthful male voice stopped her. "Hi, Ms. Fioretti."

Linda turned to see Michael Cantrell, dressed, as usual, in baggy jeans and a huge shirt. His baseball cap was stuffed into a pocket of his pants, and Linda knew that when he put it on again, its visor would be shading the back of his neck instead of his eyes.

"Hello, Michael." Linda smiled. "I hear you're entering a project in the fair."

Michael grinned. "Sure am."

"That's wonderful. What's it all about?"

"Uh, I want it to be a surprise, Ms. Fioretti."

Linda smiled again at the fourteen-year-old. He was tall and lanky with the angular build of a boy growing so fast his flesh couldn't keep up with his bones. Like his father, Max, and his uncle Guy, Michael had dark hair and blue eyes. The

Cantrell brothers were handsome men and Linda could see the same good looks developing in Michael.

Plus, he was smart. His grades were phenomenal. He was taking advanced courses in science and math because he was too far beyond the normal ninth-grade level.

The first time Linda had met Michael she had wished he were interested in art so he would be in one of her classes. But he was a scientist, like his uncle Guy, and Linda had heard from several sources, Guy himself, for one, that Michael spent a lot of time in Guy's home, getting involved in his uncle's inventions and ideas. Linda thought it wonderful training for a young man so taken with science to have someone like Guy in his family.

All the while, she had been very curious about the project Michael would bring to this year's science fair.

"You're not even giving out hints?" she asked teasingly. Michael's cheeks got red, and she knew that she had put him on the spot. "I'm only kidding, Michael. You have every right to keep your project a secret."

"Uh, thanks, Ms. Fioretti."

"Well, I should get to work. See you later, Michael." Linda left the boy and headed toward Guy.

"I want tuna fish," Samantha Kingsley declared emphatically.

"You *always* want tuna fish," Tag responded. He'd been looking for something to fix for their lunch, and obligingly he got out a can of tuna. It was healthy food and Samantha loved it. He didn't love it, but since they were going to have hamburgers for dinner, a tuna sandwich for lunch wouldn't kill him. "Get the bread while I mix this stuff," he said.

Samantha could barely reach the bread box, and Tag had to force himself to stand by and let her do it without his help. The hardest part of parenting, he was beginning to realize, was giving your child room to grow and do things for herself.

Sammy was five years old and a tiny little thing, so adorable that Tag's heart melted every time he looked at her. She had light brown hair with wispy curls that touched her shoulders and big hazel eyes; she had his eyes, Tag knew, same color, same shape. But Sammy's eyes contained something that his did not: sadness. She had still been an infant when her mother died, and while Tag knew Sammy loved him with all of her little heart, she wished that she had a mommy. Other kids did. Why didn't she? Even though Tag answered every question Sammy asked about her mother, he knew his answers didn't quite fill the void in his daughter's world.

"No mustard, Daddy," Samantha said.

Tag chuckled. He had merely moved the container of mustard to reach the jar of mayonnaise. Sammy's sharp eyes missed very little.

"Aw, heck, I thought you'd like some mustard in your tuna today," he said.

Samantha giggled. "You're teasing me."

When the sandwiches were made, he put them on paper plates, along with a few potato chips and a slice of dill pickle, and brought them to the table.

Samantha scrambled up into her chair while Tag poured two glasses of milk.

"Mmm, good," Samantha said after her first bite.

"Simply delicious," Tag said dryly after his first bite. "Hey, small fry, we might have a guest for dinner today."

"Who?"

"A very nice lady I met yesterday. I'm painting her apartment. Her name is Linda Fioretti, and she's a teacher at the high school."

"Okay." Samantha took a drink of her milk.

"I think we'll have barbecued burgers. What do you think?"

"Does she like burgers?"

"Everyone likes burgers. Don't they?"

Samantha shrugged. "Guess so."

"Maybe I should go to the store and buy some warthog. Maybe she would like barbecued warthog better than a burger."

Samantha giggled a second time. "You're teasing me again."

Tag grinned. "Sometimes I just can't help myself. That's 'cause you're so cute when you giggle."

"Oh, Daddy, you're funny."

"So it's all right with you if we have a lady over for dinner?"

Samantha nodded and took another bite of sandwich. "We should have ice cream for dessert," she said with her mouth full.

"You are absolutely right. Which flavor goes with barbecued burgers?"

"Strawberry."

It was Samantha's favorite. "Yes, I believe you are right again. Strawberry it will be. We'll go to the store after lunch, okay?"

"Okay."

Tag hadn't expected any other answer.

Linda returned home around two. She walked from carport to apartment building humming under her breath. After much discussion and thought, the final layout for the fair was planned in a way that gave each entrant equal visibility, or as close to equal as Linda had been able to make it. She was satisfied with the results of her labor, and so was Guy. He had thanked her profusely before they went their separate ways.

Unlocking her apartment door, she smiled because she could hear Tippy dancing around on the other side.

Alfred woke up, realized that Linda was home again and at the same moment saw the snake. It was a tiny thing, a little tan garter snake that began slithering away the second the huge beast in the bushes opened its eyes. Screaming at the top of his lungs, Alfred jumped straight up and plowed a new trail through the bushes.

At her door, Linda heard the screams, looked for their source and saw a grown man running from the bushes at the back of the lot. She realized after a second that he was shouting, "Snake! Snake!"

"What kind of snake?" she called, but the guy was still running and apparently didn't hear her. The kids playing nearby came up to her.

"Who's that guy?" one boy asked.

"I don't know, but he's yelling something about a snake." Linda began frowning. There was something familiar about the screaming runner.

"Let's go find it!" the boy said, and the children all ran to the bank of bushes to search for the snake.

"Be careful," Linda called to them. "It could be a rattler."

It wasn't. The kids were disappointed. "It's just an old garter snake," the apparent leader of the group said as they left the poor snake to its own devices. "And it's not even a big one."

Forgetting snake, bushes, frightened running man and everything else about the incident, the kids went back to their games.

Linda stepped into her apartment and absentmindedly greeted Tippy the way she usually did. But her thoughts were on the grown man who had been so frightened by a little garter snake that he'd run off shrieking like a wild person. Had he been *in* the bushes? They were dense and scratchy and even the neighborhood children walked around them. Why on earth would a grown-up do something that children sensibly avoided?

And he *was* familiar, although she couldn't say with absolute certainty that he was the same man who had knocked twice on her door and then run off when she opened it. Was he also the one who had walked into her apartment yesterday? And the person who had done some sneaking around the building last night? What in heaven's name was going on? Did he just haunt this apartment building or was he doing the same to the other apartment complexes on the street?

Linda had been planning to wear her green slacks and blouse when she went to Tag's house, but they had gotten a bit soiled at the gym, so she went upstairs—with Tippy following, of course—to change clothes once again.

Pondering the ambiguities of a strange man hanging around the neighborhood—was he dangerous or merely simpleminded?—Linda took a quick shower. Without giving much thought to what might be appropriate clothing for a visit to a man's carpentry shop—and perhaps for eating a burger with him and his daughter—she pulled on a full-skirted, Hawaiian-print sundress. With sandals on her feet, she brushed her long hair and fluffed it around her face. A little lipstick and a little blusher finished the job. She was ready to leave again.

But first she would take Tippy for a short walk. He probably had to go outside by now.

It was Alfred's big chance. The kids had either gone indoors or to the other side of the building. Linda, with Tippy on his leash, left the apartment and walked down the street.

But Alfred was already in his motel room, still feeling all creepy crawly because of that horrifying snake.

"My God, my God," he groaned hoarsely every time he thought of how close to a painful death he had come today. He had to get hold of that book and out of Montana before he lost his mind.

Or his life!

In good weather Tag worked in his shop with the door open so he could keep an eye on Samantha playing in the backyard.

During winter months he brought her inside to the corner playroom he'd built expressly for her use. She was rarely out of his sight, although he had come to rely on Rumor Rugrats, the preschool and nursery started by Susannah McCord, his soon-to-be sister-in-law. She and Russell, Tag's oldest brother, were presently in China. After a lavish party to announce their engagement, they had traveled to the country to finalize the adoption of a young Chinese girl. When they returned with their daughter, they would be married.

Today Sammy wasn't Tag's only concern. He kept looking at his driveway and at the street, watching for Linda. She *would* come, wouldn't she? Darn, he should have set a time for her arrival. He could have asked, "What time is best for you tomorrow?" He could have said, "I'm going to be on pins and needles all day until you get there." He could have said, "I'm not sure what to call this feeling I have for you, but it already seems to be a permanent part of the man I am."

Tag shook his head wryly. He should *not* have said anything more than he had. He had invited Linda to look at his work and have an informal meal with him and Sammy. Anything else would have been overkill, possibly a turnoff for a woman with Linda's intelligence. She had said yes, that she would come by, and he should stop acting like a lovesick half-wit and believe she kept her promises.

His current project was a headboard for Samantha's new bed. About a month ago Tag had decided she was ready for a full-size mattress, and the little girl loved the grown-up bed he had bought for her. But he hadn't purchased a headboard. That, he would build himself. It was reaching the finishing stages, and today he worked on smoothing the wood with fine sandpaper until it felt like satin to his fingertips.

This kind of work was perfect for a man with a lot on his mind. Linda was at the center of his thoughts, but why wouldn't she be when she was the first woman he'd met since

Mel's death who reminded him that he was still young, still virile and living like a monk?

Tag had grown up in the loving, wealthy household of the Kingsley family, and from an early age he hadn't wanted to get involved in the family business, which included the MonMart chain of retail outlets and a large cattle and horse ranch. Carpentry was his passion, and around the time he'd broken the news of his career choice to his father, he'd also learned his high school sweetheart, Melanie, was pregnant.

To support his burgeoning family, Tag studied carpentry as an apprentice and took any job he could find. He'd known early on what was important in life—his daughter Samantha, his wife Mel and his work.

Unfortunately, Mel's substance abuse problem, which had begun in high school worsened, and she died of a drug overdose. Tag felt as if he'd failed both Mel and his precious daughter. He'd lived in a cloud of despair ever since.

Meeting Linda seemed to have parted the clouds and let the sun in. Small wonder he was excited about her coming by today, he thought.

When he heard a car pull into the driveway, his heart skipped a beat. Dusting his hands with a clean cloth, he stepped out of his shop. Samantha immediately left her toys and went to stand by her daddy.

Linda got out of her SUV and sent a smile to father and daughter. "Hello," she called.

"Hello," Tag said, and taking Samantha's little hand in his began walking toward the incredible woman in the brightly colored dress who had not only kept her promise to come by but had arrived looking ravishingly beautiful. Every feeling that had been born yesterday intensified in Tag's system. He knew pretty much what to call that burning ache: he was falling very hard, very fast for Linda, and God help him if she didn't feel the same about him.

She walked toward him and Sammy as they walked toward

her. Linda's gaze darted from Tag to his daughter and back again. His child was beautiful and so was he. A choking sensation rose in Linda's throat; something serious was happening to her, something that she was afraid to label or even attempt to understand.

"Thanks for coming," Tag said. "This is Samantha…or Sammy. Samantha, this is Ms. Fioretti."

Linda bent over to be closer to the beautiful little girl. "Hello, Samantha," she said softly.

"Hello," the child said shyly.

The feelings flooding Linda's system almost brought tears to her eyes. This child touched her soul, and if love at first sight was more than just a dream devised by romantics, then it had just struck her straight in the heart.

"I would like it if you called me Linda," she said.

"Okay."

Linda straightened and deliberately looked beyond Tag and Sammy, as she feared her eyes might be just a little too shiny.

"You have a very nice place," she said. Then she spotted the sign above the wide door of the carpentry shop. "Carpenter for Rent," she read aloud. Smiling again, she looked at Tag. "Are you really for rent?"

"For the right person, any time of the day or night," he said softly.

A tingling thrill went up Linda's spine. He meant her, she realized. He meant that she was the right person and that he was available if she wanted him.

"Sammy, I'm going to show Linda the shop. She's interested in some bookcases. I'd like you to go back to your dolls for a while, sweetheart. We'll take care of business first, then we'll make those burgers."

Tag had spoken to his daughter, but his eyes were saying a thousand other things to Linda. What was so unusual about this exchange was that she couldn't seem to break eye contact with him, although, in all honesty, she wondered if she really wanted to. The air seemed electrically charged. With each breath she took, the stirring sensations in the pit of her stomach became more pronounced.

"Okay, Daddy." Sammy smiled shyly at Linda, then turned and ran off to her sandbox.

"Tag, she's wonderful," Linda said in a voice made husky by emotion. "You're very fortunate to have her."

"I know." The pupils of his eyes became darker. "You're so beautiful you take my breath."

She felt her face color. "Maybe…maybe we should…I mean, maybe you should show me your shop."

"Did I embarrass you? That wasn't my intention. You *are* beautiful, Linda. I thought so yesterday, and seeing you again…." Tag stopped and bit down on his lower lip for a second. There was a slight frown between his eyes. "I'm sorry. I've just never met anyone like you before. Probably because there *is* no one else like you."

Linda studied his face, looking for a lie, searching for something that would scare her off. All she saw was intense admiration and the open, honest expression of a man saying what was in his heart. Her own feelings swelled and turned into words.

"I've never met anyone like you, either," she whispered.

Tag looked into her eyes for a long, sexually charged moment then took her hand. "Let's go to the shop."

Linda felt dazed. His hand around hers was big and warm and felt like a connection to life itself, to all of the things she had never experienced. She was real and Tag was real, and what was happening between them was more real than the building they entered together.

Inside, virtually alone with him—although Sammy was only about twenty feet away from the opened door of the shop—she moistened her lips with the tip of her tongue and saw Tag watching the perfectly natural gesture with yearning eyes.

She gently disengaged her hand from his and began looking around. There were all sorts of tools and workbenches, and she saw a headboard on one of them and then a child's play area in the far corner.

"For Samantha," she said quietly. "You're a protective father."

"Comparable to a she-bear with cubs," Tag said with a slight grin.

"It's very clean in here. I think I expected sawdust…and… Oh, there's the furniture you've finished." She left him to walk over to an elegant dining table with a Sold sign on it. "You actually built this?" she asked in amazement.

Tag nodded. "Sure did."

"You're not just an ordinary carpenter, you're a craftsman, an artist." Linda moved to some chairs and then a coffee table. "Oh, these are all wonderful."

"Glad you like them. What I like is you."

Linda sucked in a startled breath.

Tag moved directly in front of her and put his hands on her waist. "I don't need a year to decide on whether or not yesterday was a red-letter day, Linda. I knew it only minutes after meeting you. And I'll tell you something else. I don't say things like that to every woman I meet. You can ask anyone in this town and they'll all inform you that I'm pretty much a loner. Once in a great while I go down to Joe's Bar and have a beer or two. That's about the extent of my social life."

Linda probed the depths of his eyes. "Tag, you must have had women friends along the way," she said softly. "You've been widowed for five years. Men don't live without female companionship for that long a time."

"I'll tell you about every woman I ever knew if you want me to. Do you?"

She shook her head. "No, of course not."

"I don't want to hear about the men in your past, either."

"But there weren't any. Other than my husband."

"Linda, Linda," he whispered. "Do you realize what's happening here?"

She knew he was going to kiss her. His face came closer to hers, and she almost felt his lips on hers.

But then they both heard Samantha calling. "Daddy? Where are you, Daddy?"

They quickly broke apart. "There you are," Samantha said, and smiled when she saw her daddy.

Tag went to his daughter and picked her up. "Let's go make those burgers, okay, sweetheart?"

"Okay, Daddy," she replied happily.

Chapter Five

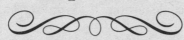

Linda loved Tag's house. Modern-rustic, she called it—only in her own mind while wondering if there was any such thing. But what else would one call a house with every modern convenience that had the feel of a cozy cabin? In particular she loved the childish drawings—held in place by fruit and vegetable magnets—covering the door of the refrigerator. It was clear that Tag was a loving father to his little daughter.

The floor plan of the house was simple and sensible and would accommodate a larger family than Tag's, all very impressive, but what delighted Linda most was the crafts-manship that Tag had lavished on his home. He was indeed a master carpenter, and Linda confidently ordered two book-cases with dimensions to fit the now vacant wall space in her compact living room. She looked forward to the day she could start unpacking her books, and she told Tag she would order three more bookcases for her bedroom if the first two were well-done.

If anything was missing from Tag's house, Linda mused, it was a woman's touch, which indicated to her that Tag was not involved in a serious relationship. Most women would love putting their mark on a man's home, and the fact that no female had done so gave Linda a surprisingly warm and satisfied feeling. *Now, if I were going to decorate this house, I would…*

It was a pleasant little fantasy, quite harmless, Linda felt. After all, she was only mentally adding colors and textures, not visualizing herself as part of the happy family picture so easily drummed up in her imaginative brain.

After a tour of the house Linda asked, "May I help in the kitchen?"

"You can help me set the table," Samantha said excitedly before Tag could answer. "I *always* set the table, don't I, Daddy?"

"Almost always, yes," Tag said with a loving smile for his daughter. "But Linda's our guest. We don't make guests do the work, do we?"

"I forgot," Samantha said with downcast eyes.

There was something about Tag's child that tugged at Linda's heartstrings more than most children did. After pondering it, Linda decided that Samantha's eyes contained a distant unhappiness and longing. The conclusion gave Linda a start. Why would a tiny girl who obviously adored her father, as he adored her, carry such a burden?

Linda smiled at the child. "I would like very much to help you set the table."

Samantha's eyes lit up. "You would?"

"Yes, I would." Linda shooed Tag away. "Tag, you go and do whatever daddies do at dinnertime and Sammy and I will take care of the table-setting."

Tag wanted to hug Linda so badly he barely kept himself from doing it. "Thank you," he said with sincere emotion, and then walked to the kitchen, whistling. It was a happy tune, and while he fashioned ground sirloin into patties for the grill, he thought about Linda and how perfectly she fit into his household.

* * *

During dinner Linda noticed the way Tag included Sammy in the conversation, and she was impressed by the girl's behavior. Obviously, the child was used to adult companionship, which, considering Linda's own childhood, gave her pause. She would hate to learn that Sammy rarely spent time with other children, for that was one of the oddities of Linda's early years and had taken her ages to get over. If the opportunity arose to talk to Tag about how crucial it was for children to associate with other children, she would take it. Not that she had the right to preach about how a man she hardly knew should be raising his daughter, but certainly she could bring up the subject in a tactful way.

Linda tried but couldn't quite finish the huge burger Tag had fixed for her. "It's delicious," she told him with a smile. "But I can only hold so much."

Tag polished off his last bite, and, since he had made a much smaller burger for Samantha, she finished hers. Picking up the bottle of very good red wine that he and Linda had enjoyed with their hamburgers, he poured a little in Linda's glass, then got to his feet.

"Sammy and I are going to clear away the dishes. You are to sit there and wait for dessert."

"Dessert! Tag, I really couldn't eat another bite."

"It's strawberry ice cream," Samantha exclaimed, looking startled that anyone would refuse dessert, especially ice cream.

Linda smiled. "I have the feeling that strawberry just might be your favorite flavor."

Sammy nodded earnestly. "I love strawberry. Do you love strawberry?"

"As a matter of fact I do."

Tag could see how taken Sammy was with Linda. He had hoped his daughter would like Linda—and why wouldn't she, when Linda seemed to know exactly what to say to a five-year-old? Grateful for the bright light that Linda had added to his and Sammy's lives, he dished up bowls of ice cream and carried them to the dining room table.

"Okay, ladies," he declared. "Dig in."

Sammy giggled and Linda smiled. It was possible that not only was she falling for Tag but for his precious daughter, as well.

Linda was impressed when Tag announced, at a reasonable hour, that it was bedtime. They had all been sitting in the living room, and he picked up his daughter, gave her a big hug and then grinned at Linda. "I always tuck her in. Do you mind being left alone for a few minutes?"

"Of course not." Linda got up from her chair. "Maybe I should go."

"Please don't. I won't be long. Sammy, say good-night to Linda." The little girl held out her arms, and Tag said to Linda, "She wants to kiss you good-night. Is it all right?"

"It's definitely all right," Linda murmured and moved close enough to father and daughter for Sammy to press a sweet kiss to her cheek. "Good night, sweetheart," she said to the child. "Pleasant dreams."

"See you shortly," Tag said quietly and left the room carrying Samantha.

Linda returned to her seat on the sofa with questions jumping around inside her head. Why was Tag Kingsley causing her to experience such unusual feelings? He would have kissed her in his shop if Sammy hadn't run in when she did. What's more, Linda knew she would not have stopped him. Would she stop him if he wanted more than a kiss?

She plucked a magazine from the coffee table and flipped pages without seeing ads, articles or photos. There was a tingling in her body that blocked concentration and made her feel incomplete and anxious.

She thought again of the possibility of falling for both Tag and Sammy. She could easily love the little girl. That was a given. But the idea of falling in love with a man she'd only met yesterday was too bizarre to accept. She was, after all, a calm, collected, mature woman, not some hyperactive nymphomaniac.

Restless, Linda got up and roamed the room. She stopped to look at the photographs on the long, ornate mantel. Samantha, at various ages, was portrayed in many of them, and Linda figured the very attractive people she didn't recognize were members of Tag's family.

Thinking about the Kingsleys, wondering exactly where Tag fit into the family, Linda wandered over to an entertainment center that contained a large television set and some very expensive-looking electronic equipment. She began looking through the CDs and approved of Tag's eclectic taste, which ran from country to classical and almost everything in between. It was, she realized, one more thing to like about him.

"She's asleep."

CD in hand, Linda turned. "She's precious, Tag. I believe Sam has captured my heart."

"How about her daddy?"

Linda's blood quickened, and she mustered a somewhat nervous smile. "I think I had better take the Fifth on that question."

"Which CD are you holding?" Tag closed the space between them with two steps and took the CD from her hand. "I like this album, too. Let's put it on."

While he stacked the CD player with that disc and some others, Linda moved to sit on the sofa. She watched Tag and admired his long legs, narrow waist and broad back. He has a great butt, she thought, startling herself, a woman who had never before even noticed the shape of a man's behind.

Her aberration struck her as funny, and when Tag finished with the CD player and walked over to sit beside her, she was holding back a laugh.

He turned, with his arm along the top of the sofa. "Something's tickling your funny bone. Care to share it?"

"I can't." Her eyes glittered from pure enjoyment. She liked him, she adored his daughter, and she had never spent a more pleasant afternoon and evening in her life. And even though he hadn't actually touched her hair, she could feel his hand back there, causing all sorts of delicious thrills to dart here and there throughout her body.

"Because the joke's on me?" he asked with a grin.

"No, because if I told you about it we would both be embarrassed."

"I don't embarrass easily." He brought his head closer to hers, finally lowered his hand to her hair and said in a soft, husky voice, "You're beautiful in so many ways I couldn't begin to list them all. Is it really possible for anyone to be so perfect?"

"Oh, Tag, I'm not perfect," she said quickly, breathlessly, wondering if she should permit this to go on. His fingers in her hair were doing sinful things to her sense of order, and his voice, warm and husky, was just as bad. Or just as good.

"You are to me," he whispered. Tipping her chin with his free hand he gently turned her face to look into her eyes. "Where have you been all my life? It's not a line. I mean it heart and soul. You're the woman I've wanted to meet for a long time. You're all woman, from the top of your head to the tips of your toes. And you're also smart, bright, talented—"

Linda broke in. "Tag, you're making me into some kind of…of… I don't even know what to call it, but I guarantee you that I'm really very ordinary."

"No, you're not," he murmured as he brushed her lips with his. "You are so delicious-looking in that dress I could eat you up."

Linda tried to make light of the serious emotions dizzying her mind. "Sort of like strawberry ice cream?"

"Ice cream is cold. You just might be the warmest human

being in all of Montana." Tag settled his lips on hers and she didn't pull away. His blood began racing through his body, and he suddenly wanted to make love to her so much that he hurt.

Linda was sinking into another world, one that promised pleasure and passion and all the things she had thus far missed in her thirty-two years. In truth, she had begun to doubt that feelings like these even existed outside of romantic novels. Learning the most important facts of life at her age was damn sad, she thought vaguely, and parted her lips for Tag's tongue. She gasped when he explored the underside of her bottom lip and then teased her tongue.

His left hand played with her hair and his right hand caressed her body, moving slowly from her waist to her breasts to her throat and back down again. His touch was magical, arousing her to recklessness, and she began her own exploration, starting with his firm chest.

Tag was elated at her responsiveness. He had hoped… After all, a man didn't really know how any woman would react to a pass, however sincere his intentions.

"You're wonderful…wonderful," he whispered raggedly.

"Oh, Tag, I really don't know what I'm doing."

"We're both only doing what we must."

"You…don't understand."

"Kiss me again and maybe I will." He took her lips again and poured his feelings into it. She kissed back with abandonment, and he became so infused with thoughts of love for this incredible woman that he almost blurted out every one of them. But even overcome with desire he maintained enough common sense to realize that the word *love* didn't belong in this scenario, this first romantic encounter. There would be many more. Of that he was certain. They were perfect for each other, and Linda must see that as clearly as he did or she wouldn't be in his arms.

He slid his hand down her thigh to the hem of her dress,

slipped under it and stroked warm bare skin until he reached her panties. He heard her breath catch in her throat, and then she tore her mouth from his.

"Wait…wait," she stammered.

He knew she was trying to say no and his heart sank. "Why should we wait, darlin'?"

"It…this is too soon…too fast." She felt awkward, with no confidence at all in her opinion that something was amiss in such overwhelming passion. "You don't know me," she whispered. "Tag, we only met yesterday."

"A sentiment that isn't worth the powder it would take to blow it to hell. Linda, I'm backing off, but I'm not giving up." He took his hands off her and held them up so she could see his gesture of sincerity. Then he slumped back against the sofa, feeling as though he'd just made a terrible mistake and wondering how a man could make quick and permanent amends.

Linda sank into the corner of the sofa to get herself together. "I'm sorry," she said without looking at him. "I like you, but I'm not good in this type of situation. I don't have enough experience to…to be good…or even to know what I should or should not be doing."

"Believe me, you were doing just fine." He turned to look at her. "Something happened between us right after you opened your door yesterday. It hit me like a ton of bricks, and I think you felt the same shock wave. Linda, the length of time we've known each other means squat. If I told you everything that passed through my mind since I sat here next to you—actually from the moment I first saw you yesterday—you'd either run like hell or stand up and haul me to the bedroom."

Her mouth fell open. "How do I respond to something like that?" She scooted to the edge of the sofa cushion. "I think I should go home now." Pushing herself up, she rose to her feet.

Tag jumped up, his expression anxious. "Are you mad at me?"

"No, but I think I should leave now. Thank you for dinner." Linda looked around. "What did I do with my handbag?"

"It's on the dining-room hutch."

Linda walked from the living room to the dining room and retrieved her small bag. Tag followed her to the back door, then rushed around her to put his hand on the knob before she could.

"Tell me you're not going home angry," he said with lines of anxiety furrowing his forehead.

"I already did that." Her eyes beseeched him. "Tag, what do you want from me?"

He saw nothing wrong with total honesty. "The same thing you want from me, Linda."

"And you know what that is when I don't?"

He found that a little hard to believe. "How could you *not* know?"

"If you had known me longer than one day you wouldn't have to ask. That's what I've been trying to get across to you, apparently without success." She sighed. "I'm afraid I might have given you the wrong idea about my morals, even though I can't imagine when it happened. Maybe I've been too friendly, coming to your house today, when we only just met. I've made more friends in Rumor than I ever did in California. The town has something to do with it, and the people, of course. But there's more to it than that. I've changed, for the better, I believe, but…"

She stopped for a breath. "I'm not explaining myself very well, probably because I'm really just beginning to *know* myself." She saw the dismay on Tag's face. "Let me put it this way. I'm different now. There are hordes of reasons—all stacked on top of each other—and I've been trying to get to the bottom of them and figure out who, exactly, Linda Fioretti really is."

"There's nothing wrong with the Linda I'm looking at right this minute."

"That's your point of view, Tag," she said softly. "Surely you've faced confusion about yourself at some point in your life."

Tag suddenly stood straighter. "How did you know that?"

She had wounded him, which hadn't been her intention. Besides, what on earth was all that blather she'd handed him about finding out who she really was? Nothing even close to that big fat lie had ever entered her mind. She *knew* the kind of woman she was today, she'd known herself in California.

Hadn't she?

Feeling as dumbfounded as Tag appeared to be, she tried to undo whatever hurt she had caused him. She laid her hand on his cheek.

"I'm sorry," she said gently. "Today was wonderful."

He put his hand over hers and kept it pressed to his cheek. "But then I ruined it by behaving like a horny kid. Linda—"

"No! You didn't ruin anything!" She tugged at the restraint of her hand. "Please, Tag. Let me go home."

He studied the ocean-green depths of her eyes. "If I could only make you understand—"

"I don't need to understand everything tonight, Tag." *As if I could! The reason for all the gibberish I used on him was his power to move me. To make me feel something hot and heavy when he kissed and touched me.* "I'm not going anywhere. Are you?" she said with all the bravado she could muster.

He drew a relieved breath. "Of course not." He let go of her hand and opened the door for her. They walked to her car and he opened the driver's door.

She got in and started the engine. Then she smiled at him. "Well, I'll say good-night now."

Tag leaned into the car and gently brushed her lips with his. "Good night. I'll see you in the morning."

A thrill of enormous magnitude shot through Linda's body. Oh, yes, he definitely had the power to move her. But why did that scare her? *Lady, you've got a whole lot of soul-searching to do!*

"But I...I won't be at the apartment in the morning," she stammered breathlessly.

"I'll be there before you leave for school."

"What about Samantha? Who cares for her while you work?"

"I take her to Rumor Rugrats. She loves going there."

"Oh, the nursery school. Of course." There went her worry that Samantha lived only with adult companionship. That was welcome news. "Well, good night again," Linda said.

Tag shut her door and stepped back from the car. He watched as she backed from the driveway into the street and then drove off. His feelings for Linda were deep and sure; he believed he would only fall harder the longer he knew her. He also believed that she felt something for him.

That should be enough for a meaningful relationship. But it hadn't been, at least not tonight.

Maybe things would look brighter in the morning.

They often did.

Alfred could hardly believe what he was seeing: Linda Fioretti's SUV pulling out of the driveway in front of him. Alfred had left his own car parked at the motel and walked the five miles to town because he had learned that an inconspicuous place to leave his vehicle while casing Linda's apartment was all but impossible to find in this horrible excuse for a town. Not that there weren't some vacant lots and open spaces within the town limits, but people around here were bold enough to ask point-blank why he would drive over ruts and through ditches—risking damage to his car—to park in a stand of pine trees.

Watching Linda's taillights getting smaller, Alfred cursed under his breath. She hadn't been home, she'd probably taken that miserable mutt with her, and he'd missed another opportunity to grab that journal and get the hell out of Montana. He felt like crying, like lying down on the asphalt and bawling like a baby.

Clenching his jaw, he turned around and began the long, frightening trek back to the State Street Motel. Trees crowded the highway, black trees with tentaclelike branches. An owl hooted and Alfred jumped as though he had just touched a hot stove and then began running. He sensed something behind him and he ran full tilt, as fast as he could, to escape a mauling from the bear that would probably eat him alive.

"No, no, go away," he screamed and ran faster.

If he had been an Olympic contender, he would have won a gold medal, as he ran the entire five miles in less than ten minutes. Finally, safe inside his room, he locked the door so the bear couldn't get in and then fell on the bed. It took him more time to slow down his wheezy breathing than it had taken him to run all the way from town.

Cursing passionately, he gathered his meager courage, peered outside to make sure no bears were in sight and crept from his room to the pay phone. He had Paul's number almost dialed when he stopped himself. Paul would either laugh or yell at him. Paul didn't want to hear any more complaints about Rumor or stories about bears. Paul wanted results.

Slamming the phone back on the hook, Alfred returned to his room. His stomach was killing him and he chewed a handful of antacids before undressing and crawling into bed.

He lay there feeling sorry for himself. Paul had never been to the wilds of Montana. How could he possibly grasp the horrors that came from all directions?

Alfred drew some comfort from the fact that Paul would probably run from a bear in the black of night, too.

Which man in his right mind wouldn't?

Chapter Six

Student projects were winding down. Walking among the easels in her classroom, Linda stopped to speak to each young artist.

"Wendy, your clouds are good. But if you use a bit more gray on their undersides, they will become much more true to life. The type of clouds you are portraying above that landscape need to billow."

"James, that old house really appears to be falling down. You have an excellent eye for perspective."

Linda had ten students in this class. In all, she taught four classes—one for each grade—all of them focused on the techniques of the most common mediums used in creating pictures—oil, acrylic and watercolor on canvas and paper. It was the format she had stepped into for this school year, but she had high hopes for subsequent years. Art wasn't just about creating a canvas; it was about history and the great artists that had, through the ages, dared to spread their wings and take chances with their individual expressions.

It was an important message that Linda was aching to teach Rumor's youthful artists, and she was working on a presentation for the school board for next year's curriculum.

If approved, her classes would incorporate art history, art therapy and, of course, hands-on experimentation with paints and brushes. And drawing. Heavens, most of the kids she taught knew next to nothing about drawing.

Linda left the students to their projects and went to her favorite perch in the room, a wide windowsill below a bank of tall windows. She sat on the sill and looked outside, aware of the quiet chatter and occasional laughter of her young charges. They were nice kids and she didn't believe in heavy-handed discipline. If they talked to each other a bit while working on their paintings, where was the harm?

Sighing softly, Linda's thoughts drifted to last night's episode on Tag's sofa. How did he have the power to make her feel so much when no one else ever had? Since her wedding night she had, at times, considered herself frigid and didn't particularly give a damn about it. Then along came a man who had changed her tune. And instead of thanking him for opening her eyes to a whole new world, she had run away like a child afraid of the dark while babbling nonsense about trying to figure out exactly who she was.

It was a crock and she knew it. She'd been positive from the day she arrived in Rumor that she had found a place of peace and serenity, and she sure as hell hadn't been sitting on her balcony at night worrying about what made her tick. Truth was, she'd been proud of the new life she had made for herself, and the courage it had taken for her to finally get out of her bad marriage and far, far away from her ex. And then she'd met Tag.

Frowning, Linda chewed on the inside of her lower lip. Tag. What in the devil was she going to do about him? She had to figure it out before she saw him again, but so far today a solution had eluded her. She had made sure to leave the apartment this morning before he got there, and she was worried about getting home before he quit for the day. She couldn't *not* see him for very long, she knew that, but maybe tomorrow she would be better equipped emotionally to deal with the only man who had ever truly made her feel like a woman.

That, of course, was what had her going in circles.

With a wince she recalled how she had prattled on about the silliest things. Why would it matter to him that she had made more friends in Rumor than anywhere else? It was true, of course. She was on good terms with Donna Mason, who owned the Getaway, which was Rumor's one spa and a great place to unwind, and she knew Valerie Fairchild, veterinarian, quite well, as she took Tippy to Valerie's animal hospital for shots, checkups and grooming. She had also met and liked Jilly Davis, owner of Jilly's Lilies, a small one-room store filled with plants, cut flowers, ribbons and balloons.

Then there were those acquaintances related to her job—all of the high-school teachers, of course, plus Dee Dee Reingard, president of the PTA, and most of the teachers' spouses. Guy Cantrell was her favorite friend at school and she knew his wife, Wanda. She was a pretty woman with a rather shrewish personality, perhaps the one person Linda had met in Rumor that hadn't been friendly to her.

Of course, there was that oddball, whoever he was, that obviously roamed the streets of Rumor and took weird notions to knock on people's doors for no reason.

In the next instant Linda recalled meeting Susannah McCord, who owned the nursery school, Rumor Rugrats, where Tag took Samantha.

For the first time since moving to Rumor, Linda understood how closely linked its residents were. Everyone knew everyone else, and these people were marrying each other, dating and keeping the pot stirred with friendships, serious relationships, breakups and every other fate that could befall a community of human beings. The same interaction occurred in large cities, of course, but it wasn't so blatantly obvious as it was here.

That progression of thoughts led Linda to wonder again about Tag's way of life. She didn't doubt that he was one of *the* Kingsleys, but if he was in the inner circle, so to speak, why was he living in town and working as a carpenter? Didn't the other members of the family live on the Kingsley Ranch, about ten miles from the center of Rumor?

And she might never learn more about Tag after behaving like a gibbering idiot before leaving his house last night. He couldn't possibly still like her after that humiliating display of immaturity.

She couldn't put her head down and openly suffer over the memory, not with ten sharp-eyed kids in the room, but the thought of Tag not liking her was actually painful. And, damn it, what was wrong with *her* liking him? What was wrong with finally warming up and responding to a man's passion? What a coward she really was, she thought sadly. What Tag had made her feel last night was pure romance. Passion and fire and romance. It had scared the living daylights out of her.

"Ms. Fioretti?"

Linda turned from the window. The kids were cleaning brushes and putting things away. A glance at the clock on the wall told her why. The bell would ring in a few minutes and school would be out for the day.

She shaped a smile and went to stand near her desk at the front of the room. "Is there anyone who thinks they might not be able to complete their project before the end of the year?"

The kids looked at each other, shook their heads and told her no. Linda smiled. "Good." The bell rang and everyone began leaving.

Linda always straightened her classroom before going home, and she was almost finished when Guy stuck his head in.

"Hi. Seen anything of Michael?"

"In an art classroom?" she asked dryly. The only place Michael hung out was the science lab. But Guy knew that better than anyone; she didn't have to remind him. "Why, what's up, Guy?"

"He wanted a ride home. I think he said his bike had a flat. He usually works with me in my home lab after school and he's really excited about… Well, I doubt you'd be interested. If he wanders by and you see him, would you tell him I'm waiting in the parking lot? I'll load his bike in the trunk of my car, so both, uh, me and his bike will be waiting."

Linda couldn't suppress a small chuckle. "Sure, Guy, glad to."

Suddenly eager to see Tag, to somehow let him know that she really was a grown-up and capable of dealing with adult issues, she retrieved her purse from a desk drawer and left first her classroom and then the school.

When she passed Rumor Rugrats, though, the only route she could take to get to her apartment from the high school, she spotted Tag's truck in the nursery school's parking lot. Her heart sank. He was already picking up Samantha, which meant he was through working for the day. If she wanted to see Tag, she would have to knock on his door.

And she couldn't do that. She might be on the verge of a breakthrough as far as her stunted development toward the opposite sex was concerned, but she wasn't quite ready to drop in on a man.

The older children were outside playing in the fenced yard behind the building. It amused Tag that Sammy was considered one of the older children, for she had only turned five a month ago. But since there were cribs and playpens on the premises for the care of infants, he understood the terminology.

Sheree Henry and Dee Dee Reingard were on duty. "Hello, ladies," Tag said with a friendly grin.

"Hello, Tag," Dee Dee said. "How are you?"

Although he'd been undergoing all sorts of new and

confusing feelings, he gave Dee Dee the standard answer to that much-used question. "Fine, and you?"

"Couldn't be better. I love working here with the children. Donna Mason runs back and forth between the Getaway and this place, when she has time, but you can imagine how busy she is with the expansion of her spa. Goodness, the ladies of Rumor can hardly wait for Donna's salon to open. Aren't you doing some of the remodeling for her?"

"Right now she's got plumbers out there putting in sinks and such. She said she would need me in about a week." Donna and Susannah were best friends, and Tag could easily understand Donna trying to help out at the nursery while Susannah was in China, however busy she was herself.

Tag had a soft spot for Dee Dee, as many folks in the area did. Her husband had once been sheriff, but was now in prison after killing his lover. Dee Dee held her head high and did her best to stay involved with friends and neighbors, same as she had before the tragic event, but sometimes she looked as though the burden of that scandal was more than she could bear. She was a wonderful mother to her kids—still had one in high school, Tag was certain, a boy who was on the football team—and the whole town knew that Dee Dee had always been there for her offspring. Obviously, from her work with Susannah's nursery and preschool, she was also there for other people's offspring.

"Your little Samantha is a darling," Dee Dee said.

"Yes, she is," Tag agreed.

"Quiet sometimes, though."

"Yes, she has her quiet moments." Tag didn't want to get into a discussion about the possible reasons for Samantha's sometimes introverted behavior, so he started for the door that opened onto the playground. "I need to get going," he said to Sheree and Dee Dee, and then opened the door and called, "Sammy!"

"Daddy!" Excited to see him, she slid off the swing and ran over to him.

He swung her up into his arms and felt her squeeze his neck while she kissed his cheek. "Time to go home, sweetheart," he said to her.

"Okay, Daddy. Bye," she called to her little friends.

Sheree smiled and waved at Samantha. "Bye, honey."

Tag grinned and said, "Bye, honey," back to her, which caused the teenager to blush.

"I didn't mean you," she said.

"I know you didn't. See you tomorrow, Sheree." He carried Samantha out to his truck and put her inside, making sure she was properly buckled in.

Then he drove away thinking of Linda. In truth, he had thought of little else all day. His jaw tightened and so did his gut. He had moved too fast last night, thinking because she had kissed him back so passionately that she was with him all the way. She hadn't been, and it was damn humiliating to remember her actually having to say no before he got the message.

Well, he knew that message by heart now. Her leaving for work so early this morning could only mean one thing: she hadn't wanted to see him.

Fine. He'd lived a lot of years without Linda Fioretti.

"How about a little trip to MonMart before going home?" he said to Samantha.

"Yes!" Samantha loved going to MonMart. "Can we see Grandpa?" The administration offices were on the second floor of the building, and Stratton Kingsley kept candy in his desk for tiny visitors.

"If he's there, sweetheart. Never know about Grandpa. Sometimes he has things to do at the ranch."

"We could visit him there."

"Yes, we could. But not today. We're going to MonMart for groceries, okay?"

"Okay."

* * *

After entering her apartment and greeting Tippy, Linda checked to see which room Tag had painted today. It was her studio, and he had considerately moved all her completed canvases to the hallway and covered the unfinished one on the easel with sturdy plastic that wouldn't adhere to the painting. He had also left the window open, she noticed and she decided to leave it open at least until bedtime.

She admired the bright new walls, then went to her bedroom to change clothes. A few minutes later, wearing jeans and a sweatshirt, she went downstairs and got Tippy's leash. He danced around, as usual, ever eager for a walk outside, and when they left the apartment Linda made doubly sure that the door was locked.

At the street she turned left. Turning right would take her past Tag's house, and it was unfortunate that a right turn now felt like an infringement on his privacy.

Linda walked at a good pace, stopping only when Tippy had to sniff at something along the road. There was nothing upbeat about her spirits. The realization was unnerving. She could not live like this, she thought, going to work earlier than she should and even avoiding walking past Tag's house so he wouldn't think she was spying on him. She was miserable. It was painful to recall the marvelous sense of peace she'd felt so strongly only a few days ago. She hadn't been at peace, she'd been naive! My God, did one short-lived amorous encounter actually have the power to vanquish the blinders through which she'd viewed life and love for thirty-two years?

State Street curved to the right a short distance from Linda's apartment. It was lovely and quiet, because the town ended near the curve. The country silence had drawn Linda from the first, but today there was a breeze and she could hear the rustling and crackling of leaves and underbrush in the woods on each side of the road.

One careless cigarette tossed from a car could destroy all

this beauty, Linda thought with unusual uneasiness. That was only the breeze causing the sounds she was picking up, wasn't it?

Never had she been leery on this road. For that matter, she'd never had cause to be uneasy over anything in or near Rumor. Well, maybe that eccentric guy had shaken her a bit, but wasn't it really her own imagination scaring her where he was concerned? Obviously the guy was weird but wasn't he also harmless?

Linda stopped walking and pulled on the leash to stop Tippy. Something—or someone—was in the woods! The pleasant breeze did not have big feet, which sounded exactly like what she was hearing tromping through dry grass.

"Okay, Tippy, time to turn around," she muttered. The sounds didn't follow her, and before she reached the big curve, she felt some of the tension leave her body. "Hey, pal, what went on back there?" she said to Tippy. "How come you didn't bark and throw a fit? Afraid of bears, are you?"

But had it really been an animal she'd heard or could it have been the oddball stalker she seemed to have acquired?

A stalker? "Oh my God," she whispered. Who would do such a thing? Paul? No, it was almost laughable to put her ex in that scenario. He'd barely given her the time of day when they were married; he certainly wouldn't interrupt his self-centered life to follow her to Montana, just to give her a scare. And he really had nothing to resent her for, since she had sent him a certified check for half of the sale price of their Culberton house and furniture. No, Paul Fioretti was not in Montana. Besides, the moron who had knocked on her door was not in any way a familiar face, and she would have instantly recognized Paul, whatever his disguise.

Regardless of common sense, the thought of a stalker was off-putting, and Linda was relieved to get home again. But the relief gave way to fury. Damn it, she was *not* going to live in fear! Stalker, indeed. All she'd heard coming from the woods was dry brush and leaves tossed about by a playful breeze.

And she was also not going to live in fear of running into Tag. In fact, she was going to encourage his attentions. Peace and serenity, my left foot, she thought disgustedly. What she needed was a hot, steamy romance.

Tag Kingsley seemed to be just the guy to provide the fuel for that fire. She would definitely be there tomorrow morning when he arrived to paint yet another of her rooms.

Turning the air blue with passionate, inventive curses, Alfred began limping toward his car, which was parked in an almost invisible cut in the trees that he had gratefully happened upon. It was much closer to Linda's apartment than his motel, and his plan had been to hike the shorter distance and hide out until she got home from school and took that accursed mutt of hers for a walk.

Well, she'd done exactly that, but he had nearly fainted when he spotted her coming around the curve in the road and realized his timing was off. Diving for the woods, he'd made a clean getaway; she'd walked right past him. He'd figured this was the long walk he'd been praying she would take. Seeing success in his immediate future, he'd chuckled under his breath.

But his glee was premature. He had been in the process of sneaking through the trees and brush with the intention of angling back to the road at the big curve, behind Linda, but there was no way to move an inch in these damnable woods without making noise. Everything was dry and crunchy, and every step he took made a crackling noise. To him the noise was as loud as a thunderclap, and he prayed it didn't carry clear to the road and Linda's ears. Actually, there was more danger in the mutt hearing him, and he tried even harder to move like James Bond on the trail of a criminal—smoothly, silently, eyes missing nothing, weapon in hand. Although, of course, Alfred had no weapon. Still, he could play the part. What did Bond have that he didn't? Pleased with the simile his agile imagination had devised, Alfred remained intent on his mission.

Then he tripped over something and went flying. The crash reverberated through his own dizzy head, and he sat up and looked for the tiny, invisible object he'd missed with his laser-like eyes. It was a log. *A log!* A fallen tree that was bigger than Alfred.

He swore and struggled to his feet. No way could Linda not have heard that crash. He found an opening in the trees to peer through and saw her turning around and quickstepping back the way she had come. Alfred ground his teeth together in frustration. His stomach hurt and now so did his left ankle.

That was when he began hobbling to his car.

Linda turned off her lights at ten that night and went outside to sit on her balcony for a few minutes before retiring. Tippy trailed her, and immediately lay down in his favorite spot near her feet.

Wishing Tag had come by to talk about the painting of her apartment, if nothing else, Linda looked up at the glorious night sky and sighed. She had caused the ache in her chest herself and maybe she deserved to suffer. Tag had made his intentions very clear. Look at the lovely things he'd said to her before kissing her, telling her how beautiful she was and how smart and talented.

Well, she didn't feel very smart right now and she had *never* felt beautiful. Talented, yes, but certainly not to the degree Tag believed her to be. But that wasn't the point. Unless he was especially good at false sincerity and handing out phony compliments, *he* believed he saw those traits in her—beauty, brains and talent.

Linda sighed again.

But she didn't intend to spend her remaining days and

nights on earth sitting around alone in the dark and sighing over stupid mistakes. She had a surprise planned for Tag's arrival tomorrow morning. Hopefully, he would get the message without her spelling it out, but if he didn't, she was prepared to apologize for her adolescent behavior and let him know that she would like to pick up their burgeoning relationship where she'd stopped it cold last night.

It would be a bold move, and she wasn't completely at ease about it. On the other hand, was she proud of her past aloofness and hands-off coolness with every man she'd met before Paul?

"No," she whispered. She wasn't proud of much that had occurred before her divorce.

Her future was strictly in her own hands. It was *not* going to be a repeat of the past. She deserved any happiness she could make for herself, and she was going to begin that new regime in the morning.

With Tag.

With Samantha.

With Rumor and her teaching career.

There wasn't a reason in the world why life shouldn't be sweet and wonderful in this great town.

Chapter Seven

Before Tag could fit the master key Heck had given him into the lock on Linda's apartment door, it flew open.

"Good morning!" she said brightly.

When Tag's surprise diminished, he realized how glad he was to see her. Who cared if she had avoided him yesterday? She was friendly again and looked pretty as a picture in a blue-and-white dress. He liked that she wore dresses; he was back to liking *everything* about her, in fact.

"Good morning," he replied with equal cheeriness. "How are you this morning?"

"I'm just fine. Please come in." Tag stepped in and set the toolbox he'd brought with him on the floor. Linda shut the door. "There's a fresh pot of coffee in the kitchen and some wonderful pastries I picked up at MonMart's bakery. Would you join me?"

"Sure would." Tag followed her into the kitchen and saw the small table set for two. The sight touched him, reviving his hopes.

Moving too fast had scared her off. She was obviously giving him an opportunity to prove he could spend time with her without grabbing her like a horny, wet-behind-the-ears kid. Should he talk about it? Bring it out in the open so they could both talk about what happened?

"Please sit down," Linda said, going for the coffeepot. She filled the two cups on the table and set the pot on a trivet near the napkin-lined basket of treats between the two place settings. Then she took her seat.

"Do you have time for this?" Tag asked as he brought his cup to his lips for a sip of hot coffee.

"I wouldn't be sitting here if I didn't," Linda said with a smile. "I have a thing about punctuality. Here, have some Danish." She moved the napkin aside so he could see the pastries.

"I had breakfast, but I do love fresh Danish." He took one.

"Me, too." Linda helped herself and took a bite. "Mmm, good." She set the pastry on the small plate in front of her. "I owe you an apology."

"I'm the one who should be doing the apologizing. Linda—"

She held up her hand. "Please, no. You did nothing wrong the other night."

"And you did? No, sweetheart, I got way out of line." Tag looked away for a moment, then shook his head. "Now, why did I start things all over again by calling you sweetheart? Linda, you make me act like someone else. No, that's not it. You make me feel things...." He stopped and frowned. "I don't know what to say to you. Every thought in my head comes out way too personal."

"Maybe not," she said softly. "I'm pleased you like me. I like you, too."

Tag felt like jumping up and dancing around the room. But he remained on his chair and tried to look mature and capable of dealing with anything.

"I'm pleased that you're pleased," he said calmly, though his heart was pounding in his chest like a jungle drum. Everything in the tiny kitchen suddenly seemed sensual, especially the stunningly beautiful woman sitting across the table from him.

Linda laughed. "I am *not* going to say, 'And I'm pleased that you're pleased that I'm pleased.'"

Tag smiled, too, but he didn't really feel like joking. He felt like walking around the table, taking Linda into his arms and kissing her until they were both wild as the animals inhabiting the jungle where those drums kept pounding, pounding, pounding.

Linda glanced at her watch. "I'm going to have to leave."

"You could skip school today and play hooky with me," Tag said, keeping the tone of his voice light and playful even though he was praying she would take him seriously. A whole day together? What an incredible idea. Tag's mouth went dry just from envisioning the possibilities.

"You're quite the kidder," she replied with a laugh and got to her feet. "Don't rush right to work. Sit there and enjoy the coffee and Danish."

But Tag was already on his feet. He watched as she picked up her purse from the counter and then took the rest of the Danish from her plate. "I'll finish it during the drive to school," she told him and started for the doorway.

Tag let her walk past him but then followed her to the front door. "Have a good day," he said quietly.

Linda turned and looked him in the eyes. They were brimming with messages, none of which were as simple as "Have a good day." She juggled her purse and pastry with her left hand and laid her right on his cheek.

"I think I'm reading your mind," she said softly.

"Nothing would thrill me more. Nothing that could happen, that is, while we're fully clothed."

She nodded. "Yes, I am definitely reading your mind. Are you going to be here when I get home this afternoon?"

"Should I be?"

Linda could feel the same nervousness that had ruined Sunday night creeping up on her again. "Um, I'm not sure how to answer that."

Tag saw in her eyes what was happening. She was trying so hard to be either more than she was or less than she was. He wasn't sure which description fit her best, but her reluctance to answer his relatively simple and certainly straightforward question was all about morality, and the kind of woman she perceived herself to be. At least the way she had typecast herself before they met.

He gently took her hand from his cheek. "You don't have to say anything. I know you like me as much as I like you. You're just not ready for more than friendship. It's all right. I'm in no hurry, even though I tried to rush you to the finish line the other night. As for my being here this afternoon when you get home, it depends on how fast I can paint the living room."

Linda couldn't tear her gaze from his. He was so incredibly wonderful that she felt all emotional and weepy, and for the first time since they met she believed in their friendship and Tag's ability to go slowly, whichever direction their relationship went.

"Thank you," she whispered. Clearing her throat, she spoke in a stronger voice. "I really must go."

Tag bent forward and pressed his lips to hers. After a few seconds he broke the kiss and raised his head. He saw her swallow and make motions of composing herself.

"Don't worry. Nothing's mussed," he said, wishing heart and soul that he ended up being the man that mussed her hair for the rest of their lives. He opened the door for her, and she hurried through it. He watched her every step. "One of these days," he said under his breath, absorbed by the feminine swaying of her body as she walked. Then she rounded a corner of the building and was out of sight, and he shut the door, told himself to get a grip, mustered up a whistle and set to work.

* * *

The day seemed to creep by for Linda. She caught herself staring off into space much more often than any teacher should. She wasn't a kid, and she shouldn't be daydreaming about a man during working hours. For that matter, she probably shouldn't be thinking longingly about Tag at all; if she was so fascinated by him, she should do something about it.

But that was easier said than done. It was an awful feeling, and Linda wondered if the painful sensation of being torn apart was the normal result of falling for someone. At thirty-two she was learning and experiencing things most people learned in their teens. She felt abysmally unequipped to deal with her emotions concerning Tag, but her body was a woman's body and it cried out for the pleasures of an adult relationship.

By the end of the day she was a nervous wreck. It was Tuesday, and usually on Tuesdays some of the teachers met at Joe's Bar for a glass of wine or beer and a few laughs before going home. The first time Linda had been invited to join the small group she had been her normal hesitant self about making new friends. But she had reminded herself of the new life she was trying to build in Montana and had bolstered her courage and gone to Joe's. She had been pleasantly surprised. Everyone had been easy to talk to, no one had gotten out of line with personal questions and she had gone home after about an hour feeling pretty darned good about the more outgoing and friendly person she was becoming.

Today, on her way to the parking lot and her car, three different teachers asked if she was going to stop at Joe's. She hemmed and hawed and said, "Maybe. I have to run home for a minute, but then maybe I'll go to Joe's."

Of course she had to run home; Tag might still be there. Suffering tightness in the pit of her stomach during the drive, Linda looked for Tag's truck at Rugrats and breathed slightly easier when she didn't see it. But, when she reached her apartment complex, she realized he wasn't there.

Disappointed enough to cry, she parked, went to her apartment to look after Tippy and then returned to her SUV and drove to Joe's.

Tag had finished painting Linda's living room at two. He debated starting on another room, but when the whole apartment was fresh with new paint, what excuse would he have for stepping foot inside Linda's place? As long as he still had work to do in her apartment, he would be able to see her. His hopes, of course, went a lot further than spending a few minutes together before she left for work.

This whole thing amazed Tag. He'd lived without a serious relationship for five years, and all it had taken to change him from a contented man to one that almost constantly thought about sex and love was meeting one sweet-looking lady. True, Linda wasn't easy to get to know, but the more distant she became with him, the more he wanted her.

Tag used Linda's phone to call his mother at the Kingsley Ranch, then drove to Rugrats and picked up Samantha early. The little girl bounced with excitement when he told her they were going out to the ranch to see Grandma. He stopped at his house so they could gather a few of Samantha's things, at which time Tag mentioned that Sammy would be staying with her grandparents this evening. "Is that okay with you, sweetheart?" he asked.

"I love visiting Grandma and Grandpa, Daddy."

"I know you do, darlin'. And they love visiting with you."

They then made the twelve-mile drive to the ranch. Tag always felt a quiet sort of thrill when he drove the long tree-lined driveway from the ranch's entrance to the main house, his parents' house, the house he'd grown up in. Both of his brothers had homes on ranch property, beautiful homes that exceeded Tag's in cost and elegance. But he never had an urge to follow in Russell's or Reed's footsteps; he was happy with the house he'd built with his own two hands.

The elegant log home in which Stratton and Carolyn Kingsley resided came into view, and Samantha announced, as she always did, "There's Grandma's house, Daddy!"

"Yes, there it is, sweetheart," he said automatically as he frowned over the condition of the pastures visible from the driveway. The grass, normally a brilliant, breathtaking green in June, was brown and yellow. If the area didn't get some rain soon, ranchers were going to feel the financial pinch of having to feed hay long after the usual winter feeding season had passed. And the fields were ripe for a wildfire, Tag thought. He uneasily glanced up at the sky; for rain they needed clouds, but clouds also produced lightning, and one lightning strike could start a fire that might destroy thousands of acres of timber and grassland.

He parked and helped Samantha out of the truck. Carrying her bag, he took her hand and began walking toward the house.

The door opened and his mother stepped outside. Beautifully dressed in a teal pantsuit, with her auburn hair and makeup in perfect order, Carolyn Kingsley, at age sixty, was a remarkably beautiful woman.

"Tag," Carolyn said with a loving smile for her youngest son. "And Samantha. How are you, darling?" She bent from the waist to give Samantha a hug and a kiss, then straightened and kissed Tag on the cheek. "Come inside."

As they went in, Tag asked, "How've you been, Mom?"

"Just fine, thank you."

"Have you heard from Russell and Susannah?"

"Russell called just last night. Heaven only knows what time it was in China. I believe there's almost a twenty-four-hour difference in time zones. It's already tomorrow there. When your father and I did serious traveling, the abrupt changes in time were difficult."

"So what did Russell have to say? Are they getting things done so they can bring the baby home with them?"

Carolyn smiled. "Indeed they are. They're so excited, Tag. Susannah got on the phone for a few minutes and she is absolutely delighted with their whole trip, and, of course, the idea of having that adorable child for their very own. Russell said they should be home in about a week."

"Well, good for them." He grinned. "Have you been planning a big wedding, Mom?"

"I would like a big wedding, but that's not what they want. Before they left for China they told me they are planning a simple ceremony at the Rumor Community Church."

Tag nodded his approval. "I don't blame them a bit. In fact, I admire their decision."

"You would," Carolyn said with a knowing expression. It wasn't phony, either. She knew all her children through and through. Each one possessed his or her own personality, although Russell was very much like Stratton. Tag, from childhood, had demanded independence; Reed was her wild-card child, with his hand in a dozen different pots at any given time; and Maura, beautiful, lovable Maura, was her only daughter.

Tag let his mother's remark pass, for he knew she hadn't meant anything derogatory by it. She accepted him as he was, and he loved her for understanding him, faults and all. Not everyone in the family always had, although that chapter of Kingsley history seemed closed these days.

"I brought Sammy's overnight bag, just in case."

"Just in case, my eye. If you are out late, please do not drive clear out here and wake this precious child from a sound sleep. You can pick her up in the morning. Is that all right with you, Samantha? Would you like to stay overnight with Grandpa and me? We always have a good time, don't we?"

"Yes, Grandma," the little girl said.

Only Tag heard the quiet note in his daughter's voice. She loved her grandparents, but she loved him more, and he knew she would rather sleep at home. But he had to get out once in a while, and he never left Samantha with a stranger. She was as safe here with her loving grandparents as she was in her own home.

Still, he realized that a five-year-old didn't always understand the obvious, and he knelt in front of his daughter and gave her a big hug.

"I promise that I'll be here bright and early in the morning to take you to school," he said to her. She loved Rumor Rugrats and playing with the other kids, and since Tag had never told her it was really a place for working parents to leave their children, Samantha had believed from her first day there that she was going to school. There were some classes, of course, simple lessons about letters of the alphabet, numbers and colors, and Sammy was always bringing home drawings, so it was apparent to Tag that the children were encouraged to express themselves with paper and crayons.

That was one thing Tag intended to talk to Susannah about when she got home from China; why not have a real artist give the kids some pointers on drawing and coloring? He'd thought of that when he'd first seen Linda's studio and recognized her talent, although he hadn't yet mentioned the idea to her. Tonight might be a good time to bring it up, in fact.

"Okay, Daddy," Samantha said, visibly brightened by his promise.

After another hug and a kiss, Tag stood. "I'll see you in the morning, Mom."

Carolyn took Samantha's hand and they walked Tag to the door. "Have a good time, dear," Carolyn said.

"Thanks, Mom." Walking to his truck, he waved at Samantha before getting in. And during the drive back to

Rumor he kept thinking of his mother's good wishes. *Have a good time.*

Why did something that shouldn't even take effort to attain seem to be keep hovering just out of reach? He would love to have a good time with Linda. He would love connecting so solidly with her that they became a couple, with everyone in town knowing and accepting the significance of their relationship.

Still pondering the mysteries of life and love, Tag turned left on Main Street and left again on State Street. He pulled into the parking area of Linda's apartment building, but almost immediately saw that her carport parking space was empty. Was she still at school? The time was iffy on an answer to that question, as he really wasn't familiar with her work schedule.

"Okay, we'll just go and see if your rig is at the high school," he said out loud.

It wasn't. In fact, there were only a few cars in the school's parking lot. "Hmm," he murmured. Leaving the lot, he slowly drove back to Main Street and decided he would go home for a shower and then return to Linda's apartment. She was probably shopping at MonMart and would be home by then.

After a shower, shave and a change of clothes, Tag dialed Linda's number and got her voice mail. He almost said something, then changed his mind and hung up. She *still* wasn't home! He started to worry and remembered the peculiar guy who had walked into Linda's apartment the first day Tag had gone there. She had sworn that she'd locked the door, but it had seemed obvious to Tag that she couldn't have. Now he wondered if he hadn't been a little too quick to doubt her memory. Weirdos and criminals showed up in Rumor every so often same as any other place.

With his heart in his throat, Tag hurried from his house and, walking past his truck, jumped into his SUV, which he used when he didn't have to haul tools and building supplies.

He drove a little faster than he should have, pulled into the parking lot of Linda's apartment complex once again and stared at her empty carport space through narrowed, suspicious eyes. This time he parked in a visitor's space, got out and practically ran to her front door. He tried the knob but the lock was engaged. He used his key to get in and then walked through the apartment, calling, "Linda? Are you here?"

Tippy was there and excited to see him, but Linda wasn't.

Mumbling under his breath, he returned to his vehicle and then sat there wondering where in hell she was. Not that everything she did was his business. But he *wanted* it to be his business, damn it!

Slapping the steering wheel, he started the engine and drove away. He was passing Joe's Bar, which he'd done a good half-dozen times today, as it was almost directly across the street from his house, when he spotted Linda's SUV in the busy parking lot. Startled, he took a second look and felt as though the air was leaving his body. *Should I drop in to Joe's or shouldn't I?*

He could see himself doing it. Walking in, pretending he didn't know Linda was there and putting on a big show of surprise when he saw her. Rather, when *she* saw him!

"Hell," he mumbled. She could be with a man, and wouldn't he feel like a total jackass if that were the case.

He took a sharp left into his own driveway, jerked his way out of the cab of his truck and entered the house. He felt as though his hair was standing on end, and the ache in his gut was close to unbearable. Why hadn't he factored another man into the picture before this? Had he suddenly become thickheaded, too dense to see the forest for the trees?

Tag strode from room to room, devising and discarding ideas to win Linda away from the lucky guy who had obviously gotten a lot further with her than he had. Being liked by Linda wasn't enough; he wanted to be *loved* by Linda.

Finally, his system calmed enough to permit clearer thinking. Her companion at Joe's could just as likely be female as male, and he shouldn't jump to conclusions.

Then Tag remembered the guy who had walked into her apartment that day—just opened the door and walked in. Regardless of Linda's vehement denials, it made sense that the man had a key. Maybe *he* was the one who rang her bells. Maybe *he* was over at Joe's right now, sitting close to Linda in a booth and…and….

Tag gave his head a shake, denying a scenario that caused him far too much pain to dwell on for long. Besides, the man who had walked in that day had been a strange-looking bird, and how could a woman of Linda's caliber find *him* attractive?

In the next heartbeat he came to a decision. He went to the nearest telephone and dialed her home number. This time he left a message on her voice mail.

"Hi, Linda. Tag here. I know it's short notice but I was wondering if you'd have dinner with me tonight at the Rooftop Café. Or, if you'd prefer, we could drive to Billings, which has some great restaurants. Give me a call when you can. You know the number."

He hung up, wandered the house some more, then found himself at a front window. Joe's Bar wasn't directly across State Street—the bar was on the northeast corner of State and Main and Tag's house was at least one large lot down from the corner on the west side of State—but he could see the place fairly well by craning his neck. He located Linda's SUV in the parking lot, then despised himself for acting like a jealous, slightly demented lover when he had no right to judge anything she did.

He had an excuse for behaving that way, though, he told himself as he forced himself from the window: His damn heart felt shattered.

The group of teachers—four of them today—exited Joe's for

the parking lot after an hour of kidding around and laughing over each other's stories about the pranks, jokes and personalities of their students. Linda walked with Shelby Peterson, the English teacher, to their vehicles, which they had parked side by side. Linda liked Shelby, who was also divorced and about her own age, although they hadn't actually compared birth dates. Shelby lived in Whitehorn and made the daily commute to Rumor. No big deal, she said.

Shelby had a rather wry way of putting things, which made Linda laugh. Like herself, she lived alone, but Shelby owned a house and claimed to loathe apartments. In fact, that was the topic under discussion as they walked to their respective vehicles. "People coming and going at all hours drove me up the wall," Shelby said about her one attempt at "living in a box with windows," as she put it. "Really, Linda, you should consider looking for a house that suits you. Rumor might have a shortage of homes for sale, but I'm sure you'd find something to your liking in Whitehorn or Billings. Mortgage payments are comparable to rent, and you get a tax break on the interest. Besides, real estate almost always appreciates."

"It makes sense," Linda agreed. "I'll give it some thought." They had reached their cars. "See you tomorrow, Shelby."

"Right."

Linda got into her SUV. Recalling some of Shelby's comical remarks about her ex-husband made Linda smile. She wished she could think of something funny to say about Paul.

Chapter Eight

Tippy practically turned himself inside out with excitement when Linda got home. "You're lonesome, aren't you?" she said as she knelt and hugged her little buddy. "How about a walk before dinner?" Tippy yipped, as though saying, "Hurrah!"

Laughing, Linda went upstairs to change clothes. She dropped her washable cotton dress in the clothes hamper and pulled on jeans and a sweatshirt. After finger-combing her long hair back from her face, she secured its bulk with an elastic band at her nape. She returned to the first floor and took Tippy's leash from the foyer coat closet, where she'd been keeping it since Tag entered her life.

Hooking the leash to the dog's collar, Linda led him outside, securely locked the door, tucked the key into a pocket of her jeans and began walking.

She had not even thought about checking her voice mail, nor did she see the sheer curtain move aside at the window of a first-floor apartment at the front of the building as she walked past it. The seventy-three-year-old woman who lived in that apartment, Mrs. Clara Raymond, watched Linda take a right turn at the street, then dropped the curtain back in place, making sure it hung straight. People-watching was a favorite pastime of Clara's, much more interesting than television soaps or talk shows, and it gave her something to talk about. Tomorrow, when she and Alice Alden, her dear friend, sat and sipped coffee at the Calico Diner, which they did nearly every day, she could bring up Linda Fioretti again. Clara loved discussing Linda, and Alice loved talking, period. They had been friends for forty years and got along famously.

Linda didn't stay on State Street, which would take her past Tag's house. Instead she went left on Main and walked toward the Getaway. But she thought about Tag and wondered if she was back to being her boring old self, a woman who wouldn't knock on a man's door uninvited for all the tea in China. Hadn't she turned over a new leaf just this morning, even flirting with Tag, letting him know quite clearly how she felt about him?

So why the teeter-totter act? she asked herself, and sighed because the truth was so silly. He hadn't been at the apartment when she'd gone home the first time, and maybe his absence had meant something, such as, "I really don't want to see you again today."

"Your inexperience is showing again," she mumbled under her breath, realizing how a lack of experience with men could work against a woman. Darn, she thought, if I could just once stick to a plan instead of vacillating all over the place, I might get somewhere with Tag.

But why hadn't he been there? She'd counted on seeing him the whole darn day.

Maybe Tag is no more dependable than Paul when it comes to dates and being on time, or giving a damn about your feelings!

Linda's heart skipped a beat, leaving what felt like a hole in her chest. Was Tag considerate when it suited him and indifferent when it didn't?

While Linda walked briskly, Clara Raymond noticed the man approaching the door to Linda's apartment. He looked over his shoulder several times, as though watching for someone, and then, when he reached the door he seemed a bit confused. At least that was how he appeared to Clara, who was, after all, only able to see his back.

Good neighbor that she was, she decided to help him out. She hurried from her apartment and strode spryly toward Linda's place, calling, "Young man! Hello!"

Alfred jumped as though he'd just touched a hot stove. Who was that busybody? Why was she screeching at him? This was his chance. He could have Paul's journal in his possession in minutes, return to the motel for his things and leave this burg in the dust. It would be, without a doubt, the happiest day of his life.

Clara descended upon him. "You must be Linda's beau. I've seen you around here before. She's not home. She took Tippy for a walk. You might be able to catch up with her. I saw her leave, and she went right at the street. My, you look pale. Are you feeling all right? We haven't had a flu bug in these parts since about February, I believe it was, but you never know, do you?"

Alfred tried not to look directly at her. All the same, he'd seen enough to notice her resemblance to his grandma Wallinski. In some ways little old ladies all looked the same to him. It was the way they wore their gray hair, short and tightly permed. Also, many of them wore gold- or silver-rimmed glasses, exactly like those perched on this one's nose.

"Uh, thanks," he mumbled, and started walking away.

"I'll tell Linda you came by," Clara called out cheerfully.

Alfred put his head down and kept going. Disappointment was eating another hole in his gut. That old bat should be told to mind her own business, and if she hadn't looked like his grandmother he would've turned the air blue with a tirade she would never have forgotten.

"Aw, hell," he muttered. He couldn't swear at old ladies, even though that one was going to make it even harder for him to get near Linda's apartment by telling her that he'd been at her door. Damn it to hell!

Linda and Tippy approached the Getaway and slowed down. The spa had impressed Linda during her first visit, and she considered stopping to get the kinks worked out of her tightly wound body.

She was almost past the place when she heard a woman calling her name. Turning around, she saw Donna coming out a side door. "Well, hi," she called back. "How are you?"

The two women walked toward each other. Donna Mason was thirtysomething, Linda estimated, tall and willowy, with short blond hair and intense blue eyes. Linda had admired her at their first meeting; she seemed so in control of her own destiny, extremely confident and slightly aloof. Her ambition was evident from her success with the Getaway, and now she was expanding the business to include a salon.

"I'm busy every moment of every day and I love it. How are you? How's the art world?"

"Fine and fine. When's the grand opening?"

"Next week, if everything goes according to plan. Right now, plumbers from Billings are putting in new pipes and sinks. When they're done, Tag will put the finishing touches on each of the manicure and hairstyling stations. Do you know Tag? Tag Kingsley? Have you met him yet?"

Linda tried to ignore the more rapid beating of her heart, caused solely by hearing Tag's name. "He's in the process of painting my apartment."

"Oh, yes, that's right. He mentioned something about a contract to do the whole complex. He's a terrific guy, don't you think?"

"Terrific," Linda agreed, and quickly changed the subject. "So have you found some good beauticians?"

"Three very good beauticians. Two live in Billings and the other lives in Whitehorn. I don't know if they'll move here or not, but the commute to either place isn't that bad." Donna glanced toward her car. "Sorry to cut this short, but I have to go and check on Rugrats and then get back here and check on the plumbers and… Well, I'm sure you get the picture."

"That's right, you're keeping an eye on the nursery for Susannah while she's in China. Did I read that in the paper or did someone tell me about it?"

"Heaven only knows around this place," Donna said dryly but with a smile. "I love Rumor and every gossip who lives here, but I know my life is an open book for anyone with the desire to turn the pages. You're in the same boat, I'd be willing to bet. Unmarried women are favorite topics of discussion in any small town. Think of the possibilities they present." Donna grinned rather devilishly. "I say let 'em talk. I've not yet spent a sleepless night over anything anyone ever said about me, and I doubt I ever will."

Linda's vision clouded for a second. Were people really talking about her just because she wasn't married? Had Donna heard derogatory remarks about her? What could they be? Dare she ask?

Donna interrupted her discomfiting thoughts. "I have to get going. Try to make the grand opening, Linda. It'll be fun."

Linda managed to pull herself together. "I'm sure it will, and yes, I'll try to make it. Good luck, Donna."

"Thanks."

They parted company and went in different directions. Linda decided that she had walked Tippy long enough and she turned around to go home. Her heart was beating unnaturally fast, and she felt strangely out of breath. Donna's take on the local gossip was disturbing. Linda didn't like thinking that she might be the topic of the day for some people, nor could she imagine what portion of her quiet way of life would pique anyone's interest. Heavens, she hadn't had a real date, for instance, since she moved to Rumor. And surely, her having dinner at Tag's house on Sunday hadn't raised eyebrows. Or had it?

A bit confused—and uneasy—about small-town grapevines, Linda rushed Tippy along. She was unusually relieved to reach her apartment complex, and she hurried up the sidewalk toward her door.

"Yoo-hoo! Linda, wait a moment, dear."

Startled, Linda turned around to see who was calling out to her. "Oh, Mrs. Raymond. Hello. Is anything wrong?"

"Oh my, no." Clara tittered. "I have something to tell you. You know how I love watching the children at play. Sometimes I take my knitting and sit in a lawn chair to see them better and hear their happy little voices. They weren't playing outside my window today, but I happened to be looking out at a propitious moment and saw your young man at your door."

Tag! Oh my God, Donna was right! Nothing goes unnoticed in Rumor. Linda drummed up a weak smile. "Thank you for telling me."

"I'm not through yet, dear. When I saw him, I hurried outside to tell him that you had left with Tippy only a short time ago and that he could easily catch up with you, if he so desired. Did he find you? He rushed away after I had only gotten out a few words."

A creepy-crawly feeling suddenly traveled Linda's spine. Clara Raymond probably knew everyone in town, and she hadn't said, "Tag Kingsley came by." She'd said, "I saw your young man was at your door."

"No," she said slowly. "He didn't find me. Tell me, Mrs. Raymond, have you seen him before?"

"Oh, yes, several times."

"So you know his name."

"Well, no. He's new to town, same as you, dear."

"I see." Linda didn't know whether to laugh or cry. That man, whoever he was, had come to her door again. That weird little man who was both comical and frightening was indeed stalking her. For what reason, for God's sake? She was positive that she had never set eyes on him before Rumor, so why on earth would he even know she was alive, let alone attempt to…?

Attempt what? He'd had several opportunities to harm her, but had run away.

"Well, thank you, Mrs. Raymond," she said with a forced smile.

"You're quite welcome, dear. Do stop in and have a cup of tea with me sometime. I know you're busy right now, what with the school year drawing to a close, but after that you should have plenty of time for your friends."

"Yes, of course. Thanks again." Linda pulled Tippy along and finally reached the peace and quiet of her apartment. After freeing Tippy from the leash, Linda all but collapsed on the living-room sofa. What in heaven's name was happening? The serenity she'd been so thrilled to find in Rumor had slipped and slid away until it had vanished completely. Now everything was topsy-turvy, and how had it happened without her cooperation, knowledge or approval?

"Damn, damn, damn," she moaned and covered her head with one of the decorative pillows she had added to her sofa. A new possibility brought her to a sitting position. Maybe that guy had lived in this apartment before her. Maybe he'd forgotten something in it, or in his feeble mind, *believed* he'd forgotten something and merely wanted to get into the apartment and look for it.

"Now you're really reaching," she muttered in self-disgust. Anyone with a lick of sense knew that items left in an apartment were removed before the next renter took possession. That idiot should be stalking Heck, not her!

Pushing herself to her feet, Linda went to the kitchen to check the contents of the refrigerator. Not that she was all that hungry, but it was dinnertime and it was something to do.

Linda pulled out some cheese for a sandwich, then eyed

the telephone and decided to check her voice mail. The message from Tag brought tears to her eyes. She could be eating dinner with him right this minute instead of contemplating a cold cheese sandwich.

"All right, that does it," she said out loud, and after locating Tag's home number, she dialed it.

He answered on the second ring. "Hello?"

"Tag, I just now got your message. I'm terribly sorry. I was gone and—"

"Yes, I know you were gone. You just now got home?" Visualizing her in Joe's for that long a time hurt like hell. Maybe he didn't have the right to ache over anything Linda did, but he couldn't fight pain with common sense.

"Yes, but—"

"It's okay, forget it."

"But I don't want to forget it. You asked me to dinner. Is it too late to say yes?"

"Well, I already ate. Haven't you?"

Linda eyed the cheese on the counter and gave up. "Yes, I had something. I'm just so sorry about missing your call."

She sounded so forlorn that Tag forgot all about the reason she'd missed his call. "I could pick up some dessert and bring it by," he said hopefully. "You see, Sammy's at the ranch for the night and I'm a free agent. I was planning on… Never mind, forget dinner, but how about that dessert?"

"The ranch?"

"My folks' place."

"Oh, yes, the Kingsley Ranch." She really should try harder to think of Tag as one of the wealthy-beyond-imagination Kingsleys, but he was such a down-to-earth guy, and he lived such an ordinary life, that it was difficult putting him in that picture. Besides, when she did manage to do so, she became all addled and uneasy. She would much rather take Tag at face value, which was priceless in her estimation.

She wasn't going to worry about that now. "Bring some

dessert if you want to, but give me twenty minutes for a shower, all right?" She'd spoken in a low, husky voice that startled even her. What would it do to Tag, or would he notice?

He noticed. He felt the sensual timbre of her voice in every cell of his body, especially when she added, "If I don't answer the door right away, I'll still be upstairs. Use your key to come in."

"Be there in twenty." He hung up, checked his watch, then stood there with his blood rushing through his body and his heart pounding. Springing into action, he hurried to his bedroom to get a few things, then out to the truck. Driving to the Calico Diner, he bought two pies, one banana cream, one apple. Both were guesses; he had no idea what kind of pie Linda preferred.

With the boxed pies on the seat of the truck, he checked his watch again. He would arrive at Linda's door right on time.

Excited, though nervous and anxious, he drove the short distance and parked in a visitor's space. It was getting dark, and he looked up at the window and balcony of Linda's bedroom. The lighted window seemed warm and inviting, exciting him further, and he stopped gawking, took the pies from the seat and walked around the building to reach her front door.

He had no idea that he was being watched by Clara Raymond, nor would he have cared if he had known. Truth was, he was used to Rumor's citizens keeping track of him and everyone else in the area, and he wasted very little time wondering or worrying about what he might do that someone would find interesting enough to pass on.

When Linda didn't answer the doorbell, he balanced the pies in his left hand and dug the key Heck had given him from his pocket with his right. He let himself in and shut the door.

"Linda?" he called.

"I'm up here," she called back. "I'll just be a few more minutes. Make yourself at home."

"Thanks." Tag brought the pies to the kitchen and then went to the foot of the stairs and looked up. The thought of Linda all warm and dewy-skinned from her shower was too vivid an image to ignore or pretend it didn't matter. He took the stairs two at a time and stopped just short of her bedroom door, which she'd left open.

He rapped on the woodwork and asked, "Anybody home?"

"Tag!" Linda whirled away from the closet, where she'd been trying to decide what to put on. She was wearing a comfortable cotton wrapper, almost sheer now from uncountable launderings. He looked wonderful to her, so big and strong and manly, so handsome, and she knew she wasn't going to berate him for too much boldness tonight. She walked toward him.

"Am I too early?" he asked.

"I think your timing couldn't be more perfect." She stood in front of him and laid her hands on his chest. "I'm dressed for the occasion, wouldn't you say?"

His blood pressure soared. He had hoped, but had he really expected this kind of welcome? She was hardly dressed at all. Her wrapper wasn't transparent, but it was close. Sucking in a deep breath, he put his arms around her and held her so close to his own body that he could feel the sweet curves of hers.

"Linda, sweetheart," he whispered thickly. "I'm getting some powerful messages from you."

"And I from you. Oh, Tag." She turned up her face and stood on tiptoe to kiss his lips.

He reacted spontaneously, bringing her closer still and all but devouring her lips and mouth. It was a kiss of such intense passion and desire that Linda's legs got weak. She clung to him for support and for the thrills of combined pleasure and agonizing need darting throughout her body.

"Tag," she managed to whisper hoarsely between kisses. "I'm completely under your spell."

"My spell?" She almost smiled, but instead whispered, "Oh, Tag, dear, wonderful Tag. You make me feel like someone living a fairy tale. Is this really me?"

"It's you, sweetheart, never doubt it." He untied the sash of her wrapper and slipped it off her shoulders. Stepping back just a few inches, he filled his eyes. "I knew you'd be this beautiful," he said raggedly. He touched her full breasts and gently caressed her nipples.

"I want to see you," she said. He quickly obliged her by pulling his shirt over his head. "Your jeans, too," she said breathlessly.

He unbuttoned and unzipped them and then slid both his jeans and underwear down to his ankles, where he kicked off first his shoes and then the clothing. He yanked off his socks and then stood there and let her look at him.

"See anything you like?" he asked with a wickedly teasing light in his eyes as he watched her eyes move up and down his body.

"You're…incredible," she whispered.

His lips tipped slightly. "So are you. Come closer."

They both moved closer, and their next kiss included the wildly arousing sensation of hot bare skin against hot bare skin. Then their lovemaking took on another dimension. Tag picked her up and carried her to bed. He laid her on the mattress and followed her down.

She spread her legs for him and then moaned sensually when he rubbed against her most sensitive spot and kissed her hungrily at the same time. Her mind was dazed, but still able to form a few questions: Was she going to regret doing this tomorrow? Next week? A year from now?

"Tag, we need protection. I'm not using anything."

"I have it. Don't go away." He left her just long enough to get the small foil packets he'd put in the back pocket of his jeans before leaving his house, just in case. He dropped one on the nightstand and used the other.

He returned to Linda's arms and in seconds felt as though there'd been no interruption at all. He loved kissing her mouth and spent long delicious minutes exploring. Her responsiveness was exciting; she was all woman, just as he'd told her. It didn't take long, hot kisses to prove her complete and utter femaleness; he'd sensed that about her from the start.

But he needed those kisses. The intensity of his passion astonished him. The smoothness of her skin and the tantalizing curves of her body amazed him. It was as though he'd never really made love before, that every other interaction he'd had with women had been child's play and insignificant. This was *very* significant, more meaningful than any other adult act of his life. Its meaning was quite clear to him: He was in love. He'd fallen in love with Linda the second he had laid eyes on her.

He almost told her. The words were in his throat, traveling from the core of his heart to his lips, and it took all the willpower he possessed to keep from saying them. She scared easily. Dare he forget Sunday night and how she had broken away from his arms? He had gone too fast that night and she'd run away. Tonight she had come to grips with the reality of their need for each other. But baring his soul just might destroy everything. He couldn't take that chance.

Linda was so feverish from his kisses and caresses that she could no longer lie still. There were mysterious forces at work, things she didn't quite understand. Tag knew things about her. He knew her body better than she did, and how could that be?

His body was a work of art. Even though her brain was fuzzy from feelings she had only read about before this, she knew that his body was perfectly proportioned. The live male models she had drawn uncountable times in college classrooms had not been as perfectly formed as Tag.

"Oh, please," she moaned. "Tag. Tag."

He heard the gravelly plea of her voice. He felt her wetness between her legs, and he knew they were both ready for the ultimate pleasure. He didn't plunge into her, although it took almost superhuman effort to keep things slow and easy with so much testosterone raging through his system. He'd never wanted a woman more.

But this wasn't just the hottest sex he'd ever experienced, he was also in love with this incredible lady. With his mouth on hers he gently slid into her. Surprise bolted through him; she was almost unnaturally tight. In the next heartbeat, though, the pleasure of their shared movements overcame even the ability to form a complete thought.

Linda's hips rose when his did and fell back each time he pushed into her. She was dazed and dazzled and so over-whelmed with all that was happening to her that she couldn't contain her emotions and they expelled themselves in the form of tears. Moaning, she dug her fingertips into his back, and she heard herself moan again with each thrust of his body. She couldn't seem to silence herself, nor did it really matter. Nothing mattered, nothing but the feelings building in the pit of her stomach. Something necessary to life itself, so it seemed, was just out of reach, and she had to have it. She lifted her hips higher and wrapped her legs around him.

"I need…I need…" she stammered hoarsely.

"Darlin', we're riding the same wave, believe me," Tag mumbled. He buried his face in the glorious mass of her hair on the pillow, burrowed his hands beneath her hips to raise them even higher and released all the stoppers he'd placed on himself to make sure she got as much joy out of this as he did.

He knew the exact moment she went over the edge. Grateful and proud that he had satisfied her, he sought his own release.

When it came it was a stunner, and he fell forward feeling weak as a newborn kitten.

They lay like that, intertwined, breathless and unmoving, for a very long time.

Chapter Nine

Linda learned something else that evening; the aftermath of great lovemaking was almost as pleasurable as what had come before it.

But not quite. As deliciously relaxed as she was, she knew that nothing else could compare with the kind of sexual gift Tag had just bestowed upon her.

He raised himself to an elbow and looked into her eyes. "Everything okay?" he asked softly.

"You have no idea," she murmured, then smiled a little over what she perceived to have been a rather ridiculous reply. "Sorry, guess you were there, weren't you?"

"Every step of the way, sweetheart." He began rearranging her hair on the pillow, spreading it around her head and pleasing her because he so obviously liked what he was doing. He smiled. "You have the most incredible hair. The color, the length. Why don't more women wear their hair long like this?"

"Maybe because it's a lot of work."

"Takes longer to dry than short hair, right?"

"Much longer."

He played with her hair a few minutes more then asked quietly, "May I stay all night?"

Linda hadn't thought of that, but decided that she probably should have. With Samantha at her grandparents' ranch for the night, there was no reason for Tag to hurry home. "Maybe," she said and saw a devilish twinkle come into his eyes. "You're not planning on a good night's sleep, are you?"

Tag arched an eyebrow. "Sleep? What's that?"

She couldn't help laughing, but it was short-lived. In an instant she became serious. "I'm not sure I should tell you this, but I..." Her spurt of honesty faltered as the memory of stumbling over her own words at his house on Sunday night assaulted her senses. Honesty was priceless to her, but so was privacy. Was it necessary for Tag to know that he had brought her sensual side to life tonight? Someday, perhaps, depending on how things went for them, but not this soon, she decided.

Tag dipped his head to move his lips over her face. "You what, sweetheart?"

"It's not important," she murmured.

Everything about her was important to Tag, but he realized that she wasn't ready to share "everything" with him. Again he reminded himself to take it one slow step at a time.

Lovingly he traced the line of her jaw with his forefinger. His thumb caressed her cheekbones. "You are seriously beautiful," he said softly.

"Oh, Tag, I'm not," she said with just a hint of a shy and girlish smile.

He loved this side of her. "Hasn't anyone told you that before?"

"Of course not."

Was she serious? "Not in all your life?" he persisted.

"Not in all of my thirty-two years."

A loud and disturbing warning bell sounded in Tag's head. He was six years younger, and self-preservation or simply his ample supply of horse sense told him that Linda wouldn't like being that much older. It was a subject to avoid.

"That's really hard to believe," he said. "There must be something wrong with the men in California."

"Men are men," she said quietly, then peered deeply into his eyes again. "There are exceptions, of course," she added. "You seem to be a major exception."

"Thus far, you mean?"

"Thus far is as far as we are, isn't it?" She reached up and gently swept a lock of his hair to the side of his forehead. "You're a remarkably handsome man."

"Aw, shucks, ma'am," he said, feigning embarrassment.

She laughed. "You know you're good-looking, don't you?"

"Been a doll all my life," he drawled.

"A modest doll," she retorted. "How old are you, doll-face?" She thought he would laugh over that silly endearment but he seemed to freeze up instead.

He recovered quickly, though, and answered, "About the same as you. We're a perfect match, sweetheart. Say, did I mention the pies sitting on your kitchen counter?"

"You really did bring dessert? What kind of pies?"

"One banana cream, one apple. Should we have some?"

"Yes!"

They scrambled out of bed, wrapped sheets around themselves and went downstairs. Tippy went with them, and Linda stopped to reassure the little dog.

In the kitchen they dished up slabs of pie and poured glasses of milk. "Mmm, this is great," Linda said after her first bite of banana cream. Her cheese sandwich eaten on the run hadn't been much of a dinner, and the pie hit the spot. Especially since it was delicious. "Who made these pies?"

"Someone at the Calico Diner."

"And they sell whole pies. That's good to know." Linda

took a swallow of milk. "You know, I learn something new about Rumor nearly every day."

"And I'm sure Rumor learns something new about you nearly every day," Tag said dryly. "The *Rumor Mill* publishes all the local news that's fit to print. Rumor's gossip mill isn't quite so fussy."

"Why on earth would anyone gossip about me? I mean, I know people talk around here. I heard that from the first. But my lifestyle shouldn't raise anyone's eyebrows."

"You're young and attractive. Actually, it's the attractive part that whips the gossips into a lather."

"And you've felt the brunt of those wagging tongues yourself?"

"Oh, yes. Not for a while now, but when the town gets wind of you and I showing interest in each other, those tongues will go into overdrive, believe me."

Linda set her fork on her plate. "That picture isn't exactly comforting."

Tag shrugged. "Just act like you couldn't care less. Actually, you *shouldn't* care. Let it all roll off your back as though you never heard a word. That's if you happen to hear a word."

"Donna Mason said something similar."

"Donna marches to her own drummer and doesn't give a damn what anybody thinks or says about it. I like her style."

"Have…have you dated her?"

"Donna? Heck no. We're friends. Since you brought it up, maybe you wouldn't mind talking about your past. No, that came out wrong. The term *your past* sounds like a person is concealing deep, dark secrets. I guess I'm just curious about, well, you know."

He was hemming and hawing, not at all characteristic of the way he had behaved around her up to this point. Linda knew exactly what he was beating around the bush about, though. She had said very little about her marriage and divorce. He was curious about her past relationships.

She slowly picked up her fork and took a small bite, giving herself a moment to decide which way to go. Tag wasn't just anyone, she told herself. They had created a bond this evening that would mean something to her for the rest of her days. He'd taught her things about her own body that she should have known long before this. He'd taken her to the stars in her own bed, and if anyone had a right to know a few facts about her past, he did.

"I was married right out of college," she said quietly. "And divorced just before I moved here."

"You were married a long time. Long enough to have kids. What happened there?"

"Intense disappointment happened. I wanted children very much, he didn't."

"I'm sorry," Tag said. The pie on their plates and the milk in their glasses were gone. He got off the stool, tucked the sheet more securely around himself and brought the dishes to the dishwasher.

Linda watched him. "You don't have to do that."

He closed the door of the dishwasher and returned to take her hand and urge her from her stool. "I doubt that putting two small plates and two glasses in your dishwasher shortened my life any. Come on, sweetheart, let's go back to bed."

Moved over a simple kindness, Linda batted her eyelids in an attempt to stave off threatening tears. "Yes," she whispered. "Let's go back to bed."

They climbed the stairs arm in arm.

Linda woke slowly and heard the shower running. Tag had beaten her to the bathroom. She glanced at the clock and saw how early it was. She had plenty of time to get ready for the workday ahead.

Stretching lazily, she thought about the long, delectable night of lovemaking and togetherness, and smiled in utter contentment. Was this warm, mellow feeling significant? Had she fallen in love last night? Were hours of shared emotion and pleasure a strong enough foundation upon which to build a lasting relationship?

There was no question about her being gun-shy. One bad marriage was one too many. If she ever married again, everything would have to be perfect, or as close to perfect as human interaction could get. She knew the importance of sex now, and for just a moment she let herself wonder if she would have been more tolerant of Paul's flaws if their sex life had been good.

But she didn't linger on thoughts of Paul for long. Tag was her man now, and she stretched again and counted the times they had made love during the night. Giggling like a schoolgirl, wondering if her face was as flushed as her body felt from her very hot memories, she snuggled deeper into the blankets. They smelled of Tag. They smelled of sex.

A sudden image of him naked and wet in the shower invaded her brain and made her gasp. Last night he'd told her to be bold, to just let go and do whatever came naturally. It seemed natural to her this morning to join him in the shower, and she threw aside the blankets and padded barefoot and naked to the bathroom door.

With her heart pounding, she opened it and saw Tag's form behind the frosted-glass shower door. She eased over and slid the door back. Without a word, she stepped inside and wrapped her arms around him from behind.

Tag was already aroused. He'd *awakened* aroused, and the only reason he hadn't woke Linda was that he'd brought her awake so many times during the night.

He turned around and enclosed her in his arms. The shower water beat on his back. "I can't get enough of you either," he said huskily, summing up her assertiveness in one intuitive sentence.

She merely nestled closer to his wet and slippery body, letting go, as he'd directed her to do in the night, and cherishing the rising tide of desire again.

He dropped kisses all over her wet face, then settled his mouth on hers. It was a hot and hungry kiss, and in seconds he lifted her from the shower floor. She hooked her legs around him and he slid his hard manhood into her. Every time they made love Linda thought it couldn't get any better, but each time it did. They weren't using protection this time, and she didn't care. Her body burned like a wildfire. He was right; she couldn't get enough of him.

They climaxed together, their voices bouncing off the bathroom walls. Breathing hard, Tag lowered her feet to the floor and looked at her. He'd wanted to tell her how deep his feelings went for her so many times, but he'd managed to stifle the urges. He felt it again, the need to say "I love you," and to hear those words from her beautiful lips.

But after a moment of studying the emotion in her eyes, he once again became leery of scaring her off. It was amazing to him that he'd lived for twenty-six years without falling so hard before this, but he couldn't alter history, and the truth was that his love for Melanie had been kid stuff compared to what he felt for Linda.

A startling barrage of guilt hit him then. Mel had been his wife, his very first love! And now he was thinking that he hadn't really loved her? What he'd felt for Mel and what he felt now for Linda were incomparable.

He touched Linda's face, brushing her wet hair back from her cheek and forehead. "You're beautiful and…and…" *And I love you*.

Maybe he couldn't say the words, but they were in his eyes. Linda sucked in a startled breath. Their lovemaking was incredible and she'd been thinking about love and permanency and all sorts of romantic fantasies, but something told her it was too soon for them to be discussing the serious side of their burgeoning relationship.

She raised on tiptoe and kissed his lips. "You're beautiful, too. Were you finished with your shower when I came barging in?"

"Sweetheart, you can barge like that anytime you take the notion, and yes, I was finished. Why? Trying to get rid of me now?"

"Stay if you like, but I need to put some shampoo on this wet mop of hair."

He quit kidding around. "All right. Honey, I hate leaving so soon, but I promised Sammy that I would pick her up this morning so she could go to school."

"Then you must do it, of course. We'll see each other again. You happen to have my address," she said teasingly. "And another room to paint, I believe?"

"I'll be finishing your place today, Linda."

"Don't look so forlorn about it. You don't need an excuse to see me."

He hugged her tightly for a long moment, then slid the door back and stepped from the shower. "I'll get dressed and be on my way," he said while reaching for a towel.

Linda shut the door except for a tiny crack to peer through, as she'd been getting chilled with it wide open. "Can you and Samantha come for dinner tonight?"

Tag's eyes lit up. "You bet we can. I like Sammy to eat around five or five-thirty."

"No problem. I usually get home around four, but I might go by MonMart first. So let's say five-thirty, okay?"

"Okay, great." Dried off, Tag leaned forward and pushed the door back again just enough to give her a kiss. "See you later, light of my life."

He left Linda wondering about that endearment, which seemed very special to her. For one thing, she could describe him in the same wonderful way, as he had truly become the brightest light in her life. Humming happily, she squirted shampoo into her hand and began washing her hair.

* * *

Alfred's heart was jump-started that morning by someone pounding on the door of his room. Warily he crept to the door in his underwear. "Who's there?" he asked, deliberately deepening his voice so the person outside would know he wasn't anyone to mess with.

"Ya got a phone call. You're supposed to call a guy named Paul, on the double."

"Oh. Okay, thanks." Alfred heard the messenger walking away, and he grabbed his pants and pulled them on. Nervously he put on his shoes and found his cleanest dirty shirt. He'd been wearing the same clothes over and over, and since Rumor didn't have one of those coin-operated laundries where a guy could do his own wash, he was going to have to risk a drive to that big store on the other side of town to buy some new ones.

Finally dressed, he hurried out to the phone booth and placed a collect call to Paul's office number. Nervously clearing his throat, he said a bright, cheery, "Hi, Paul," when his boss came on the line.

"Hi, my fanny. What's going on there? Why aren't you back here with that book?"

Alfred's bravado vanished like a puff of smoke in a gale. "Uh, I'm, uh, trying real hard, Paul," he stammered. "I ain't hanging here 'cause I like the place."

"Well, why in hell don't you get the job done and get out of there? I think you *do* like it. I think you met some girlie and have been having a high old time on my dime."

"That ain't true, Paul." Wounded to the quick, Alfred almost burst into tears. "Let me tell you again what I'm up against. There's some big guy hanging out in Linda's apartment. There's her dog that barks loud enough to wake the dead. There are snakes in the bushes near the building. And now one of the old ladies that lives there comes outside to talk when she sees me."

Paul let loose with a string of profanities that came close to curling Alfred's thinning hair. Wincing, he held the phone away from his ear until Paul wound down.

"A dog and an old lady? Now, those two are really scary threats! I can see why you're cringing in terror instead of getting the job done. What breed of dog does Linda have? A rottweiler? A Doberman? A pit bull?"

"Uh, no. I don't know what it is, but it's a fierce little mutt."

"A fierce *little* mutt? How little?"

"About…about a foot high."

"A foot high? You moronic SOB! If I ever get the notion to put you on another job, may lightning paralyze my tongue before I can get the words out of my mouth! Now, you listen to me, and listen well. I don't care about the snakes and old ladies. I don't care if a bull chases you clear to North Dakota and gores your cowardly butt every step of the way. I don't care how many foot-high dogs are guarding Linda's door. God help me," Paul groaned. "What am I gonna do? Alfred, I swear on my mother's grave that if you were in reach I'd choke the life out of you with my own two hands. Instead of getting arrested for it I'd get a medal, because I'd be doing all of mankind a service. You are, without a doubt, the most useless piece of dog dung on the face of the planet. Now, are you going to get that freakin' book or not?"

By the time Paul asked that final question, Alfred was shaking like a leaf. And there were tears in his eyes. "I'll get it," he promised while just barely holding back a sob. Paul hated him; he would never be one of the guys. "I'll get it," he repeated sadly.

"See that you do!"

The phone had been slammed down in Alfred's ear. Downcast and sorrowful, he shuffled back to his room. Paul just didn't understand, he thought forlornly. No one who hadn't been to the wilds of Montana could possibly understand what he was going through.

* * *

By 10:00 a.m. the inhabitants of Rumor were all going about their various activities. Linda was in her classroom, trying to stay focused on art and her students instead of daydreaming about Tag and last night. Samantha was sitting cross-legged on a mat with a circle of other children at Rumor Rugrats, engrossed in the story being read out loud by Dee Dee Reingard. Tag was painting Linda's bedroom, with the furniture covered by drop cloths, and thinking about his job schedule; he could easily finish Linda's apartment today and possibly get another unit done before Donna needed him at the Getaway.

Guy Cantrell was working in his home lab, as his first Wednesday science class at the high school started at one o'clock. Michael had ditched his morning classes to work with his uncle; the two of them were trying not to be too elated, although being on the verge of perfecting a formula that would benefit all of humanity probably rated *some* elation.

Alfred Wallinski sat huddled in his ratty little motel room and chewed on his fingernails. He *had* to get that book for Paul, but how?

Stratton Kingsley was at his desk in the administrative offices of MonMart, doodling on a pad of paper and thinking about a dozen different things—family matters, the ranch and fluctuating beef prices, and his latest venture, the retail business, the very store in which he was presently ensconced, MonMart. At the ranch, his wife, Carolyn, was on the phone with the national chairwoman of a worthy charity, discussing the annual drive for donations.

And in the Calico Diner, Alice Alden and Clara Raymond sat in their favorite booth and smiled at each other.

"Well, don't you look like the cat that just caught the canary?" Alice said teasingly.

"Wait until you hear," Clara replied with a smug little twinkle in her eyes.

Every waitress in the place knew the ladies' order; they didn't have to ask, but simply brought over a pot of coffee, a container of fresh cream and two cups and saucers whenever Mrs. Alden and Mrs. Raymond came in.

The ladies each prepared her coffee then took a sip. "Mmm, wonderful," Clara said.

"As always," Alice agreed. "Now, tell me what's going on before I burst."

"Well, yesterday was almost too much for my heart to take. The first thing that happened was that odd-looking young man showing up at Linda Fioretti's door again when she was gone. I can't figure out how they communicate—besides the telephone, of course—because she's never home when he goes there. Anyhow, I decided to be kind and help him out this time, and I went outside and told him that Linda had just taken Tippy for a walk, and he should be able to catch up with her. Can you believe that he was hardly even polite to me? Some people have no gratitude at all."

"That's so true, Clara. Times are different from when we were that age."

"Indeed they are, Alice." They each took a swallow of coffee. "I just can't help being disappointed in Linda. She seems so ladylike and…" Clara paused for a breath. "Tag Kingsley stayed in her apartment all of last night. He left early this morning."

"No!"

"I'm afraid so. Two beaus are fine, of course, but I can't imagine overnight visits from both."

"Oh, she wouldn't!"

"Alice, I've told you about seeing that impolite young man going to her door after dark. If her porch light and interior lights aren't on, however, I can only see so much from my window, so I can't say for sure if she let him in. And you know I would never say something that I don't know as fact."

Alice patted her friend's hand. "I know, dear. Neither would I."

Two of the waitresses stopped working long enough to whisper to each other. "Who are they tearing apart today?" one asked.

"Now, that's mean. They don't intend anything malicious, and I think they're sweet."

"Sweet as honey," the woman drawled. "Okay, fine, forget my sarcasm, but do tell me who these honeybees are dissecting today."

"Linda Fioretti, Tag Kingsley and one other guy whose name they don't know. That strikes me as strange. I would've sworn they knew everyone in town. Anyhow, it seems that Tag spent last night with Linda. Apparently, Mrs. Raymond witnessed his arrival and departure. She lives in the same building as Linda does, you know."

"Well, now, isn't *that* an interesting tidbit? Who's the other guy, do you suppose?"

"Haven't a clue. Have you noticed any strangers hanging around?"

"The only strangers I've seen around here are the occasional tourists dropping in for ice cream or a burger."

"Same here."

"Hmm. Makes for some intriguing speculation, doesn't it?"

"Yes indeedy."

Chapter Ten

Linda hurried from her kitchen at the first peal of the doorbell. She opened the door for Tag and Samantha and was nearly unbalanced by the little girl's exuberant rush to hug her legs. "Linda!" the child exclaimed.

"Sammy, it's so good to see you." Deeply touched by Samantha's affection, Linda knelt to give her a real hug. "I'm so glad you're going to have dinner with me."

"Me, too."

With her arms still holding Tag's daughter close to her heart, Linda looked up and saw a strange expression on his face. Confusion? Perplexity? Disapproval? A mix of all three?

But then their eyes connected, he smiled at her and everything seemed to be all right. Gently breaking the hug, Linda stood. She ached to kiss Tag, and her gaze lingered on his mouth for a moment.

"Welcome," she said huskily. "Dinner's almost ready. Why don't you and Sammy sit in the living room while I finish up in the kitchen."

"We will, thanks." Tag realized that he should have foreseen the frustration of being so close to Linda and having to keep his hands in his pockets. Memories of last night didn't help, but he couldn't shake them. All day he'd looked forward to seeing her this evening, and not until the second that Sammy had eagerly thrown herself at Linda had the reality of the situation sunk in.

Linda went to the kitchen, and Tag, troubled and wondering why he should be feeling so uneasy, brought his daughter to the living room. "We'll sit on the sofa," he told her, which they did. They had just gotten settled when Tippy showed up in the doorway.

"Hey, Tippy, come on over and meet Sammy," Tag said eagerly, welcoming an opportunity to suspend concerns that pinched and poked but remained too vague to pinpoint. Uneasiness had struck hard when Samantha had thrown herself at Linda in that startling display of affection. It was all food for thought, possibly some very serious thought, Tag realized, but he gladly pushed it to the back of his mind for the time being.

"Daddy, a doggie! Oh, he's so cute." Sammy started to get down from the sofa, but Tag laid a restraining hand on her arm.

"Let him come to you, honey. He has to get to know you in his own way. That's always the best way to meet a new dog." Tag hadn't seen Tippy behave so cautiously before and wondered if it was because Sammy was a child. Maybe a child had abused him. Linda had talked as though the dog had been badly mistreated but had admitted having no knowledge of the abuser. "Just give Tippy a chance, Sammy," he said quietly.

Sure enough, Tippy began slowly walking toward them. "See? He's coming over," Tag said. "Just sit nice and still and let him sniff you. He can tell by sniffing you if you're a nice person or someone to fear."

"He doesn't have to be afraid of me, Daddy. I would never be mean to a doggie."

"I know you wouldn't, sweetie, but he doesn't."

Tippy finally got near enough for Tag to pet him, but as much as he seemed to enjoy Tag's attentions, he still kept a wary eye on Samantha.

Some kid had done a number on Tippy and the dog was guarded around small people. He continued to pet him while talking to Samantha. "He's warming up, sweetheart. You watch. He's very curious about you and it won't be long before he moves around my legs and sniffs you."

Samantha could just barely sit still. "I wish we had a doggie like Tippy," she said. "He's so cute, Daddy."

Tag had heard that wish more times than he could remember, but the situation was the same as it had always been. The two of them were home at night and on Sundays—sometimes during the week, but not always. A dog would be alone much of the time. Tag had never figured he needed a guard dog, which he wouldn't have on the place anyway because he wouldn't risk Sammy's safety with a vicious animal. A small dog, one about Tippy's size, was more of a house pet, which meant that someone had to take him outside several times a day. He didn't have the time and Sammy was too young for that much responsibility.

Finally Tippy crept around Tag's legs and sniffed Sammy's shoes. Her feet were barely over the edge of the cushion, which was what probably caused him to jump up on the sofa. Sammy started laughing when the dog first sniffed then licked her face.

"Daddy, he's kissing me!"

"Yes, he is. Okay, you can pet him now. He likes you."

Linda came in. "What on earth?" she said with her hands on her hips when she saw Tippy on the sofa. She nearly dressed him down for doing something that was strictly forbidden, but then she realized that he was making friends with Samantha, and the child was giggling and hugging him. It was such a moving sight that Linda just stood there and smiled.

In one way or another, Sammy was the center of attention

throughout dinner and the short time Tag and she stayed afterward. Linda had genuinely enjoyed the child's innocent chatter, and in her estimation the evening was a success. However, the restraint between Tag and herself felt as wide as the Grand Canyon. They looked at each other with yearning eyes, but that was about all they could do.

Everyone, including Tippy, said goodbye at Linda's door around seven-thirty, and she and Tag gazed longingly at each other one more time. Just before he left, though, he took her hand, squeezed it and said softly, "I'll call you later, okay?"

"Please do."

Linda got ready for bed, but every cell in her body was waiting for the phone to ring. The apartment was dark, except for her bedroom, when the phone finally rang, and Linda sat on the bed to answer.

"Hi, sweetheart," Tag said in her ear after her hello. "Are you all right? Tonight was tough on the nerves."

"I'm fine. You have a child and she has to be part of our relationship. Besides, I believe she really likes me, Tag, and think if she didn't?"

"She does like you," Tag said, and paused because his earlier concerns, vague then, were suddenly in his face and clear as glass. Maybe Samantha liked Linda too much. He had high hopes for this relationship, but what if something he hadn't yet anticipated occurred and Linda suddenly dropped him? It was misery to think about, but it could happen, and if Sammy was emotionally tied to Linda, she would be devastated. She was already walking that treacherous path because she didn't have a mother.

My God, is that why she likes Linda so much, because she's already thinking of her as the mother she longs for?

"Tag? What's wrong?"

"Um, nothing, sweetheart." *Nothing I can talk about right now.*

"You sound…troubled. Is Sammy all right? She seemed to have a good time tonight."

"She did. Never doubt it. She's wild about Tippy…and you."

"Well, I'm a little wild about her, too."

Outside, skulking in the dark shadows of the building and nearby trees, Alfred peered up at the lighted window in Linda's apartment. It was the only one spilling light and he suspected the room was Linda's bedroom. Was she up there or wasn't she? He was so upset and anxious over Paul's anger today that he would do just about anything—short of breaking in when Linda was home—to get his hands on that journal.

But there was only one way to see into that second-story window and find out if Linda was home or not. Did he have the nerve to climb a very tall pine tree? Alfred's heart began pounding fearfully and a shudder shook his body. He had never climbed anything higher than a three-step utility ladder. Linda could have gone somewhere and taken the mutt with her. This could be it, the big chance he'd been hoping and praying for.

He forced himself to the foot of the tree that was nearest the lighted window and began the physically grueling climb, using his arms, thighs and knees to hang on when there wasn't a branch sturdy enough to bear his weight, slight as it was. He hugged the tree in abject terror whenever he looked down; he was afraid of heights and escalators and elevators and… and Montana! He felt like bawling, but decided he could do that later. Right now he was on a mission—one that would do James Bond justice.

Putting on a tough expression and deliberately muttering a choice curse, he forced himself up the branches until he was level with the window. But he wasn't facing it squarely and could only see a small portion of the bedroom. He moved cautiously and maneuvered himself around the tree to get a better view. His foot slipped and he began falling.

Horrified screams accompanied his fall as he hit one branch after another and scraped his skin on the bark of the tree. He hit the ground with a thud; the wind had been knocked out of him and he lay gasping for air.

Inside, Linda exclaimed into the phone, "My God, what was that?"

"What was what, Linda?"

"A horrible crashing sound. A voice, too, I think. Tag, hold on, I've got to take a look outside." She set the phone down and hurried over to the window. There was nothing to see, beyond the usual pitch-black, nighttime shadows. Frowning, she returned to the telephone. "There's nothing. I can't imagine—"

"Call the sheriff."

Tag sounded so gruff and demanding that Linda was taken aback. "I'm not sure that's necessary," she said slowly, surprised that he would speak that way to her. "There are things going on around here all the time. I've heard noises at night many times."

"Call the sheriff! Linda, if Sammy wasn't sound asleep, I'd be over there faster than you could dial the phone. But I can't leave her alone in the house. This should be checked out. What if some crackpot is trying to break into your apartment? Or someone else's apartment?"

"No one is trying to break in, for goodness' sake. Tag, I don't understand your attitude."

He covered the phone with his hand and groaned. He couldn't leave Sammy alone and he couldn't bundle her up and haul her with him to check out a possible burglar, or worse. Old feelings of guilt assaulted his senses, burrowing deep, hurting like hell. He should have protected Mel; he hadn't and she had died. A man should protect the woman in his life; he wasn't going to make the same mistake with Linda.

"Hang up and call the sheriff," he said again, practically shouting.

"Now, that's just about enough of that," Linda said sharply. "What is wrong with you?"

"Hang up and call the sheriff!"

Linda hung up all right. She slammed the receiver down so hard she hoped it deafened him. When in God's name had Tag turned into a demanding, querulous jerk?

She climbed into bed, snapped off the lamp, angrily punched her pillow into shape and settled down for the night. Or *tried* to settle down. Every nerve in her body felt shredded and aching. After all that had passed between them last night, and even the pleasant dinner they had shared this evening, how could he talk to her like that?

Fifteen minutes later she still hadn't closed her eyes. There'd been no more crashes outside, no more mysterious shrieking voices, barely any sounds at all, in fact. She couldn't begin to guess what had caused those noises, nor did she want to stay awake all night trying to figure it out. Good heavens, she thought disgustedly, someone was almost always coming or going in an apartment complex, and why had Tag made such a big deal out of it?

A minute later her doorbell rang. Genuinely startled, she switched on the lamp, got out of bed, grabbed a robe and pulled it on as she went downstairs. Maybe it was Tag at her door—with Sammy, of course—although she couldn't imagine him hauling his sleeping child out of bed at this hour. Tag might not be as perfect as she'd been thinking before that ridiculous phone conversation tonight, but he was quite possibly the best father she'd ever met.

She turned on the outside light and peered through the peephole in the door. It was a deputy! Two of them! Linda saw red. Tag must have called the sheriff's department after she'd hung up.

She opened the door and said a decent hello. She couldn't take out her fury at Tag on the deputies who were, after all, only doing their job.

"Are you Linda Fioretti?"

"Yes, and this is my apartment." Linda's heart sank. The deputies' cruiser had been left with its red lights flashing, and windows were lit up throughout the complex. Some residents were even coming outside to see what was going on. Tag's unnecessary overprotectiveness had culminated in the interruption of everyone's rest. She was furious.

"We checked the grounds, ma'am, and if there was an intruder in the area he's gone now. We'd like to come in and walk through your apartment."

"What?" Linda's eyebrows drew together in a stunned frown. "For what reason?"

"We were told you live alone. Are you alone now?"

"Of course I'm alone!"

"We'd like to make sure. Of course, you can refuse to let us come in. We don't have a warrant."

"Thank you for letting me know that. Write it in your report that I refused to let you in. Believe me, there is no intruder lurking in my apartment and threatening my life."

"All right, but may I ask why you had someone else call for assistance rather than do it yourself?"

"I didn't *need* assistance!" Linda took a calming breath. "I appreciate your consideration, but I told Mr. Kingsley that there were noises at night around here all the time. There was no reason to call for help. He should not have taken it upon himself to make that call."

"Apparently, he thought differently. Well, if you're sure everything's all right, we'll leave and let you go back to sleep."

Yeah, right. "Thank you," she said, and as the deputies left her front door, she shut it and made sure it was locked.

Steaming, she went back upstairs, then sat on the bed and glared at the phone. At the moment, she would like nothing better than to give Tag hell, to shriek in his ear her enraged opinion of his gall. Did he think she was some kind of moron, incapable of differentiating between a noise at night and true danger?

The truth was that she was so furious she was afraid to place that call. She would say things neither of them would be able to forget, and jerk of the year or not, she still had serious feelings for Tag.

But Tag had no such compunction, and when a reasonable amount of time had passed, he called Linda.

She was in bed, the lamp was off, and she let the phone ring four times before gritting her teeth and reaching for it in the dark.

"Hello," she said coldly.

"Did they come?"

"They came and managed to wake up the entire neighborhood. Thank you so much for your interference. Good night." She hung up before she said more. In fact, maybe what she'd said in a few words might have been too much.

Linda sighed and hoped not. If she never heard from Tag again, she would hurt for a very long time.

But, damn it, he shouldn't have called the sheriff!

Alfred moaned with every painful step, but he had to walk to the spot where he'd left his car. He was bruised, scraped and scratched from the top of his head all the way down to the relative protection of his shoes. Nothing seemed to be broken, though. He could walk, he could move his arms and hands, and turn his head from side to side. He'd taken a beating in that fall, but he wasn't in jail, which was where he would probably be if he hadn't forced himself to get the hell away from that tree the second he'd been able to breathe without gasping.

Gritting his teeth over this fiasco of a night, Alfred forced one foot ahead of the other. Next time he would know that even one light burning in Linda's apartment could mean that she was home. Why hadn't that miserable mutt of hers done any barking, though? Dogs didn't need to see a man to know he was just outside and climbing a tree.

Cursing every tree in Montana, Alfred pondered Tippy's silence. Was Linda's dog so used to his scent by now that he no longer considered him a threat? Alfred suddenly felt as though he had stumbled upon a really important fact in this most difficult of missions.

No, he thought with his chin raised defiantly, he hadn't stumbled upon that fact, he had *deduced* it, brilliantly.

"Next time," he whispered. "Next time." He was infused with a confidence that had been sadly lacking thus far in his covert operation.

But he still hurt like hell.

Tag came awake at 4:00 a.m. Predawn silence always seemed heavy and nearly audible to him. He hated waking that early even on a good day. The knot in his gut was advance notice of a *not* so good day in the making.

Crooking an arm beneath his head, he stared at the dark ceiling and thought about last night. He honestly would never have believed that such nasty sarcasm could have come out of Linda's mouth before she'd laid it on him in that final phone call. So she wasn't *all* sugar and spice, was she? She had numerous good points, but she didn't like being crossed any more than anyone else did.

But that was where Tag got stalled every time he thought about it. What had he done that would anger her so? Didn't she recognize good intentions when they arrived in the form of lawmen? Didn't she understand that his feelings for her included a powerful need to keep her safe?

"Linda," he whispered, worrying himself into a sweat because their relationship could be at an end over something that made no sense in the first place. Why on earth had he taken her startled reaction to an outside noise seriously when she had not? He heard outside noises around his place at night once in a while, but they weren't loud crashes or voices right next to the house.

And now that he thought of it, hadn't she been rather cavalier when he'd told her about that guy walking into her apartment? She'd said she had locked the door and no one but Heck had a key, the same one, presumably, that the burly super had given him so he could come and go as needed.

He was finished with Linda's apartment. He no longer had a reason to step foot into her unit and the timing couldn't be worse. If there was just one wall that still needed painting, he could go over there and maybe kid her out of being mad at him.

But he wasn't going to crawl or beg. "No way," he muttered as he gave up on any more sleep and got out of bed. He'd let the whole thing lie for a day or so and see what Linda did. Maybe she was already sorry for lashing out at him, and maybe she would call or come by, in which case he would forgive her immediately and everything would be great.

And if she did nothing? If he heard not one word from her?

Tag's heart sank. It really *could* be over for them.

Clara was animated as she related last night's events to Alice. "Tag brought his daughter to Linda's place at five-thirty, and they left at seven-thirty. I expect they had dinner together, a simple enough occasion, and yet the inclusion of Samantha somewhat alarms me. She's such a darling child, but she's only five years old, Alice. Do you think it's proper for a child that young to accompany her father on dates?"

"Perhaps they didn't think of it as a date, Clara."

"Nonsense. Tag spent an entire night with Linda. They certainly wouldn't revert to being mere acquaintances after something like that. Alice, how old do you think Linda is?"

"Well, I haven't seen her as much as you have, but I would guess she's in her late twenties or early thirties."

"My opinion exactly. And how old is Tag?"

"Let me see." Alice had an amazing ability to recall dates, and she could figure out the age of nearly everyone in Rumor with some simple math. "Russell is thirty-five, Reed is thirty-two. Tag has to be twenty-six."

"I knew it! He's five or six years younger than Linda. Alice, this entire episode, or whatever it should be called, is becoming quite upsetting."

"Clara, do their ages really matter?"

"I'm surprised at you, Alice Alden! Haven't we agreed many times that the best romantic partnerships are those in which the woman is at least three years younger?"

"Good grief," one waitress whispered to another in passing. "Now they've got Linda Fioretti, that super new art teacher, robbing the cradle." When she brought fresh coffee to the ladies' table, however, the subject had been changed.

"I heard the strangest noise and got up," Clara said. "Even though I couldn't imagine what had caused it, Alice, I don't mind admitting that it gave me the jitters. Anyway, I peeked out my window and saw a person limping away. I think it was a man, but he…or she…was wearing dark clothing and stayed away from even the glimmer of any light. Fifteen minutes later, up drives a sheriff's car. Two deputies got out, walked completely around the building and then went to Linda's door."

"To Linda's door! Whatever for? She wasn't outside making frightening noises, was she?"

"Heavens, no, but from what I overheard, Tag had called for assistance and asked them to check on Linda. Alice, there are some very odd forces at work in Rumor lately. Actually, I could say strange things began happening when she moved in, even though I would never say an unkind word about a soul. But we cannot forget that as nice as Linda is to talk to, she has two young men hot on her trail, which leaves room for, well, for speculation. Tag is a homeboy, but that other young man isn't. Do you suppose he was the person who limped away before the deputies arrived last night?"

Linda put in a terrible day. Her head started aching the moment she awoke and remembered the events of last night. It was still aching when she got home from school that afternoon. Barely stopping to greet Tippy on her way into her apartment, she hurriedly checked her voice mail and learned there was none; Tag hadn't called.

Now what? she thought sadly. Should she phone him? She *had* been brusque when he'd called last night, and maybe he felt she owed him an apology.

But, darn it, she'd had every right to get upset over the law ringing her doorbell and waking up everyone in the building! And over nothing, besides a piddly little noise. What kind of namby-pamby coward did he think she was?

No, she was *not* going to call. Stubbornly walking away from the phone, she mentally threw the ball in Tag's court.

The future or the end of their relationship was up to him. She had kept her marriage together for almost ten years by playing the obedient wife; she was *not* going to walk on eggshells for a man ever again.

And if Tag should decide to call, she just might tell him exactly that.

Chapter Eleven

Tidying her classroom during the silence that followed the stampede of students leaving for the day, Linda sighed heavily just as Shelby Peterson stuck her head in.

"That sounded ominous," Shelby drawled as she walked on in. "Smile, girlfriend. This is Friday."

Linda showed a weak smile. "So it is. And in a very short time school will be out for the year. The kids are practically bouncing off the walls with exuberance. Do you remember being so excited about the end of a school year? I don't think I was."

Shelby sat on Linda's desk, setting her purse next to her thigh. "Well, I sure was. For me, the last day of school was almost better than Christmas. A whole summer to look forward to? It was freedom, fun and fantasy, all tied up and handed to you in one adrenaline-pumping package. It was a great feeling, Linda. I remember it very well."

"Hmm," Linda murmured, still not able to recall feeling quite that way. Not about anything, she realized when she really thought about it. There was only one luminous spot of excitement in the otherwise gray days of her entire life, and his name was Tag Kingsley. And she had not heard one word from him since Wednesday night.

A painful sadness brought tears to her eyes, and she turned away from Shelby to blink them back while sorting cleaned and dried paintbrushes by size and storing them in a supply cabinet. But if there was an emotion Linda truly despised, it was self-pity. She had refused to indulge in self-pity while growing up in the disorganized household of her parents, and again during a marriage that had gone wrong within hours of saying "I do." To let it overcome her now, when her life was finally in order, was unthinkable. She had even been happy before meeting Tag. Damn him, for the first time in her whole crappy life, she had actually been happy!

"Well, guess I'd better head for home," Shelby said, and slid off the desk. "Got big plans for the weekend?"

"I think I'm going to hang some pictures. I told you about my apartment getting a new coat of paint."

"Fresh paint is great in whatever domicile takes our fancy, but have you done any thinking about buying a house?" Shelby began easing toward the door.

"I've thought about it, yes, but I haven't talked to a Realtor or done any looking on my own. A house would be nice, all right, but maybe I'm not quite ready to make that move. You've seen my apartment. I'm really very comfortable there."

"It's not a question of comfort, Linda, it's the financial advantage of paying down a mortgage instead of paying rent."

"I know that's sound advice, but I'm just not in a move-again mood, I guess." Linda took up her purse. "I'll walk out with you."

"Moving is a pain, I can't deny that," Shelby said, picking up the thread of their conversation as they walked out to the school's parking area. "All that packing and unpacking. Just thinking about it makes my back ache."

Linda's thoughts went to the speed with which she had

packed her things in the Culberton house. Her back hadn't ached a bit. She'd been almost dizzy with relief over finally being divorced, overjoyed because she would never have to see Paul again or listen to another one of his lies. How could he have been so dense to not know that *she'd* known he was lying?

Those memories reminded Linda of how really good she had it now, even with the pain of losing Tag nipping at her insides. With slightly higher spirits urging her back to normal, she decided that she was not going to mope around all weekend.

"Shelby, how about coming to my place for dinner tonight?"

"Hon, I'd love to, but I have plans. Some cousins from Arizona are visiting my mother, and she's got this big family-dinner thing going on tonight. Thanks for the invite, though."

"You're welcome. We'll do it another time."

"Sure will. Well, here's where we part ways." Shelby touched Linda's arm. "Something's not quite right, isn't it? I can see it in your eyes. I'm sure Mom has all sorts of things lined up for the family this weekend, but I could probably break away for a few hours, if you'd like to talk about it."

"Oh, no, Shelby, everything's fine," Linda hastened to say. Talk about Tag? About making love with him and actually, for the first time, feeling what every woman *should* feel with the right man? "I'm just…a little tired."

Shelby raised a dubious eyebrow, but she accepted Linda's explanation. Her reservations were apparent in her next question, though. "What are you going to do all summer?"

Linda drew her eyebrows together in a frown. "That question has been bothering me off and on. I'll do some painting, of course. There are incredibly scenic spots within driving distance, if I decide to turn out a few landscapes. What will you do?"

"About the same as I do every summer. Take care of any

requirements the state might have to maintain my Montana teaching certificate and then do volunteer work at the White-horn Hospital and at a convalescent home."

"Shelby, that's wonderful." Linda was truly impressed with her friend's generosity.

"Well, if you get bored and don't want to tie yourself to a regular job, try volunteer work. I've met some great people that way."

"I just might do that. Thanks for the tip."

"You're very welcome. And if you change your mind about having a heart-to-heart over the weekend, you have my home number. See you on Monday, if not before."

"Bye," Linda called as they went in different directions, each to her own car. The second she was away from Shelby, her eyes began stinging again. She feared a dismal weekend was ahead, as she couldn't hang on to a good mood to save her soul.

Shelby peeled out of the parking lot and Linda dawdled behind. There were houses between the high school and the corner of Logan and Main, where she would turn left to head home, and she glanced at them as she slowly drove past. A house *would* be nice, she thought listlessly, but it had its disadvantages, make no mistake. There was always some problem coming out of nowhere in maintaining a house…a leaky faucet, a cracked window, shingles blown off the roof during a storm, weeds, weeds and more weeds. The list was endless, actually, and since Paul had rarely been home long enough to do more than invent a lie about what he'd been doing during his latest absence, Linda had learned to do a lot of the household fix-it jobs herself. So it wasn't that she wasn't able to deal with the responsibilities of home maintenance; the question was whether she wanted to.

Of course, if she had a man with a brain and any affection at all for their home, she would definitely choose a house over an apartment.

Tag immediately flashed into her mind and she sighed again.

Noticing that she was directly in front of Rugrats, she pulled over to the side of the road. Samantha was probably in there, she thought, and felt a terrible burning behind her eyes. It wasn't news that she loved Tag's child; she hadn't dwelled on the fact before, but that didn't make it any less true. Samantha had worked her way into Linda's heart at their very first meeting. Sam was a naturally loving and lovable little girl, and Linda ached from just thinking about her. Staring at Rugrats, she wished she had the right to walk in and see her.

But she had no rights at all where Sammy was concerned. It all seemed so unfair. Tears trickled down Linda's cheeks, and she dug out some tissues and dried her eyes.

She drove home then without further delay. After all, she had Tippy waiting for her...and maybe, just maybe, Tag had called and left a message on her voice mail.

This is getting ridiculous, Tag thought on Saturday morning. Why couldn't he just call Linda and get it over with? They weren't a couple of kids, for God's sake, playing a stupid game of whoever-calls-first-loses.

And yet something kept stopping him. He'd never thought of himself as unfairly mule-headed, but he was so wounded over Linda's reaction to his heartfelt concern for her safety and security that night that he couldn't seem to say "To hell with it" and dial her number. If stubbornness was at the bottom of his seemingly irrevocable reluctance to eat crow, then he was a lot more mule-headed than he'd known.

But so was she, damn it. Wasn't she even a tiny bit sorry that she'd lambasted instead of thanked him for calling out the troops Wednesday night?

"Guess not," he muttered. "Sammy? I'm going out to the shop. Take your dolls and come with me." His thoughts returned to Wednesday night. He wouldn't even leave Sammy alone in the house during the day. He sure as hell would never apologize for not doing it at night when she was sleeping.

Not even to Linda.

Alfred applied ointment to his scrapes and bruises again and fell back on his bed with a groan. After two days and nights, his body still ached from that terrifying fall. He would never climb another tree for as long as he lived. Actually, he could be dead right this minute instead of moaning and groaning in this awful motel room, he realized, and he didn't want to die in Montana. He wasn't prepared to die anywhere, but to face the ultimate penalty in this godforsaken place would be the cruelest blow fate could bestow on him.

But then he thought of a blow that might be worse—Paul Fioretti's fury.

Shuddering fearfully, Alfred turned his thoughts to that journal in Linda's apartment. He had to get hold of it, somehow, someway. A plan. He desperately needed a plan, one that would work.

Why couldn't he think of one?

Linda did some housecleaning on Saturday morning, just to be on hand should Tag show his face, but by early afternoon she gave up on that happening, took her paints, easel and a couple of canvases and drove out to Lake Monet.

It was an incredibly beautiful day, with hardly a breeze to disturb the serenity. Nature's quietude was more soothing than man-made silence, Linda decided as she set up her easel in a particularly pretty spot. In mere moments she was ready to begin creating her personal interpretation of the lake's unique colors.

But she stood before a blank canvas with palette and brush in hand and bit down on her bottom lip. Her heart simply wasn't in this, she realized unhappily, and she put her things in the box on the tailgate of her SUV and walked to a large rock on a rise. She sat with her arms around her knees and stared almost unseeingly at the lake.

She had never been in love and had never felt the anguish of a broken heart. It hurt, it hurt like hell, and it was all caused by something so silly.

Well, maybe it hadn't been silly; she'd truly been embarrassed by the incident, and Tag should not have put her through something so unnecessary.

But still, the whole episode hadn't been as bad as one of Paul's lies, which she had put up with for almost ten years. Linda narrowed her eyes on the quiet waters of Lake Monet as a new and disturbing question popped into her brain: Was she taking out past frustrations and misery on Tag simply because she had vowed so ardently to never again be walked on by a man?

"Oh Lord," she whispered while her heart sank clear to her toes. Thinking rationally, there was no comparison between Paul's endless deceits and what Tag had done, but her instant anger could be explained as an involuntary reaction to the possibility of Tag assuming the alpha-male role and treating her exactly as Paul had, as a mindless, helpless female.

Did Tag really think of her that way? She had trusted in his compliments, believed he'd meant them, when they could have been no more than a smooth line of patter to get her into bed.

Linda put her head on her knees and cried softly. There had been uncountable moments of emotional agony to deal with during her lifetime, but none had hurt quite this much.

Hours later, eyes dry and emotions controlled, she broke down her easel and drove home; she had made a decision about Tag. She would be sticking her neck out, but even another stinging slap to her pride would be better than the awful nothingness engulfing her daily existence.

It was, she felt, a good decision. Well, maybe *sensible* was a more accurate word than *good*. At least she would learn exactly where she stood with Tag.

"Unk, you've done it! It's going to work!" Michael Cantrell's blue eyes were as big as saucers and shone with youthful excitement.

"Appears so," Guy said calmly, frowning because as much as he knew about biology, chemistry, physics and all of the other related sciences, he couldn't quite figure out why his formula might work. "Let's not celebrate yet, though, all right?"

"But…"

"Michael, you haven't said anything to anyone about this, have you?"

"Heck, no. Told you I wouldn't, and I won't. Dad's on my case about why I'm over here so much, but I just said you were helping me with some physics equations."

"I don't like you lying to your dad, Michael."

"I'm not lying. You *are* helping me with physics, biology and all that stuff."

"I suppose one could interpret our association as such," Guy said dryly, then abruptly changed tones. "But your dad is my older brother, and I hate him thinking that I might be trying to steal his only son."

"You've never tried to *steal* me. We just think alike." Michael looked around Guy's home laboratory. "And I love your lab."

"Max would rather you loved *his* lab."

"The whole house is a lab, but it's all computer stuff. I like computers and Dad's experiments with virtual reality and all of his great games and things, but I like it over here a whole lot more. Anyhow, when are you gonna test the formula? It's ready for testing, don't you think?"

"Almost, Michael, almost. There are aspects to it that I

can't quite prove, which means I'm not yet positive of the outcome."

"You can test it on me. I'm volunteering right now to be the first human to use your formula."

"Don't even think it," Guy said sharply, a tone of voice he rarely used with anyone, let alone his beloved nephew. "And don't you ever get any ideas about trying it out someday when I'm not here, understand?"

"You don't need to get mad."

"I'm not mad, Michael." Guy worked up a small grin. "Maybe a *little* mad, but not angry."

Michael grinned. "You're a hoot."

Linda dialed Tag's number with a less than steady hand. His phone rang, and rang, and rang, and then his answering machine clicked on and she heard Tag's voice. "Don't hang up. Your call is important. Please leave your name and number after the beep."

Linda slowly put down the phone. She couldn't talk to a machine, not about this. She would try again later.

"That finishes it," Tag said, giving the bookcase a final dusting with a clean cloth. He had worked all day in his shop, with Sammy and the radio for company, and he had completed the second of the two bookcases that Linda had ordered for her living room. He would deliver them tomorrow...or *attempt* delivery. Considering the current cold front coming from the direction of Linda's apartment, she might tell him where she'd prefer he shove his oak bookcases.

It was a hell of a painful situation. A stupid situation was more like it. He got along with people; he normally didn't make enemies by showing concern for other human beings.

But he shouldn't forget that Linda was not a born-and-bred Montanan, as he was, and maybe Los Angelenos had different standards toward friends and lovers than he did. How would a man who'd never lived anywhere but small-town Montana know what a city woman expected from a relationship?

He dusted his hands with another cloth and called it a day. "Hey, small fry," he called out to Samantha. "Let's drive out to the ranch and bum dinner off Grandma. What d'ya say?"

"Yay!" Samantha jumped up, dolls and toys forgotten.

Linda phoned twice more, once at six and again at eight. Since Tag was so conscientious about Samantha's bedtime, she concluded that he simply wasn't answering the phone because it might be her on the line. Then, too, she mused, he could have caller ID on his phone, in which case he would *know* who was calling the second his phone rang.

She called for Tippy and they went upstairs. After changing into her nightgown, she lay on her bed—waiting for total darkness so she could sit unseen on her balcony—and made herself miserable again by wondering if Tag was out with another woman.

Turning to her side, she dug her fingers into the pillow and whispered, "Damn," while a few tears spilled from her eyes.

Clara Raymond had company, which was customary for Saturday nights. Alice and she took turns preparing dinner and then they played cribbage, sometimes until the wee hours.

"It's a lovely night," Clara said. "Warm enough to leave those windows open. You're not chilly, are you, Alice?"

"With my hot flashes?" Alice chuckled. "How many old ladies still suffer hot flashes?"

"Oh, they're so awful. I remember how it was, believe me."

"Yes, but you got over the darn things." She laid down a face card from her hand and said, "Ten."

Clara played a five and counted. "Fifteen-two." She moved her peg on the cribbage board two holes.

Alice played a five. "Twenty for two." She moved her peg two holes.

Clara played another five. "Twenty-five for six. Now don't tell me you have the fourth five!"

Alice did, and she played it with a triumphant giggle. "Thirty for twelve and I believe that puts me out!"

"Clearly you're tonight's champion," Clara said. "But I'll get you next week. Now, how about a nice cup of tea?"

"Lovely," Alice replied.

They were sipping hot tea and nibbling delicious homemade sugar cookies when they heard a noise from outside. Their eyes met.

"See?" Clara said quietly. "Odd noises almost every night. I would bet my entire savings account that they're coming from the back of the building, where Linda's apartment is located."

"Dare we take a look?"

"Dare we *not* take a look?" Clara said wryly. "Sit still while I turn off the lamps."

In the dark they peeked through Clara's window screens. "There's someone over there, near that big tree," Clara whispered. "Do you see him?"

"Yes! Oh my goodness, should we call the sheriff?"

"Alice, he's just one of Linda's boyfriends."

"Well, I can't see Tag Kingsley sneaking around like that!"

"Of course not. It's the other one." The dark form vanished. "He's gone, probably into Linda's apartment. And don't ask me why he acts like a sneaky thief instead of a beau, because I don't understand half the things young people do today."

"Well, neither do I, but that man's behavior strikes me as peculiar. I'm not sure we should just write it off as normal for romantic trysts these days. You could be in danger, Clara."

"Nonsense," Clara scoffed. "I still have Henry's .45, and

I wouldn't hesitate to use it if someone dared to invade my home."

"If you heard him," Alice said. "If he came in after you were asleep, you wouldn't hear him."

"I'm a light sleeper, Alice, and that weapon is close at hand when I retire. Don't worry, this old bird can take care of herself just fine."

Alfred stood directly under the balcony that he had finally figured out was attached to Linda's apartment. He was sort of spaced out, though, because he'd driven to Billings—a darned painful trip—seen a doctor, told him about being forced to go up a tree to lop off its top—dangerous in a windstorm—and losing his balance. The doctor had been sympathetic about his injuries and given him some antibiotic cream to use on his bruises and pills to ease the pain and help him sleep.

He'd taken one of the pills before leaving Billings and had arrived back at his motel feeling light-headed. But he'd been able to move around without groaning and had decided to get this miserable job over with so he could go home.

Thus, he stood there, weaving back and forth a bit, and worried about the height of the balcony from the ground. The tree incident was indelibly etched on his brain. Finding footholds and climbing up to that balcony would be worse than climbing a tree, which he wouldn't try again for a million bucks.

But what if he had a ladder?

Weaving dizzily, Alfred pondered the logistics of the problem: Go to MonMart and buy the ladder; somehow transport it in his car; bring it here after dark; carry it from car to balcony.

It *might* work.

At midnight Tag began yawning. He'd been surprised and pleased by his family's exuberance when he and Samantha had arrived at the ranch. Reed and Maura had been there. The whole family had been beaming from ear to ear.

Carolyn explained. "Russell phoned a couple of hours ago. They were so excited they could barely contain themselves, but they finally managed to tell me their good news. All the paperwork is finally finished and approved, and he and Susannah have Mei. They'll be home on Tuesday and asked me to make sure the Community Church is still available for their wedding on Friday evening. Tag, I called all of you right away. Weren't you at home?"

"I was out in the shop, using the sander on and off. I can't hear the phone with that running. You must have called when it was on."

"Possibly, but you're here now and that's what matters. You'll all stay for dinner, I hope?" Carolyn's smile included all three of her children.

It had been a fine evening. Tag was a stickler about Samantha's bedtime, and he had tucked her in at the usual time. But it was time to go home now. Maura was already gone and Reed was in the process of leaving.

Carolyn didn't approve of Tag's intention to take Samantha out of a warm bed for the drive back to town.

"Please leave her right where she is, Tag," Carolyn said. "And you go to bed in your old room. We all get up early around here, and you can go home in the morning."

Tag decided it didn't matter, and he kissed his mother's cheek, said good night to his father and Reed and then went to the bedroom he had used from birth until he had moved out to marry Melanie.

As tired as he was, though, he didn't immediately fall asleep; there was too much to think about. He was happy for Russell, who would marry the woman he loved next Friday evening. The wedding was going to be a simple affair, with a family-only guest list. Tiny Mei, Susannah's newly adopted daughter, would be there, along with her new aunt, uncles, grandparents and five-year-old cousin.

Life was great for Russell right now, and Tag told himself he was happy for him. He did *not* resent his oldest brother for having what he did not...the woman he loved.

Yes, damn it, he loved Linda. A battery of emotions suddenly choked him as he lay there and tried to understand—one more time—why the perfectly ordinary steps of concern and caring that he had taken on Wednesday night had caused a seemingly unbridgeable chasm between them.

Was he going to walk away and forget Linda? Get on with his life as though they hadn't met, hadn't made love, hadn't touched each other's souls?

Determination overcame softer emotions throughout his system. "Not on your life."

Chapter Twelve

Wearing the comfy white terry robe she favored, Linda picked up her folded Sunday-morning newspaper from the sidewalk and went back inside. In her kitchen she sat at the counter with her coffee and toast, fully intending to read the paper while she ate.

But she found that she couldn't muster interest in the tidbits of news. The question taking precedence in her mind this morning was how long she should wait before calling Tag. He'd told her he never worked on Sunday, and it was possible that he was sleeping in. Did five-year-old girls sleep in? Linda wondered, and then was just barely able to swallow her bite of toast because of the massive lump in her throat. She tortured herself even more by visualizing Sunday morning in Tag's home, with Samantha bright-eyed from a good night's sleep and Tag making their breakfast.

"Stop it," she said sharply, chiding herself for such unnecessary torment. She would call shortly and Tag would answer or he wouldn't. It was as simple as that. She couldn't *make* him like her again, and if it really was over between them then she would have to forget him.

Such a simple concept, she thought wistfully, knowing that

she could never forget Tag and his endearing grins, his passionate lovemaking, his beautiful body, his teasing remarks and laughter. Only a complete fool would try to convince herself that she could forget a man like Tag, and while she knew she had done some foolish things in her life, she didn't consider herself a total fool.

Not yet, at any rate. Linda sucked in a suddenly anxious breath as another question struck without mercy: Exactly how far would she go to get Tag to talk to her? Sad and lonely and still hopeful were one thing; desperate was quite another. When did hope evolve into desperation? Were there signs she should be watching for?

Her doorbell rang. Startled, Linda slid off the stool, made sure her robe was securely closed, and made her way to the front door. She peered through the peephole and thought her heart might stop on the spot. It was Tag!

"Oh my God," she whispered tremulously, wishing heart and soul that she looked better. Her hair was still damp and uncombed from her shower, and there wasn't a speck of makeup on her face. She should be dressed, not wrapped in an old robe.

Then she remembered that although she had phoned him three times yesterday afternoon and evening, she hadn't left any messages. He was here on his own!

Inhaling deeply, striving for composure, she opened the door. One arm was above his head, propped against the frame of her door, and he looked so incredibly handsome and morning-fresh that Linda just lost it.

"Tag," she said breathlessly and reached out to curl her fingers into the front of his shirt. Backing up, she urged him forward. His eyes grew darker and took on a feverish sheen. "Where's Samantha?" she whispered.

"At the ranch. We stayed there last night." Tag made sure the door was closed and locked behind him. Linda's sensual reaction to seeing him was really all he could think of. She wasn't mad at him, and maybe she never had been, beyond those few minutes after the deputies had come calling on her Wednesday night.

"I've been a damned idiot," he said huskily as he locked her into his arms, nestling her body against his.

She fought tears of gratitude for whatever fate had brought them both to their senses, and raised her arms to his neck. "Don't think about it." He kissed her, hungrily, passionately, and she kissed him in the same arousing way.

He managed to untie her robe and then she felt his hands on her bare skin. She was so ready for this that the inhibitions that had once directed her behavior seemed to disintegrate within her, never, she was certain, to reappear. This time, kissing and touching Tag wherever she chose, there were no hurdles of morality or shyness to clear, and she wanted to caress his manhood, so she did it. After unzipping his jeans, she held him in her hand.

"You're very beautiful," she whispered against his lips. "I love touching you."

"If you keep on touching me like that, this isn't going to last very long. And I want it to last, Linda. I want to pleasure you. You're all I've thought about every day and every night since…" It was too painful to say out loud. He'd been so stupid, so dense, so childish about something that he should have put an end to on Thursday morning. He could have managed to see Linda before she left for school on Thursday, and neither of them would have gone through the hell that had nearly brought him to his knees. Now he knew that Linda had been in that same lost place with him.

"Don't say it. Don't even think about it. We can talk later. Let's go upstairs." After a second, she added with a slight smile, "To my unmade bed."

He loved her for understanding what he hadn't been able to say, and she was right. They could talk later, all day, in fact. Sammy was safe at the ranch. He was free for the rest of the day, and he was so thankful that Linda hadn't slammed the door in his face that he was weak-kneed over it.

He gazed into her eyes and whispered, "You're my darling."

"Yes, oh, yes."

He kissed her until they were both so overcome by hot and demanding emotions that kissing was no longer enough, and then he swung her into his arms and carried her up the stairs.

In her bedroom she threw off her robe and felt rosy all over from the desirous look he bestowed on her naked body. They both undressed, Tag tearing at buttons and fabric, fumbling and hurrying and breathing as though they had each run a mile.

Lying on top of the disarrayed covers, she held up her arms to him. He followed her down, fitting his form to hers, and immediately began kissing her lips, her forehead and cheeks, the soft, tender spot just beneath her chin and the sweet curve of her throat. From there his lips blazed a trail of utter delight—for each of them—to first her left breast, then the right, where he licked her nipples and then gently sucked on them.

"Tag, oh, Tag," she moaned. The aching pleasure darting from her nipples to the pit of her stomach would not let her lie still. Writhing under him, she spread her legs so that he fit in between them, in perfect position for what every cell in her body screamed for. "Do it," she said raggedly. "Do it, darling. I need you so much."

He didn't need to be asked twice. Swiftly, almost roughly, he slid into her and heard her gasp with pleasure. They moved as one entity, connected in the most elemental way, and it turned out to be hotter and faster than anything they had shared their first night together. In mere minutes they climaxed, first Linda then Tag.

They were breathing hard, and it took a while for their

hearts to slow down. Tag held her close, her back to his front, and let the scent of her hair permeate his senses. If he were any happier he would levitate three feet above the bed and float around the room.

"You are the most incredible woman on earth," he said huskily, with his lips near her ear.

"I'm so happy," she said softly. "And I never really was. Before you."

He raised his head to peer at her face. "I love being the guy making you happy, but, sweetheart, there are all kinds of happiness. Surely your art gave you pleasure."

"I didn't want to be an artist. It just happened."

"Because you were born with talent, right?"

"I guess." She turned over to face him. "I never wanted to be like my parents, so I was afraid of getting too involved in the art world. It was all they lived for while I was growing up."

"Which is why you chose teaching as a career?"

"My teaching career began here in Rumor, Tag."

"Really?"

"Yes, really."

He thought of a bunch of questions he could ask about that topic, but he wasn't in the mood to dig up old memories or events from either of their pasts. So he looked into her eyes and deliberately changed the subject, bringing it back to them and only them, as they were now, in bed, in each other's arms, as close as two people could be.

"Do you have any idea how beautiful you are?" he asked.

"I think so," she said, and he saw the small frown between her eyes.

"You *don't* know, do you? I can tell by your expression that you think of yourself as ordinary, and you're not."

She thought a moment. "If I appear extraordinary to you, it's all because of chemistry."

A teasing twinkle entered his eyes. "I thought you taught art not chemistry."

She gently slapped his arm. "You know what I meant."

"Well, don't lie there and tell me you're not special, because that's something no one could ever convince me of."

"All right, fine. Thank you for the lovely compliments." She recalled wondering if his compliments were his way of enticing women to bed, and while she wasn't thrilled with the idea, she knew it was a possibility. He was a charmer by nature, and she had fallen hard for him. Were his exaggerated appreciations of female beauty a significant part of his charm?

She hated thinking that way. They had made up. Everything was good again, and they were in bed and naked and she loved him as she had loved no other.

She began tracing patterns on his chest with her fingertips. "I'm glad you're not all hairy," she said with a smile.

He chuckled. "I wanted a hairy chest in high school almost as much as I wanted whiskers."

"Well, I'm not fond of either. A clean-shaven face and a hairless chest is a dynamite combination, handsome."

He whooped. "You don't want me to say you're beautiful, but you don't mind calling me handsome. Where's the parity in those attitudes, my sweet?"

She had to laugh. "Guess there isn't any."

He pulled her tightly against himself and kissed her lips. "Time for a replay," he whispered against her mouth, and she knew from the hard shaft of his manhood pressing into her abdomen that he intended they make love again.

She cooperated fully.

Around two Tag called to check on Samantha and to ask if it was all right if she stayed at the ranch for a few more hours. Carolyn said, "Of course it's all right. We love having her."

After he put the phone down, Tag looked at Linda, who

couldn't be more relaxed, nor put on a more satisfied expression, if she died trying. He lay down again and placed his head near hers on the same pillow.

Looking directly into her drowsy, heavy-lidded eyes, he said softly, "I'd like you to meet my family."

Linda's eyes were suddenly huge, and she jerked herself to a sitting position.

"Did I just say something I shouldn't have?" Tag asked slowly, noticing how she was covering her breasts with the sheet. Inasmuch as they had both been unashamedly naked for hours, he saw her sudden modesty as withdrawal. "You don't want to meet them, do you?"

"I...it's silly, but..." It *was* silly, but she had successfully separated Tag from the wealthy Kingsleys, and meeting them would change everything. They would become real people if she met them, and what would Tag become? He was perfect now, an honest man with an honest vocation. He worked for his living, same as she did, and lived an ordinary life, same as her. His house was beautiful but it wasn't a mansion, and he'd built it himself, which gave it immeasurable value in her eyes. If she learned that he had millions tucked here and there in banks and investment accounts? *Oh Lord.* Just the thought made her shudder.

Tag saw that shudder and was surprised. Frowning because he didn't grasp Linda's apparent reluctance to doing something so normal as meeting her lover's family—this wasn't just an affair going on between them, after all—he nevertheless hastened to reassure her.

"Linda, you don't have to meet them now. I mean, if it makes you uncomfortable we'll forget the whole thing."

She turned her head a bit, just enough to take a peek at his face. If her reluctance was causing him distress, she would make an attempt to explain her attitude, although exactly how she would accomplish that without making herself look petty escaped her.

"Are you sure?" she asked in an unsteady voice.

"For now, yes. You'll have to meet them someday, though."

"I suppose."

"They're not ogres, sweetheart. Come here." He urged her back into his arms, kissed the top of her head and then gazed off into space. Russell and Susannah's wedding would be the perfect opportunity for Linda to meet his family, and vice versa. Maybe he could change Linda's mind by then, he thought, although the big event wasn't that far off.

He'd work on it, he decided, because with his feelings for Linda getting more serious by the day, she and his family *had* to meet.

Around five, Tag used her shower and then returned to the bedroom to get dressed. Linda lay in bed, relaxed as a cat, and watched him. She loved the fluid way he moved and the rippling of the muscles in his arms and back. He was an incredible person, very male, very handsome and *hers*.

He *was* hers, wasn't he?

He turned around then and she got a full frontal view of his remarkable body. Her mouth went dry, and she felt the marvelously familiar tingle between her legs that he and only he had brought to life. She folded back the sheet and struck an erotic pose so he would see all of her. "Tag," she said softly to get his attention.

She saw the change that came over his face when he looked at her. "You want to make love again?" he asked raggedly. She could see his manhood stirring, beginning to harden.

"Do you have enough time? I know you have to pick up Sammy." Not long ago the mere thought of such boldness would have reddened her face. Now it seemed perfectly natural.

Tag didn't answer; he just stepped to the bed and lay down next to her. The hunger with which they kissed and made love was astonishing, for only twenty or so minutes before his shower they had drained themselves in a wildly passionate encounter.

Apparently not, though, Linda thought dreamily. Apparently, the well of this kind of emotion didn't easily run dry.

Physically sated again, they held each other. Linda knew Tag had to leave, but she couldn't help wishing otherwise.

"You're wonderful," she whispered while pressing a loving kiss to his chest.

"I'd like to hold you like this all night."

"I know you can't."

Tag pushed himself up to an elbow and gently brushed tendrils of hair back from her face. "There's something I've been meaning to talk to you about since the day we met."

She smiled. "Better late than never, darling."

"It's about your talent. Sammy loves to draw and color and she does pretty well for a kid her age, but I was thinking how great it would be for someone with your abilities to teach her techniques and things. And not just her, sweetheart. I was thinking more along the lines of your doing some teaching at Rugrats. What do you think?"

"Well, I don't know." Linda hesitated a moment. "Have you talked to Susannah about it? No, you couldn't have. She's still gone, isn't she?"

"Yes, but she'll be back this coming week. I wanted to get your take on the idea before I mentioned it to her." Tag got off the bed and started to dress. "Think about it. I doubt that the classes would take up too much of your time, probably only about an hour a day."

"It's not the time," Linda said thoughtfully. "I'm going to be footloose and fancy-free for months, once school is out. But teaching such young children. I'm just not sure I know how to do that."

Tag grinned. "Give them a piece of blank paper and show them the right way to draw a horse, or a dog, or a house."

Linda cocked her eyebrow. "Easy for you to say, big boy."

"Any more of that kind of flirting and I'll be back in that bed with you."

She smiled. "You make me so happy I could sing. Oh, I think I already told you that."

Tag moved to the edge of the bed, bent over and tenderly kissed her lips. "Say it anytime you wish, sweetheart." He straightened and then laughed. "I almost forgot. I have two bookcases for you on the back of my truck."

Linda's eyes lit up as she jumped out of bed. "Oh, I'm so thrilled. Let me throw something on and I'll help you carry them in."

"I can manage just fine. I kind of like what you're wearing now."

"You like my birthday suit? You're bad, mister, really bad."

They laughed together, then Tag left the room and Linda went to her closet for some jeans and a shirt that she hurriedly pulled on. She was putting on shoes when she heard Tag downstairs.

"Are you back already?" she called down.

"Back with the first bookcase, sweetheart. I think I know where you want it, but maybe you'd better come down here and make sure," Tag called out.

"Be right there." Linda skipped down the stairs, then stopped in awe. The bookcase was beautiful. "Oh, Tag, it's wonderful."

Together they situated the piece exactly where Linda had originally envisioned it. "Now I can start unpacking my books."

"I'm going out for the other one." Tag left the apartment, and Linda ran her fingers over the smooth, varnished wood of the bookcase.

"You are a true artisan," she said softly, talking to Tag even though he was outside. His love of carpentry was apparent in his creations. Why was she so worried about meeting his family? What did the Kingsleys' wealth have to do with her admiration of Tag's career? Linda drew her eyebrows together, frowning over questions that made her uneasy. She'd known from the beginning that Tag wasn't an orphan, and she should be pleased and proud that he wanted her to meet his family.

Hearing Tag returning, she forced the worry from her mind and helped him situate the second bookcase.

"They're absolutely beautiful," she said. "I love them, Tag. Can you make me three more for the bedroom?"

He kissed her. "Absolutely. I have to go, sweetheart. I'll call you later, all right? After I get home with Sammy?"

"Wonderful." After Tag had gone, the apartment seemed empty and much too silent. Linda put on some music, then went upstairs and carried down a box of books. She had used small cartons for her books so that she would be able to lift them, and the closet in her studio and the small storage shed in the carport were both crammed full.

She wasn't facing a small, inconsequential job, but finally being able to unpack her books was going to be more fun than drudgery, she thought as she slit open the sealed flaps of the box and smiled.

Alfred had become bolder about driving his car around Rumor. Actually, he had little choice in the matter. If he wanted to eat on a semiregular basis, he had to shop for groceries that wouldn't spoil overnight without refrigeration, or go to restaurants. MonMart was a huge store that sold almost anything Alfred could think of, but it also did a thriving business and there was no telling when he would run into the same shopper two or three times. He figured that would be enough to arouse questions about who he was and why he was hanging around this nosy little burg.

He slipped in and out of the Calico Diner during its busiest times of the day, usually around noon or five in the afternoon and did the same with the Rooftop Café. He couldn't be sure that any of the townspeople had caught on to the stranger in their midst, but every time he stepped foot out of his motel room, he started sweating. It was a hell of a way to live and he resented Paul Fioretti a little more each day.

On Sunday afternoon he slowly drove past Linda's apartment building and spotted the truck that her boyfriend drove. It was parked in the visitor's lot and before he was completely past it, he did a double take. Linda's boyfriend was unloading furniture! He must be moving in.

"Hell's bells," Alfred muttered, realizing his mistake in assuming the guy had been living with Linda all along. Could the situation get any worse? he wondered as his small reserve of courage shrank.

One other person noticed Tag Kingsley carrying furniture into Linda's apartment. "Well, I never," Clara Raymond declared. "Is he moving in? Where's Samantha? Oh, this is getting way out of hand. I wonder if I should call Carolyn Kingsley and tell her what's going on. Scandalous, that's what it is, just scandalous!"

She couldn't wait until tomorrow's coffee klatch to pass on *this* news, and she hurried to the phone and dialed Alice's number.

"You will never believe what I just saw," Clara said the second her friend answered. "Tag Kingsley is hauling furniture into Linda's apartment, and there's no sign of Samantha. What do you think of that?"

"You don't mean it! My word, is he moving in with her? He has that lovely house, you know. I would think if they were going to live together that Linda would move in with him, instead of him moving in with her."

"One would think," Clara agreed. "But as we've said a hundred times, Alice, people our age will never understand the antics of today's generation. I'm dreadfully shocked, and I was wondering if I should call Carolyn Kingsley and tell her about this. She's a very moral woman, and I'm certain that she wouldn't like what's going on for all the world to see."

"I'm sure she wouldn't. But what if there's another explanation? Maybe you should wait a bit, say, a day or two, and see what takes place before calling Carolyn."

"You're right. Far be it from me to make trouble for anyone."

"Yes, dear, I know how true that is."

When the phone rang two hours later, Linda smiled and picked it up, fully expecting to hear Tag's voice. Instead, she heard a stranger's deep, gravelly voice saying, "Don't you dare let a man move in with you. This is a warning. You had better pay attention to it."

Linda was so startled she nearly dropped the phone. Just in time she got hold of her wits and said angrily, "Who is this? How dare you?" The phone went dead.

She slowly set it down. Her heart was pounding a mile a minute. What on earth was *that* all about? Why would anyone think a man was moving in with her, and who would care if one did?

Linda's legs gave out and she fell onto the sofa. "The stalker," she whispered as fear built within her. That weird little man who had appeared and disappeared so many times since she moved to Rumor was now making threatening phone calls to her? Why, for God's sake? She'd never seen him before her move.

But what made him think a man was moving in with her? Surely not because he'd seen Tag carrying in a couple of bookcases.

"This is getting scary," Linda said, truly wary for the first time, because now she couldn't pretend that someone wasn't watching everything she did.

What in heaven's name should she do?

Chapter Thirteen

On Wednesday evening the entire Kingsley family gathered at Stratton and Carolyn's house. Everyone was focused on tiny Mei, slumbering peacefully in her soon-to-be father's arms. "She's still tired from the long trip," Russell explained.

"She's so beautiful," everyone kept saying, which was only the truth. "Like a China doll."

Russell grinned and Susannah laughed. "That's what she is. Or was. Now she's an American doll."

Russell reached for Susannah's hand. "After Friday evening, we'll be an American *family*."

"Yes," Susannah answered softly, speaking to Russell with an adoring expression in her lovely eyes. "Everything is ready at the Community Church."

"Yes, the church is ours on Friday evening," Carolyn said. "Pastor Rayburn has agreed to perform the ceremony, and I promise it will be the loveliest wedding ever held in that wonderful old church."

Everyone in the room believed her. When Carolyn Kingsley made a promise, she kept it.

* * *

Life had become so great, so exciting, that Linda walked around all week with a seemingly permanent smile on her face. Her students didn't notice, but her colleagues did. Shelby was the only one with enough nerve to take her curiosity directly to Linda.

"Something big is going on, lady," Shelby said in the lunchroom on Thursday. "You've been grinning like the Cheshire cat all week. Did you finally decide to be glad about the school year coming to an end?"

"There *is* something big going on, and it has nothing to do with the end of the school year." Linda's green eyes were twinkling like Christmas bulbs.

"Well, are you going to keep me in suspense, or what?"

"I suppose there's no reason not to tell you. I'm in love."

Shelby's eyes widened. "Well, for goodness' sake! Who's the lucky guy?"

"I'd rather not say just yet. I don't want it to get around town."

"How long has this been going on?"

"A week or so."

"And you think it isn't *already* around town? Believe me, kiddo, the only reason I haven't heard about it is because I live in Whitehorn."

"Oh, I really don't think anyone knows, Shelby," Linda said earnestly.

"Do you still believe in the tooth fairy, as well?" Shelby asked dryly.

Linda fell silent. *Was* the town talking? Maybe she was the only person in Rumor who hadn't heard the gossip. Her and Tag, that is. If he'd heard talk about the two of them he would have told her, wouldn't he? They saw each other every day and talked on the phone every evening. Each morning after taking Samantha to Rugrats, he came by and they made love until she had to leave for work. Then, in the afternoon, she went directly home from school and he came by again. Their meetings never lasted for very long, but Tag had a business to run and a young daughter to care for, and Linda understood and admired his dedication to duty.

Tomorrow night, though, they were going to have a real date. He had talked about it all week. "I have something special in mind," he'd said. "But don't ask what it is, because then I'd have to tell you and it wouldn't be a surprise." She was so thrilled about his surprise date that all week she had been mentally putting together the perfect outfit—something attractive and subtly sexy.

"Shelby, you're wrong in this case. We haven't appeared in public together even one time." Linda smiled. "But that's going to change tomorrow night. He has something special planned."

"Well, then you might as well tell me his name. If it isn't already all over town, as you seem to believe, it will be after that."

Linda bit her lip for a moment, then nodded. "You're right." She lowered her voice. "It's Tag Kingsley."

Shelby's mouth dropped. "Your fella is a Kingsley? Why, you sly puss. How'd you land one of the biggest fish in the sea? Oh, there has to be a story behind this. Give, girl, I'm all ears."

Laughing, Linda got to her feet and picked up her lunch tray. "Sorry, but that's all the information you're getting, you nosy Nellie."

"But you'll tell me about tomorrow night next week, right?" Shelby said as Linda walked away.

"We'll see."

Linda hadn't received any more warning phone calls, and she wondered if she had misinterpreted what had been said to her on the phone Sunday night. Life was so good these days that she wouldn't permit the word *stalker* to even enter her mind. She hadn't mentioned that word or the telephone incident to Tag because he had called the sheriff when he'd thought she might be in danger, and just the thought of another visit from the law made her cringe.

They had discussed that topic briefly. "I was worried about you, sweetheart," Tag said.

"I realize that."

"But you don't want me worrying about you."

"Darling, worry all you want, but please don't sound any more unnecessary alarms."

She was thinking about that while sitting on her balcony on Thursday evening. Had that weird little guy really been stalking her? Was he the man—the voice had sounded male— who had made that phone call? Why hadn't she seen or heard anything from him since the call? Did he think he had frightened her enough? In other words, was his modus operandi no more than silly maneuvers to frighten her before moving on to another innocent victim?

Those were new and, Linda realized, very disturbing questions. What if she had figured him out and now he was scaring the living daylights out of some other woman?

She really should talk to the sheriff, she thought with butterflies filling her stomach, but not here. Lord, no, not here in her apartment. Maybe she would work up the courage to go by the sheriff's station and talk to someone there.

But it made her terribly nervous to even think about doing that, and she was afraid that going to the sheriff just might be too much for her to deal with.

She would, however, give the idea more thought, she promised herself.

On Friday afternoon Tag didn't come to the apartment as he'd been doing. Their date was set for six o'clock, and the minute Linda got home from work she began getting ready for the big event. She could hardly contain her excitement, and she fairly bounced around her bedroom and bath with nervous energy. Tippy followed her steps for a while, then gave up and curled up on his rug near the bed.

Linda found a wrinkle in the dress she planned to wear, and she ran downstairs with it to set up the ironing board and plug in the iron. Giving the appliance a few minutes to heat, she wandered into the living room to admire her bookcases. She had filled the shelves and still hadn't unpacked all her books. There were three boxes in the studio closet and a good dozen in the carport storage area. But Tag had said the other bookcases she had ordered would be finished in about a week, and then she would have a heyday unpacking the rest.

Standing back, delighting in the sight of those beautiful bookcases filled with her beloved books, Linda narrowed her eyes. Something was amiss. The books weren't as she had placed them. She didn't alphabetize, but she always sorted by author. *And they should have been in perfect alignment!*

With her heart in her throat, Linda approached a bookcase, praying she was wrong. But several books by favorite authors were intermingled, and the alignment of volumes on every shelf was off. Not by much. No one else would notice. But she did, and the discrepancies screamed at her: Someone had rearranged her books! Why? When?

Linda glanced around, feeling as though she wasn't alone. There was nobody to see, but she still felt a presence. Someone had been in her apartment and touched her things. She felt violated.

Fear and anger struck her then. How dare someone invade her home? What else did they touch with their filthy hands, or steal? Quickly then, she hurried through the downstairs rooms to see what else was moved, or maybe missing. And when nothing looked awry on the first floor, she ran upstairs. The first thing she checked was her jewelry box. She had a few pieces of good jewelry and the rest was costume, but it was all there.

"Well, what in hell were you after?" she muttered, looking around the bedroom suspiciously. Surely someone hadn't broken in for her paintings! Hurrying to her studio, she gasped. The books from the three boxes she hadn't yet unpacked were strewn on the floor of the closet, as though someone had grabbed and dropped them. It was mystifying. Why on earth would anyone look through her books?

She walked to the bed on shaky legs. Her fingertips curled into the bedspread on each side of her, digging in as though seeking a handhold while her mind frantically sought a solution.

What was this all about? Her books weren't first editions or of any real value, except to her, but they appeared to be the only thing in the apartment that the burglar or intruder or weirdo, whichever he was, had been interested in. Could anything be more peculiar? What would the sheriff make of something so bizarre?

Tag had a key to the apartment, and so did the manager of the building. Linda simply could not see either man entering when she wasn't home and looking through her books. That idea, in fact, was utterly preposterous. Actually, the whole thing was preposterous.

Sucking in an unsteady breath, she eyed Tippy sitting on his haunches near her feet. "Where were you when this was going on?" she asked. He wagged his tail. "Some watchdog you are."

Alfred paced the small space of his motel room—back and forth, wall to wall—and chewed antacids while blinking back tears. He'd finally devised a plan so clean and brilliant it had amazed even him. He had waited for that old busybody in the front apartment to leave for her morning coffee at the Calico Diner—oh, yes, he'd figured her out—then he'd quickly picked Linda's lock and stepped inside. Tippy had thrown a fit until Alfred had tossed a handful of doggie treats on the floor, and after that the wretched little beast loved him.

He had spotted the bookcases in the living room at once and had been so thrilled he'd nearly hyperventilated. There, on one of those shelves, had to be Paul's journal. Alfred had immediately envisioned himself getting into his car, leaving this horrible place in the dust and receiving a hero's welcome from Paul when he handed him the journal.

Only it hadn't been on one of those shelves. Nor, when he'd gone in search of more books and finally found some in boxes in a closet, had it been among them. *It wasn't in the apartment!*

"Oh, God, how am I gonna tell Paul? He'll kill me."

It's not your fault! For crying out loud, Paul should have figured out that Linda had sorted through her books before moving to Montana and thrown his out! Be a man. Call him and…and…

Alfred collapsed on the bed with his heart pounding so hard he thought he was having a heart attack. He couldn't call Paul and admit failure. There must be more books somewhere in that apartment. There *had* to be.

Tag arrived promptly at six. Linda was ready, but she should have been ecstatic about the surprise evening ahead and instead she couldn't shake the awful sense of violation that had overwhelmed her a few hours earlier.

"Come in," she said quietly after opening the door when Tag rang the doorbell. "You could have used your key."

"Not tonight." He looked for a smile on her face and saw not even a hint. Something was wrong. Had she figured out what he had planned for the evening? If she had been reading her newspapers instead of stacking them in the laundry room, she probably would have. Why *hadn't* she been reading the papers? Something was bothering her, Tag knew, and he'd been sort of thinking it was the enormous feelings that had developed between them. The feelings were still there—at least his were—but with her acting so withdrawn, he wondered if something else was causing this mood swing. Something he knew nothing about. Something she hadn't told him.

"Sweetheart, you look terrific," he said brightly, hoping to transfer his good mood to her. What he'd told her wasn't flattery; she looked fantastic. Her outfit was a stunning shade of green, a dress and matching jacket. She wore high heels, and her incredible hair had been twisted and pinned into a loose knot at the back of her head. Wisps floated around her beautiful face. And there was a very subtle scent of perfume in the air. She had, apparently, gone all-out for this date.

"Linda, you're beautiful," he added a bit more solemnly. "I'm truly knocked out."

"Thank you." She eyed his suit, which had not come off of any rack. "I'm sort of knocked out myself," she said, pleased that he knew how to dress and oddly concerned that he had enough money to fly to Europe and have his clothes custom-made by, arguably, the best tailors in the world.

"I'll get my bag," she said, and walked away.

Tag checked his watch and saw that they had enough time to do a little talking before they left. He wanted tonight to be a major success, and maybe he could bring her spirits up a notch with some conversation. "There's no rush. Let's have a glass of wine before we go."

Linda stopped and turned. "You're conducting the orchestra tonight, so if you say we have time for a glass of wine, then I guess we have time."

"Why don't you sit on the sofa and let me get it."

"That's fine, if you wish, but there's no reason why I couldn't...."

"Just sit, sweetheart." Tag hurried to the kitchen.

Linda sank onto the sofa and immediately began staring at the bookcases. She hadn't returned the books to their initial arrangement, and their disarray made her heart beat faster.

Who had done that, and for God's sake, *why?* It made absolutely no sense. She suddenly wanted to tell Tag about it. She needed to talk about it. Too many unexplained and unreasonable things had been occurring. She wasn't scared to death, but she was terribly uneasy, maybe with very good reason.

Tag came in with two glasses of wine, handed her one and then sat next to her. "Cheers, sweetheart," he said, touching her glass with his. "To us and to the evening ahead. May it be everything I've hoped it would be."

Linda finally smiled, which gladdened Tag's heart. "To us and the evening ahead," she repeated, and sipped from her glass. But her smile wasn't all sweetness and light. She wanted to tell Tag about every single thing that had happened prior to today and finish her story with the book episode. He was so happy over his plans for tonight, though, she hated the idea of ruining his upbeat mood.

Maybe later on, she decided. Depending on how the evening went. Sighing softly, she raised her glass to her lips.

Tag couldn't seem to stop looking at her. She no longer seemed so down in the dumps. Relaxing had been a good idea. But it had also given Tag some very personal ideas. He took a quick peek at his watch; he had time to kiss her.

He slid across the sofa cushions to sit closer to her. She noticed and smiled at him. "Am I reading your mind?"

"Probably." He leaned forward and pressed his lips to hers. It was a gentle kiss that lasted a long time and could have turned feverishly hungry in a second, if either of them had let it. When it was over he looked into her eyes and took a chance. "You seem different tonight. Is there something I should know?"

Linda's heart skipped a beat. He had just given her the perfect opening to bare her uneasy soul. But the certainty of worrying him and worrying about what he might try to do about her problems stopped her. She had firsthand experience, after all, with his need to protect those he cared about. And he did care about her, she was as positive of that as she was of her feelings for him.

And so she let the opportunity slide past and said instead, "I'm not at all different. Except for better-than-usual clothes, a good makeup job and a fancy hairdo." She'd spoken lightly in an effort to throw him off the scent. As close as they had become, it was only natural for him to sense her inner unease. "Kiss me again," she whispered.

"I'd love to." He took her glass from her hand and set it on the coffee table along with his. This time he put his arms around her, laid her head back and really kissed her. His tongue teased her lips and she felt the heavy need she had come to know and love beginning in the pit of her stomach.

"If you kiss me like that for very long, I won't be able to stop," she whispered tremulously.

"Guess I should go sit in that chair over there," he said hoarsely. He probed the depths of her eyes. "Should I?"

"You should, but please don't." She moistened her lips with the tip of her tongue and saw his eyes become darker. "Do we have time for...for...you know?"

"Do we have time to undress and do all the things we both need and want right now? No, and I shouldn't have touched you, though it was just about all I've thought of from the second you opened your door. Linda, you're always beautiful...and sexy...but you're especially so tonight."

She thought of the word *love,* and nearly said it. It might be too soon for them to actually talk about love and commitment, but it wasn't too soon for her to know in her heart that she would love him forever.

She leaned into him and brought her mouth to his. "One more," she whispered huskily. "Just one more, darling."

One more was their undoing. This kiss was hot and passionate and decimated common sense. In seconds Tag's hand was under her dress, sliding up her thigh. She opened her legs and moaned when his fingers went beneath her panties and began stroking in that rhythmic, sensual way that she had no defense against. She didn't worry about her dress getting wrinkled or her makeup getting smeared. She had to have what he was giving her.

She reached to the front of his pants and caressed the hard bulge behind his zipper. But she didn't take him out; if they went that far they would undress completely and go for broke. His surprise would be forgotten, and they would spend the entire evening in bed. It was incredibly tempting, but so was a real date.

"Tag. Tag," she said raggedly against his lips as his fingers moved between her legs.

He only kissed her again and kept tantalizing her most sensitive spot. She felt herself going over the edge, and small, shaken moans came from deep in her throat. Her release was so strong she fell forward against him, weak and limp and not giving a damn if she ever moved again.

Tag kissed the top of her head, then chuckled softly. "You're going to have to fix your hair again, my sweet."

"I'll trade a hairdo for what you just made me feel any day of the week," she mumbled thickly.

"Liked it, did you?"

"Yes," she whispered. "I liked it a lot."

Twenty minutes later she was put back together, and they left the apartment. Clara Raymond had seen Tag go in all dressed up and had been waiting to see if Linda was going to come out when he did, wondering if she, too, would be fancied up. Linda was dressed to the nines and looked lovely, pleasing Clara, who was certain of the handsome couple's destination tonight. Almost everyone in town knew about the Kingsley wedding scheduled at the Community Church, and Tag taking Linda to the family-only event indicated some very serious intentions on his part.

But exactly what was Linda going to do about her other beau? Clara wondered. He still showed up, sometimes right after Tag left, sometimes in the wee hours of the night, once in a while when Linda was gone during the day.

It was a very strange situation and Clara couldn't quite figure it out. Surely Tag Kingsley wasn't the sort to share a woman he cared about with another man.

"Trouble's a-brewin', mark my words," Clara said under her breath and went to the telephone to call Alice. Some things simply couldn't wait until their next coffee klatch at the Calico Diner.

When they were seated in Tag's shined and polished SUV, he said, "I'd like you to close your eyes."

She stared at him in amazement. "Close my eyes! Why?"

"So you won't figure out where we're going before we get there."

"Your surprise is right here in Rumor? I'll bet you have dinner reservations at the Rooftop Café. Everyone will see us, you know. Our relationship will no longer be a private affair." She flushed slightly. "Now, I'd call that a real slip of the tongue, because I certainly don't consider our, uh, what we have together…I mean, I hate the word *affair*."

"Darlin', I knew exactly what you meant and please don't worry about it. What we have together is definitely not just an affair. Linda, you have to know I love you."

She blinked at the sudden moisture in her eyes. "Don't make me cry now," she whispered. "I'll have to go back in and repair my makeup."

Tag smiled and gently touched her cheek. "You were supposed to say, 'Tag, I love you, too.'"

"I do, darling, I do. I love you with all my heart."

"Now *I've* got tears in my eyes." Tag cleared his throat and started the engine. "Shut your eyes, okay?"

"Yes, of course." She put her head back against the headrest and shut her eyes. It was hard not to cry. She had never been happier. Reveling in the joy of it all she barely noticed the turns Tag took as he drove. It wasn't a long drive—no destination in Rumor would take more than a few minutes—and then she felt the vehicle stop and heard Tag turn off the engine.

"Can I look now?" she asked.

"In a minute. Stay put and I'll come around and help you out."

A bubble of laughter rose in her throat. If she had ever before felt so carefree and elated, she couldn't recall it. When her door opened, Tag took her arm and assisted her out.

"Keep your eyes closed for just another minute or so," he said. "I'm going to walk you inside."

A surprise party! What fun! "All right, but please make sure I don't trip over something in these high heels."

"I'll be very careful."

Linda let herself be led across gravel, then grass and finally a short sidewalk. "Here are some steps," Tag said. For some reason he was no longer comfortable with the plan that had seemed so great before he actually put it in motion.

Linda heard music...organ music! "Tag, are we at the church?"

"We're going in now, and yes, you guessed it. Go ahead and open your eyes."

She did and in her very next breath nearly fainted. They were inside the Rumor Community Church, and it was beautifully decorated with lighted candles and flowers. And there were people, all tastefully dressed, all attractive and all looking at her.

She tried to smile and nothing happened. Her chest felt tightly banded by some invisible force and she could just barely breathe. She knew exactly what Tag had done. He'd wanted her to meet his family and had figured a way to get it done. How in God's name could she be so madly in love with a man who rode roughshod over her wishes and then expected applause for his actions? She could feel his eyes on her now, sense the pride he had in himself and his originality, and actually see his hopeful smile without looking directly at him. In truth, she dared not look directly at him, for then she might say something that could never be retracted.

Then, suddenly, the hushed moment was gone, shrinking to nothing more than a memory by Samantha running down the center aisle and happily calling, "Linda! Linda! You came! You came to Uncle Russell's wedding!"

Chapter Fourteen

Bending from the waist, Linda gave Samantha a warm hug. "Oh, it's good to see you. You look so pretty in that lavender dress."

"I'm in the... I'm going to..." Samantha looked up at her father. "What am I doing, Daddy? What's it called?"

Tag smiled. "You're going to hold the bouquet after Susannah hands it to you. You're in the wedding party."

Proudly, Sammy nodded. "I'm in the wedding party, Linda."

"That's wonderful." Linda caught sight of a small, attractive woman walking toward them. Her dress was stunning, an unusual smoky lavender. She wore coordinated pumps and a necklace and earrings with gemstones the same smoky-lavender shade.

Tag strode forth and kissed the woman's cheek. "Do you know Grandma?" Samantha asked Linda.

"Not yet," Linda murmured. Her heart was beating hard and seemed to have risen to the base of her throat. She wouldn't be anything but polite and gracious to the Kingsleys, but she just might devise some slow and agonizing torture for Tag when this was over.

Tag escorted his mother the final few steps to Linda. "Mom, this is Linda Fioretti. Linda, my mother, Carolyn Kingsley."

Carolyn extended her right hand. "I'm happy to meet you, Linda."

Linda smiled over their handshake. "The pleasure is mine, Mrs. Kingsley."

"Carolyn. You must call me Carolyn. Tag said he planned to bring you here this evening. We've been hoping to meet you."

So he'd been talking about her to his family? "I confess to feeling rather like an intruder. Isn't this a family-only affair?" Linda shot Tag a look, but mostly kept her attention on Carolyn. Mrs. Kingsley was, after all, an innocent bystander in her son's sneaky, manipulative behavior.

"Primarily, yes, but there are a few especially close friends in attendance. Tag, please show Linda to the second pew. The ceremony is about to begin. Linda, I'm sure we'll get a chance to chat later on. Come, Samantha." Carolyn smiled and walked away with her granddaughter in tow.

"She's lovely and charming," Linda said quietly. "Elegant."

"Yes, she is." Tag took her arm and they walked up the aisle to the second pew, where they sat down.

Linda put some space between them, but Tag immediately moved over so their bodies were touching again. He then took Linda's hand and held it against his thigh.

The wedding party was gathering at the flower-bedecked altar. Linda tried to ignore Tag's nearness and his possessive grasp on her hand. This was neither the time nor place to tell him how disappointed, hurt and angry she was over his surprise date. This wasn't a *date* at all. He'd used the word—and taken advantage of her belief in his honesty—to manipulate her into meeting his family on his timetable, not hers.

Tag spoke in an undertone. "Do you know which man is the groom?" he asked.

"I think so," she said coolly.

"Well, the one on his right is Reed, our other brother. Russell's the oldest, thirty-five, and Reed is a few years younger. Maura, the pretty little redhead holding Mei, the little girl Russell and Susannah brought back from China, is the baby of the family. She's only twenty-two."

"Ten years your junior."

Tag started to correct her but stopped himself in time. Frowning slightly, he wished he hadn't deceived Linda about his age. Even knowing that, Tag was still reluctant to tell Linda the truth, that he was twenty-six, not thirty-two, her age. Good Lord, *Reed* was thirty-two and they sure weren't twins.

Linda was thinking of how quickly the Kingsleys had produced three strapping sons, and then had waited ten years for their fourth child, Maura. Her thoughts on that subject faded quickly, however, when Donna Mason, wearing a bluish-lavender dress preceded the bride, beautifully outfitted in a filmy off-white gown. Susannah's hair was adorned with white and lavender flowers, she carried a stunning bouquet and her beauty and glowing smile brought tears to Linda's eyes.

The soft organ music stopped when Pastor Rayburn began speaking. "We are gathered here this evening for a blessed event, the marriage of Russell Kingsley and Susannah McCord."

Linda mentally applauded the pastor's choice of words. Marriage *should* be a blessed event, she thought as emotion caused her eyes to water again. Russell and Susannah's love for each other was like a living, breathing entity in that pretty little church, exactly the way two people should feel about each other before taking the enormous step that tied them together legally and in the eyes of God.

Every emotion Linda possessed became softer as she sat there next to the man she loved and listened to and watched the lovely wedding ceremony. *Why did I force Tag to maneuver me into meeting his family? People in love* should *know each*

*other's family. I'm more to blame for this than he is. I'm glad
he's close to his parents. I wish I were closer to mine.*

It was the very first time that Linda had ever put that wish
into words. Oh, she had wished many times that her parents
had been different than they were, but they never would be.
Regardless of their eccentricities, Hilly and Vandyne Vareck
were her mother and father, the only blood family she had,
and she should at least talk to them on the phone once in a
while. Of course, they could call her, too, but maybe they
were waiting for *her* to call them.

"You may kiss your bride," Pastor Rayburn said with a big
smile.

Linda wiped her eyes and clapped with the others when
Russell and Susannah shared their first kiss as man and wife.
They held out their arms then and Maura brought them their
daughter. The congratulations began at once.

"You weren't in the wedding party," Linda said quietly.

"I could have stood at the altar with Russell and Reed,
but I begged off so I could sit with you." Tag turned his head
toward her. "Look at me, sweetheart." Linda slowly faced
him. Their eyes met. "The next Kingsley wedding could be
ours," he said softly.

Linda's breath caught. "Don't…it's…please…"

"You're fumbling, my love. I took you by surprise, didn't
I? I'm sorry. It just came spilling out. Come on, let's go wish
the newlyweds many years of happiness."

Linda was so stunned over Tag's left-handed proposal that
she let herself be led from the pew to the front of the church.
In seconds she had been introduced to everyone there, and
they were all congenial and pleasant to her.

Thus, when everyone began filing out of the church and
Tag told her that his mother and father were hosting a wedding
supper at the ranch, Linda let herself be swept along. "Come
on, Sammy," Tag called. "We're leaving for the ranch now,
honey."

Maura called back, "She's riding with me, Tag."

Tag chuckled and opened the passenger door of his SUV for Linda to get in. "Maura's making sure we have time alone. They like you. All of them like you. I knew they would."

Linda stared straight ahead as Tag got in line with the small parade of vehicles heading for the ranch. She felt Tag's hand on her knee and finally looked at him.

"Are you all right?" he asked.

"I'm not sure."

"Should I have told you about the wedding? Would you have come if I had?"

"I'm not sure of anything right now, Tag. Except for one thing. I know I feel overwhelmed, but there again I'm not sure if it's because you pulled a fast one on me tonight or because I like your family and wish I had agreed to meet them when you first mentioned it."

"Neither is a capital offense, Linda."

"A punishable crime? No, of course not. But are you and I hot for each other *in* bed and incompatible *out* of it?" Her words were intentionally blunt and to the point; were they really in love or merely in lust? Lust was so easily provable. It was too bad that proof of love was virtually invisible to others. It was probably the easiest emotion to lie about, to use to one's own advantage.

Tag was surprised by her choice of words. *Hot for each other* was not indigenous to Linda's ladylike conversation.

"I happen to be in love with you, which I told you earlier this evening," he said. "If I recall correctly, you said the same to me."

Linda murmured softly, "I know." She took a breath. "It's just that I hate dishonesty so much, and I can't help wondering if you and I are always honest with each other."

"Linda, for crying out loud."

"Are you getting angry?"

"You're making a mountain out of a molehill."

"A lie is not a molehill, Tag. You didn't tell me an out-and-out lie about tonight, but you led me to believe in something that was not going to happen."

"Well, I happen to believe that attending a wedding is as good a date as any other, probably better than most. Not only that, we'll go out tomorrow night, and the next and the next and the next, until you're so sick of eating out that you'll beg me to grill you a burger."

"Now you're laughing at me."

Grinning, Tag sent her a glance. "Would I do that?"

"Frankly, Taggart Kingsley, right now I wouldn't put anything past you."

He took her hand and held it. "I think I'm going to ask Maura if Sammy can spend the night with her. There's a whole bunch of things I'd like to do to you, with you and for you, hoping, of course, that you will agree and reciprocate the tantalizing pleasures that are sure to come."

"You're incorrigible."

"I'm in love."

Linda heaved a quiet sigh. "So am I, you big jerk, so am I."

He laughed out loud. "I know you are, darlin', and that makes me so happy I could fly."

Stratton and Carolyn Kingsley's ranch house was constructed of logs, but it wasn't like any log home Linda had ever seen. They had designed a home that sat in complete harmony with the magnificence of the Montana countryside. Linda had been inside some impressive homes in California, but the unique elegance of the Kingsley mansion actually took her breath.

Tag sensed Linda's awe the second they walked in. "If you think this foyer is something, wait until you see the indoor pool and home theater," he said in a teasing undertone.

Linda smiled and swore to take the remainder of the evening in stride.

For that matter, why did she object to wealth so strenuously? It was a tantalizing question, one she knew would haunt her until she came up with some sort of probable answer.

"This way," Tag said with a hand on her arm.

The dining room was incredible, as was the meal served by a man everyone called Harrison. He was immaculately clad in a dark suit and spoke with a British accent.

"Your parents have a British butler?" Linda whispered.

"Harrison's relatively new. He came as a couple. His wife, Mabel, is a great cook and he's sort of a jack-of-all-trades around the house," Tag replied.

"An English couple," Linda said dryly, then shot Tag a dirty look. "Why do you act all ordinary and like you have to work? You're not a carpenter, you're a big phony."

Tag fell silent. No one noticed. The conversation around the table was animated and gay. The food was delicious and there were numerous champagne toasts and bursts of laughter. Tag took a bite of lobster salad, a sip of champagne and pondered Linda's accusation. *You're a big phony.*

After a few minutes he dipped his head toward her to whisper, "You're wrong about me, and I can't believe you don't know it for yourself."

Linda slanted her gaze toward him. "I know you well enough."

"Obviously, you don't. How about us spending the night talking after we leave here? I at least deserve a chance to explain myself."

"Oh, like talking is all you'd want to do!"

"Don't be sarcastic. You're as hot for me as I am for you. But we're both grown-ups, and if we decide to talk instead of fulfilling our sexual fantasies, I'm sure we can manage."

"I could. I don't know about you."

"Really? Did you dig the high-minded conversation we had on your sofa before leaving for the church?"

Linda gasped. "That's crude!"

Reed Kingsley was on Linda's left, and he spoke to her. "How long have you been teaching, Linda?"

She gladly turned her back to Tag. "This was my first year, Reed."

The wedding cake was cut with all the ceremony and fun that went along with the ritual, and then everyone left the dining room and went to the most sumptuous living room Linda had ever seen. Tag brought her a glass of champagne.

"Would you like a tour of the house?" he asked her.

He was trying to make amends for that whispered squabble at the table, she realized. She wanted to make amends, too, but not here, not in one of these luxurious rooms. She could see it all in her mind's eye. He would lead her into some gorgeous room and shut the door, then he would kiss her and things would get out of hand very quickly, as always happened between them, and it could all become very embarrassing if someone happened upon them.

"Not tonight," she said quietly. "Donna's coming this way. Be nice."

"I'm always nice."

"Yes, nice and sneaky," she retorted before smiling at Donna. "Your dress is beautiful. You look wonderful."

Donna smiled. "Thank you. The wedding was just great, wasn't it?"

"Very special," Linda agreed.

"I'm going to go and find my daughter," Tag said. "Have you seen her, Donna?" Tag said.

"I think Maura put a cartoon video on in the TV room. That's probably where you'll find them."

"Thanks." Tag walked away, going in search of Sammy and Maura.

"You missed my grand opening," Donna said.

Linda's eyes widened. "Oh, no! I'm so sorry. When was it?"

"Wednesday. The announcement was in the paper."

Something heavy suddenly seemed to be tugging on Linda, trying to drag her down. Too much had been happening over which she had no control. Her life wasn't her own anymore; it was Tag's…and that weird stalker's. She'd been so happy living in Rumor, and now she was only confused. Her mind whirled with it all, causing a disoriented sensation, and blaming some of it on too much champagne, she lowered the glass in her hand to a nearby table and tried to show Donna a genuine smile.

"I haven't been reading the paper lately," she admitted a bit shamefacedly. What else had she missed by not keeping up with the local news? she wondered, shaken over letting life pass her by because of two men, one of whom she loved and the other…? Well, the other was a mystery, no doubt about it. Someone with a book fetish? Lord above, why her? Why break in and mess with *her* books?

"Donna, I'm terribly sorry," she said again. "I wanted very much to attend your grand opening."

"Hey, it's not that big a deal. But speaking of big deals, it looks to me like you and Tag are becoming one. I'm glad, Linda. He's been too much of a loner since…well, for much too long a time."

"Since his wife died?"

"Yes," Donna said quietly. "I'm sorry. I didn't need to introduce that subject tonight. Everyone is so happy for Russell and Susannah. Oh, she's coming over. You've met her before this evening, haven't you?"

"Once, yes."

Susannah's arrival made a threesome. "Thank you for coming, Linda," Susannah said. "Tag told the family that he was going to ask you to accompany him, but he wasn't sure you would agree."

"I really had no choice," Linda murmured, then realized what she'd said. "That sounded terrible. I didn't mean it the way it came out."

"Even if you did, don't apologize," Donna drawled. "I know how insistent Tag can be when he wants something."

Susannah laughed. "I think stubbornness is a Kingsley trait."

"It could be worse," Donna said.

"Linda, Tag said that you might be interested in teaching at Rugrats for the summer," Susannah said.

"He mentioned the idea to me, and the more I think about it the more I like it," Linda said. "But you should know that I haven't taught very young children before. In fact, this is my first year of teaching anyone of any age. If loving children counts for anything, though, it should work out."

"Well, I'm quite thrilled over the idea, Linda. The little ones who attend my nursery school adore drawing and coloring, and just think of the advantages they would gain from learning something about real art from an expert. Tag is very impressed with your work. I would love to see it one day." Susannah laughed. "When things settle down some."

"Yes, of course," Linda murmured, not all that comfortable with the prospect of Susannah judging her work, which was what a viewing boiled down to. She'd sold a couple of paintings in California, but not because she had finally decided to follow in her parents' footsteps and earn herself a name and reputation in the world of art and artists. She still had no desire for fame or fortune based on her talent, and other than Tag, no one in Rumor had seen her finished paintings. She couldn't say that, though, so she changed the subject.

"Your daughter is very beautiful, Susannah."

"Yes, she is. Russell and I became loving parents the second we saw her. Having her with us and knowing she's ours seems like a miracle." Susannah smiled. "She was getting tired at the church, and I put her down when we got here. I think I'll go check on her. It was very nice talking to you, Linda. How about us getting together right after school is out to discuss Rugrats? That's next week, isn't it?"

"School is out on Tuesday and the science fair is scheduled for Wednesday. After that I'll be free as the breeze."

"Great. I'll contact you, okay?"

"Wonderful." Linda watched her walk away then turned to Donna. "She's very nice."

"Yes, she is. We've been best friends since high school."

Tag came into the room and walked over to them. "Sammy is going home with Maura for a sleepover."

Donna grinned. "Convenient, Taggart, very convenient." She saw Linda's pink cheeks. "Don't be embarrassed by our foolishness, Linda. We've teased each other since we were kids." She began easing away. "You two have fun, you hear?"

Tag took Linda's elbow and leaned forward to whisper, "We *always* have fun, don't we, sweetheart?"

She backed off just enough to look him in the eye. "Not always, but then our individual ideas of fun don't always coincide, do they?"

Tag looked crestfallen. "You're still mad about tonight."

"I'm not." She heaved a sigh. "I don't know what I am."

"But I do. You're my darling." He looked at her for a long moment, hoping for a sign of agreement from her, then seeing only doubt and confusion in her beautiful eyes he said softly, "I think it's time we said good night to everyone. We need to be alone."

Linda couldn't disagree. They did need to be alone. Together they made the rounds, spending a few minutes with Carolyn, then Stratton, and on through the rest of the family. It took almost thirty minutes to say good-night—and another ten with Samantha—but finally they were outside and walking to Tag's SUV.

He opened the door for her, and she got in and settled herself with a relieved sigh. She couldn't fault the evening or anyone she'd met, but she was still glad it was over. She *had* been scrutinized, after all, and why wouldn't Tag's family be curious? No, she didn't blame them for any of her unease this evening; the whole thing had been Tag's doing.

He climbed into the driver's seat and started the engine. Then and only then did he stop everything else and look at her. "Tell me you're all right with tonight," he said quietly.

"I'm all right."

"The words are there, but not the heart. You're trying not to be angry, but you are." He slid over and put his arm around her, tipping her head back to kiss her lips. She closed her eyes and kissed him back. His lips moved on hers, and she opened her mouth for his tongue. She might be royally ticked at him—and she wasn't positive of that anymore—but she couldn't ignore what he made her feel.

When he finally broke the kiss they were both struggling to breathe normally. "What you do to me should be X-rated," he said raggedly.

"I could say the same about you, but didn't you mention something during dinner about us talking for the rest of the night?"

He groaned. "Are you going to hold me to that?"

"Aren't you going to hold yourself to that?"

Tag floundered a moment then gave in. "You're right. I said it, and I'll do it. But what were we going to discuss, exactly? Can you remember?"

"Of course I remember. You wanted a chance to explain yourself."

"Oh. Well, there's not that much to explain. I'll bare all during the drive to town."

"I'd rather you waited until you took me home."

Tag put the SUV in motion and began the drive. "You're inviting me in?"

"When did you start waiting for an invitation?"

Tag sent her a grin. "Guess I've been pretty overbearing, huh?"

"About as subtle as a train wreck," she retorted. "Almost from the first you let me know what you wanted."

"You wanted the same thing, only you didn't know it."

"But you knew because you're so wise and all-seeing."

"Don't be sarcastic, sweetheart. Play nice with the naughty little boy."

"Play nice? Is that what we've been doing?"

Tag took his right hand off the wheel and laid it on her thigh. "There's nothing else on this planet any nicer."

She plucked his hand from her thigh and moved it back to the steering wheel. "I think our little talk tonight will be more beneficial if you keep your hands on something besides me."

Tag chuckled deep in his throat. "I'm going to try, that's all I can promise. But you must promise something, too. You have to promise to turn off the sex appeal."

"Turn it off! Good Lord, I never turned it on!"

"Then it's just a natural part of your makeup, darlin'. If you got it, you got it. You can't hide or ignore it."

"No one ever thought I had it before," she drawled.

"Then you were associating with the wrong men, babe."

Linda let that remark lie for a moment, then said, "You are so right."

He heard the seriousness in her voice and altered his own tone. "Maybe you'll do a little explaining tonight, too."

"Maybe I will," she said quietly. After a few moments of thoughtful silence she spoke again. "Would you please turn on the radio?"

"How about a nice soothing CD?"

"Fine." When the music began, she put her head back and

shut her eyes. Her thoughts drifted. For one thing, it was almost laughable to remember how at peace she'd felt only a few weeks back. Then Tag had knocked on her door and everything had changed.

But Tag wasn't really the problem, was he? She had never been at peace when other people were telling her what to do and directing her life. First it had been her parents, then Paul and now Tag. Why did this sense of subjugation keep happening to her? She had lived her parents' life until she met Paul and then she had lived his. Lightning must have struck her without her knowledge, for she had finally gotten her fill of Paul Fioretti and done something about it.

And she'd been happy. Contented. Her new life had agreed with her, and she'd had Tippy and her job and some new friends and her painting, when she felt like working on a canvas. Then came Tag, and she had fallen for him very hard, very fast. Sex had become important. Love had become important.

But he had started driving her bus right from the get-go. Was there something about her that brought out other people's tendencies to rule the roost? Did she look and act timid or helpless and cause the people around her to get all protective and concerned? She was certainly as smart as her parents and ten times smarter than Paul, and yet they had told her when to jump and she had asked, "How high?" Why, for God's sake?

And now she was doing the same with Tag. Not intentionally, but in some subtle way she couldn't begin to pinpoint she had given him the reins that she should be gripping tightly in her own two hands. She brought out his protective side, proof of which was his calling the sheriff just because she'd heard a noise outside.

She had issues, make no mistake, and that recognition and admittance hurt like hell and brought tears to her eyes.

"What the devil is going on now?" Tag asked, abruptly turning off the CD player.

Linda opened her eyes and raised her head. They had just turned onto State Street and her apartment was just ahead. Flashing red lights lit up the neighborhood.

"Looks like someone called the sheriff again," Linda said, and a small chill went up her spine. It felt like a premonition. Had that weirdo returned to mess up her books again and been spotted?

Tag stopped the SUV at the street because the driveway was blocked by police cars. Linda gasped. Mixing with the crowd of curiosity seekers milling around was a small white dog.

"My God, it's Tippy! How did he get out?" she cried.

Chapter Fifteen

Linda jumped out and hurried toward her apartment house, made eerie by the flashing lights. She felt Tag right behind her, but at the moment he wasn't uppermost in her mind.

"Tippy!" she called, and everyone turned to look at her. Tippy's ears perked up. Spotting Linda, he wagged his tail like crazy then ran for her. When he got close enough, he took a flying leap and landed in her arms, where he wriggled happily and licked her face.

Tag ruffled the hair on the little dog's head. "What're you doing out here, pal?" he said.

Linda realized that her good green dress now bore dirty paw prints, but she didn't care. "How in heck did you get outside?" she said with another hug for her pet.

Mrs. Raymond suddenly appeared. "This is all your doing," the elderly woman said through pursed lips.

Linda's jaw dropped. "I beg your pardon."

"I just got sick and tired of seeing that boyfriend of yours wandering around this building at all hours of the day or night."

Linda was thunderstruck. "What boyfriend of mine?"

Tag was taking it all in and trying to figure out what Mrs.

Raymond was talking about. He was the only man Linda was seeing, wasn't he? On the other hand, she'd been at Joe's Bar with someone. He really didn't know what to believe, but he was getting damn upset.

"You know what boyfriend I'm talking about. You have two of them, everyone knows it, Taggart Kingsley standing right here, and Mr. No-Name. That's what I've started calling him, Mr. No-Name, 'cause he sure isn't anyone I've ever met in Rumor. He has to be new to town, which is neither here nor there at the moment. Tonight I said enough is enough and called the sheriff. It's getting so a body doesn't feel safe in her own home, even though I'm pretty well protected with my .45 and good shootin' eye."

Linda felt a ball of anger getting hotter and bigger in her midsection. "Mrs. Raymond, you are accusing me of something that isn't remotely true. Either your own imagination is warped and overworked or someone is feeding you false information."

The older woman gasped. "Sassy and snotty besides! Well, I used to think you were a nice person. Obviously, I was mistaken." She turned and marched off, head held high, back straight, the very picture of undeserved rancor.

"What is wrong with that woman?" Linda groaned.

"Is she completely off base?" Tag asked.

Linda blinked at him. "Well, she's certainly not *on* base. Please don't tell me you believe that gibberish about my having another boyfriend!"

Tag's mouth was drawn into a thin, grim line. "I've got to get to the bottom of this," he muttered, and headed off at a fast pace toward a couple of deputies who appeared to be returning to their prowl cars.

Tag knew them. "Cliff. Tommy. What in hell happened here tonight?"

"Hey, Tag. Chasing ambulances tonight?" Cliff quipped.

"No, my friend lives in this building. We just got here, drove in from the ranch. What's going on?"

Tommy interrupted. "I'm heading back to the station. You can fill Tag in, Cliff."

"Sure thing." Tommy walked off and Cliff said to Tag, "One of the tenants called in and raised such a ruckus, dispatch sent out two cars. Claimed that she'd been watching some guy sneaking in and out of the shadows and that she'd seen him quite a few times before tonight. This is the second call to this address, so even though there was no one doing any sneaking when we got here, there could be something to her story."

"I made the first call. It was Wednesday night, a week ago."

Cliff checked his clipboard. "That's right, it was. You made that call? How come?"

"Because my friend and I were talking on the phone and she heard a loud crash right outside her window. I told her to hang up and call the law, but she didn't much like that idea, so I did it for her. I would've come over here myself to check things out, but my daughter was in bed asleep and I couldn't leave her alone, nor could I wake her up and bring her with me when I didn't know what I'd run into."

"Well, it wouldn't have been real smart of you to do it anyhow, Tag. You never know what kind of moron you might meet up with in the dark. Could have been packing a weapon. You don't want to get mixed up in something like that. That's why Tommy and me get the big bucks." Cliff chuckled at his own wit then suddenly turned thoughtful. "Wonder if the two incidents are related," he murmured, adding after a moment, "Oh, well, the whole thing's probably nothing."

Tag thought of Tippy being outside when he knew that Linda *never* let him out alone, but he kept quiet. It wasn't beyond the realm of possibility that she had slipped up this evening, what with getting ready for their big date and all.

Maybe the dog had come outside unnoticed when they left the apartment. Considering the romantic interlude on Linda's sofa only minutes before, neither of them was probably thinking of much else.

"But you and Tommy thoroughly checked the area, right?"

Cliff nodded. "Sure did. If there was a prowler anywhere near this building, he's long gone, believe me."

"Well, good of you to fill me in. Appreciate it, Cliff." Tag and the deputy parted and Tag returned to where Linda was still standing, looking a bit shell-shocked and battle-weary. Tippy was at her feet now, but her dress was a maze of dirty paw prints.

"I can't imagine how long he was outside, but he must have gotten into some mud," she said.

"Come on, honey," Tag said quietly, taking her arm and steering her toward the door of her apartment. With the deputies gone, the onlookers were wandering away. The show, obviously, was over.

"Give me your key," Tag said.

Her hands were shaking, as were her legs, and she held out her bag. "Would you get it, please?"

"Sure." He dug into her small handbag and easily found her key ring. "You're really shook, aren't you?" he asked as he unlocked the door and pushed it open.

"Mrs. Raymond—and Tippy—knocked me for a loop," Linda said huskily, entering her apartment ahead of him. Tippy bounded in and began eating something off the floor. "Tippy!" she cried. "What is that?" Bending over, she identified small bits of doggie treats. Her heart seemed to flip in her chest. *She* certainly hadn't tossed treats on the floor. "Oh my God," she whispered fearfully.

"What?" Tag asked, frowning deeply.

"Come with me," she said hoarsely, taking his hand and gingerly leading him into the living room. She saw the books scattered across the floor at once. This time the intruder hadn't merely *looked* at the books on the shelves and put them back, he'd thrown them around like a maniac.

Tag stared at the strewn books. "What in hell is going on?" he muttered.

"He…he came back," Linda whispered.

"*Who* came back?" Tag took her by the shoulders and turned her to face him. "Are you seeing someone else?"

"No, I am not!"

"Then who were you with at Joe's Bar a couple weeks ago? I saw your SUV in the parking lot, so you were definitely there. The question is, with whom?"

"I was with friends! Teachers! We sometimes go to Joe's on Tuesday afternoons for a drink before calling it a day. My God, Tag, if you were so worried about who I was in there with, why didn't you come in yourself and find out?"

"I didn't want you thinking I didn't trust you."

"Not to put too fine a point on it, but you didn't!" Linda narrowed her eyes. "And at the time we had just barely met. You really have some nerve!" She jerked free of his grasp and started toward the stairs. "I'm going to change clothes," she announced curtly.

"Linda, I don't want to fight with you."

She stopped walking and turned to look at him. "I don't want to fight, either. But you've been thinking the same thing Mrs. Raymond has, that I've been seeing you and that jerk she calls Mr. No-Name."

Tag couldn't help laughing. "Mrs. Raymond is pretty funny."

Linda tried to see it his way and couldn't quite do it. "I'm sorry, but I don't think she's at all funny. With her imagination I'll bet she's one of the biggest gossips in Rumor, and I really see nothing funny in ruining other people's reputations with exaggerated or embellished stories that have only a kernel of truth to them."

"Are you saying there's a kernel of truth in her speculation about Mr. No-Name? Is he someone you've seen or talked to?"

Linda sighed. "I suppose the man she's referring to is the same weirdo that's been, sort of, haunting me."

"He's been doing *what?*" Tag's eyes were suddenly blazing with anger. "Did he cause the crash the night I called the sheriff?"

"I don't know who or what caused that crash." Linda held out her hands, a gesture of supplication. "Please give me a minute to get out of this dirty dress, and I'll tell you everything." Without waiting for his reply, she ran up the stairs and into her bedroom, where she immediately kicked off her high heels. She felt like giving up, throwing herself across the bed and bawling her eyes out. The evening had been nerve-racking—lovely and wonderful and nerve-racking, all at the same time. Part of her was upset with Tag for conning her, another part of her was thrilled to have met his family.

On top of that she had opened a door during the drive from the ranch that she would never be able to completely close again. Questions from the past had come pouring out, questions about herself, her parents, her marriage and questions about her relationship with Tag.

Then to arrive home, to the only place in the whole damn world that was truly hers, and learn that the idiot who'd been stalking her had again been inside her apartment was the final straw. He was clever with locks. Somehow Tippy had gotten out. The bastard had again gone through her books.

With those thoughts hounding her, Linda rushed down the short hall to her studio. Sure enough, the books she had picked up and returned to the boxes after his first visit were again strewn across the floor. Weakly she leaned against the wall. Why on earth was that *person* so obsessed with her books? Unless books hadn't been the only thing on his mind.

Rushing back to the bedroom she began opening drawers.

Her things had been disturbed! He had rifled through her lingerie, her sweaters, the drawer that contained folded scarves, belts, gloves and other miscellaneous items.

She stumbled to the bed and sat on it. *He's looking for something! Did he find it tonight? What was it?*

"Linda?"

Tag was calling her from downstairs. She rose and went to the door. "I'll be right down."

"I poured us a brandy. I think we both could use it."

"Fine."

She finished changing and went downstairs wearing a simple wraparound dress. She had felt no need or urge to impress Tag with something fancy or even becoming, and she had taken down her hair and just let it fall. It had received exactly two brush strokes before she said, "To hell with it," and dropped the brush on top of her dresser.

When she walked into the living room, Tag's breath caught. She always did that to him, he realized. Just seeing her stole his breath, made it hard for him to say something ordinary and reminded him again and again of how incredible she was.

He got to his feet and brought her a glass when she sat down. "Thank you," she said. He returned to his place on the sofa and retrieved his glass from where he'd set it on the coffee table. She seemed to be suffering.

"I swear to make it better for you," he said softly.

Her eyes flew to his. "You're not my babysitter, Tag!"

"Of course not, but I am your man." He studied her. "Aren't I?"

"Which means you should take care of me?"

"Yes, it does."

Linda took a sip of her brandy. "Don't even think it."

He started. "Why would you say that? Why shouldn't a man protect the woman he loves? That's a very strange attitude you have, Linda."

"I've been a victim of strange attitudes, as you put it, all my life, although I only realized tonight the extent of my subservience to everyone who ever meant anything to me." She raised her glass to her lips and eyed him over it while sipping.

"You've never struck me as subservient," Tag said quietly, although his heart was pumping harder than normal. This was an unusual discussion, a *disturbing* discussion.

"Then why do you think I need your protection?"

He got to his feet, suddenly too antsy to sit still. "You've got a stalker on your trail and you still have to ask that?"

Linda sighed. "He's not dangerous. He's had ample opportunity to harm me, if that was his intention. To be honest, he couldn't care less about me. There's something in this apartment that he wants."

Tag looked at her incredulously. "Some imbecile breaks into your home, throws your things around and your summation of the event is that there's something in here he wants? Well, since you seem to have it all figured out, suppose you tell me what it is."

"I have no idea." Her gaze went to the books on the carpet. "It makes no sense. None of my books are valuable. But he's after a book. He didn't find it the first time he did this and he came back for another look."

Tag held up his hand. "Back up a minute. This same thing happened before?"

"Yes." She took in the shocked, angry expression on his face. "Don't get all puffed up and indignant," she said sharply. "I didn't tell you about it because you took it upon yourself to call the sheriff about something that was none of your business. Someone's been telling me how to live my life ever since I can remember, first my parents, then my ex-husband and now you. I had a few months of total independence before we met, and I'm telling you now, right to your face, that I liked—no, *loved*—making my own decisions without someone's interference."

Tag was flabbergasted. He downed the rest of his brandy, then stood there looking at her.

"Should I take that to mean you'd like me to quietly disappear?" he finally asked.

"Of course not," she snapped. "Can't a man and woman be equal partners in a relationship? Why do you have to carry the weight? Why do you have to make decisions for me? Take tonight, for one very good example. You decided it was time I met your family so you manipulated me into a situation where eluding your overbearing tactics would have made me look like a fool."

She watched Tag slowly sink onto the sofa. "I was always a good little girl for my parents, and I was a stupidly dense wife to a man who was a cheat and a liar and couldn't possibly have ever loved me, judging by the way he mostly ignored my very existence. I took this treatment for years. I was so conditioned to unquestioning obedience from my abnormal childhood that I stepped into the role of subservient wife without batting an eye."

"I don't see you that way," Tag mumbled.

"Yes, you do. Or you did. You *still* think I need your protection. Well, you know what I think? I think you have a few issues of your own on your back."

"I'm only protective of you because I love you. I don't see anything unnatural about that. A man *should* take care of the woman he loves."

There was something odd in his voice and in his eyes, something that had nothing—or very little—to do with her. She took a shot in the dark.

"You're talking about your wife, aren't you?" she said softly. To her dismay he covered his face with his hands and made a sound that wrenched her heart. Jumping up, she went to the sofa, sat next to him and put her arms around him. "Tag, I'm sorry. I'm sorry." Tears flooded her eyes. "I never meant to hurt you."

"I wasn't talking about my wife, but…maybe I was." He lowered his hands and looked at her with anguished eyes. "She died from drugs because I didn't see how seriously addicted she was. I should have seen. I *should* have seen and understood and I didn't. I let it happen."

"Oh my Lord, you did not! Tag, you can't blame yourself because she used drugs."

"She was just a kid," Tag said bitterly.

"So were you."

"Yes, but I was the man and I should have taken better care of her."

Linda fell back against the sofa. "Women are weak, so men should be strong," she said in a husky, emotional voice. "That's a very sad philosophy to be burdened with, especially when it couldn't be more inaccurate." She heaved a long sigh. "We're both pretty sad cases, Tag." He turned his head to look at her and their gazes locked. "That doesn't quite fit the image you have of yourself, does it?" she said.

"Nor the one I have of you. Neither of us is a sad case. Okay, I'll admit to carrying around some baggage from years ago, and maybe you are, too, but we're good people, Linda. You've made something of your life, and you're a highly respected teacher now. Everyone in Rumor likes you."

"Not everyone," Linda said dryly, referring to her run-in with Clara Raymond.

"You can't listen to gossip or those that spread it, Linda, I told you that before. Rumor's a gossipy little town, everyone knows it and those of us with half a brain ignore it." He turned himself enough to lay his right hand on her cheek. "Don't let busybodies like Clara bother you. And if I've been playing king of the hill with you, I'm truly sorry. I'll try to change my wicked ways, okay?"

She couldn't help smiling. "I think the word *wicked* is a bit harsh. You're overbearing and always right, but you're not wicked."

He grinned. "Overbearing and always right, huh? Well, I guess I can live with that." His expression sobered. "Will you tell me everything you know about the guy who broke in here tonight?"

She sat straighter and then curled her legs under her. She talked for a long time and found herself laughing a few times. "He's funny, Tag. You should have seen him in those high heels."

But Tag didn't laugh. "He might have been funny at first, but he's starting to get dangerous, Linda. The next time he breaks in, you could be here. You could be asleep and not hear him until he's in your bedroom. He seems to have made a friend of Tippy, so he could probably get in again anytime he likes."

A chill went up Linda's spine. "You're right. He's not funny at all."

"We're going to stop him. I'm not sure exactly how we'll do it yet, but it has to be done before someone gets hurt." He took her hand. "And if that's being too protective of you, sweetheart, you're just going to have to live with that."

"All right," she said with a hint of a smile. "Guess you're going to be my knight in shining armor no matter what I say."

"I don't really boss you around, do I?"

"What do you call what you did tonight? Oh, forget it. I don't want to talk about it anymore."

"Maybe we're through talking for tonight."

She smiled at the hopeful light in his eyes and lovingly touched his face. "Maybe we are."

Alfred was lost. He'd run for his car and headed for the motel, scared out of his wits at his narrow escape. But there'd been a police car at the Beauties and the Beat strip joint, right next door to the motel, and he'd driven on past the place, entering totally foreign territory. Until that moment there'd been no reason for him to drive north from Rumor, and in the dark, on a road without traffic, the dense forest all around him seemed ominous.

He was shaking, he realized, conjuring up visions of Montana prison cells, which he'd heard were underground, without recalling the source of that information. Was it true? he wondered. Did those big Montana cops throw convicts into tiny, windowless, underground cells?

Tears flooded his eyes, and he wiped his face with the sleeve of his shirt. Then, in the distance, he spotted headlights, and his pulse went wild. In almost the next breath he saw what appeared to be an old road, if two ruts in the dirt and trees could be called a road. He made a sharp right turn and was almost immediately canopied by heavy forest. The road continued a short distance, then forked; Alfred took the left fork because it looked less used than the right.

Sweating, breathing in gasps, he drove as fast as the terrible little rutted trail permitted. There were several more turns and he finally figured out that he was driving on old logging roads. Even to a city man's eyes it was pretty apparent that these old roads were no longer used—at least not on a regular basis. He felt safe from the deputies crawling all over Rumor, but he began to worry about being so far from civilization.

He pulled to a stop and shut off the engine. The headlights beamed through thick foliage and the silence was deafening. He reached out and locked all four of the car doors. He knew that he didn't dare leave the headlights on, but the thought of no light at all out there was terrifying. Finally he took a deep breath and turned off the headlights. The darkness was so complete he felt smothered by it, and he endured it for as long as he could and then switched the lights back on.

He let out a screech, for standing right in front of his car was a huge beast with large luminous eyes staring directly at him. He made a dive for the back seat and hunkered down on the floor, shaking like a leaf, weeping crocodile tears and mumbling every curse word he knew. At that moment he hated Paul Fioretti more than he hated Montana, more than he hated wild animals and snakes and falling out of trees. More than he hated running from the law and hiding out in a forest inhabited by enormous creatures with eyes of fire.

He finally forced himself back to the front seat and started his car.

An hour later, still driving, still watching for monsters, he began to face one more horror. Every road looked the same, every tree looked the same, every damn pothole he swerved to avoid looked the same.

He was lost.

Around midnight, lying drowsy and half-asleep in Tag's arms, Linda murmured, "I have a wonderful idea."

"Hmm," Tag said.

"Are you awake?"

"Hmm," Tag said.

"Well, maybe you're not completely awake, but will you remember my wonderful idea in the morning if I tell it to you tonight?"

"Hmm," Tag said.

"Okay, it's this. I'd like to pack a huge lunch, and you and I take Samantha and Tippy and go on a picnic. You must know some great spots for a picnic, but even if one doesn't immediately come to mind, we could drive around, see the sights and find a perfect place to stop, spread our blankets and gorge on good food. Samantha and Tippy would love it, and so would I. You probably would like it, too. What do you think?"

"Hmm," Tag said.

Linda turned over and leaned over Tag to peer at his face. "Are you sleeping?"

"I don't think so. Not now, anyhow."

"Did you hear my wonderful idea?"

"Yes, and I'm all for it. Only we'll have to do it on Sunday instead of tomorrow."

"How come?"

"I've got some work to do tomorrow. It can't wait."

"Oh." Linda lay down again and nestled her back and behind into the warm curve of his body. "I'll get all the food and picnic gear ready tomorrow then and plan for a Sunday outing, okay?"

"Hmm," Tag said.

Chapter Sixteen

Saturday morning Linda awoke at 8:00 a.m. Thinking about Tag's departure at five made her smile. He had kissed her and told her not to get up. Her reply had been a drowsy, "Don't worry, I won't." She had immediately gone back to sleep.

Now, lying there being lazy, which she couldn't do for long because Tippy was sitting on his haunches next to the bed staring at her, she thought of how silent the apartment was without Tag. His ready grin and warm personality enlivened everything around him, even a stale old apartment. Of course, the new coat of paint on every wall had brightened up the place, but even that couldn't compete with Tag's presence.

Ignoring Tippy's beseeching eyes a few minutes longer, Linda let her thoughts drift to tomorrow's picnic. It was going to be such fun, she thought. She would pack a great lunch, and Sammy and Tippy would play and they all would eat and enjoy the day together. She could hardly wait.

That final thought got her moving. "Okay, okay, I'm up," she said to Tippy, who eagerly pranced around. Linda went downstairs, filled Tippy's food and water bowls, then made coffee, which would brew while she showered. On her way back to the stairs the sight of her books all over the living-room floor brought her up short. She picked up an armload and carried them to one of the bookcases. That bastard had tossed her things around. Touched them. She wiped her hands on her robe, as though that would make the problem go away, and at the same time she experienced a chilling, eerie sensation.

Was someone watching her? No one was in the apartment with her, but she couldn't shake the discomfiting feeling. He'd been in this room last night. He'd been in her bedroom last night and had gone into her dresser drawers. He'd touched her clothing in his search for…for what? What could she possibly have that someone else would want so badly? She knew that she had nothing of Paul's, for she had painstakingly made certain that every tiny thing of his had been neatly packed in cartons and shipped to his restaurant. While packing her own things, she had done a lot of weeding out so that she wouldn't be moving items she no longer used or wanted.

Her troubled gaze fell on the bookcases again. Mr. No-Name was intrigued with her books. She couldn't imagine why anyone would be, but both times that he'd picked her locks and entered her home he had gone for her books. He must have one particular book in mind, she decided uneasily, but which one? She had some aged books that she had purchased at little hole-in-the-wall secondhand stores through the years, but surely they weren't worth any more than the price she'd paid for them.

She knew what he was after, what he'd *been* after since the first time he'd shown up at her door in one of his inept disguises. He wanted a book, but he hadn't found it because it was still in a box in her storage shed. Obviously, he didn't know about the tenants' storage sheds or he would not have broken into the apartment twice; his second attempt would have been her shed.

"Maybe it was!" Jumping to her feet, Linda went to the one window in the apartment that offered a view of the carport.

Her SUV was clearly in sight, but its bulk prevented her from seeing the door to the storage shed.

She ran upstairs, yanked on jeans and a shirt and stuck her feet into some shoes without socks. Grabbing her key ring from the top of the dresser, she skipped back down the stairs. Tippy was through eating and eager to go outside.

"All right," she said with a sigh and got his leash. Outside she walked him directly to the carport and was actually surprised to see that the lock on the shed door had not been disturbed. To make absolutely certain, she used her key and unlocked it. Nothing had been moved around, none of her cartons had been opened. Exactly as she had suspected, Mr. No-Name didn't know about these little sheds, one for each apartment.

Locking it up again, Linda took Tippy for his walk. But she still felt unseen eyes on her and didn't go far. This whole thing was finally getting to her, she thought with another shiver. Maybe Tag was right. Mr. No-Name hadn't been a danger… yet.

But he could be getting frustrated and desperate, and desperate people did desperate things.

The minute Linda got back to her apartment she dialed Tag's number. She got his answering machine and hung up. Either he was working with power tools and hadn't heard the phone or he wasn't home. She would try again later.

Three hours later Linda was ready to go to MonMart to shop for tomorrow's picnic fare. She tried Tag's number again, got the machine again and this time left a message. "I have something important to tell you about that No-Name guy. I think I've figured out what he's looking for, though for the life of me I can't imagine his reason for taking such ridiculous chances. Anyhow, I'll be at MonMart for an hour or so, but then I'll be home. Please call when you can."

Linda hung up and looked around her shiny, clean kitchen with a sense of satisfaction. The whole apartment gleamed and smelled good. She had gotten a burst of energy while putting clean sheets on her bed and started a binge of cleaning that hadn't wound down until every room had been vacuumed, dusted, scrubbed and polished. Not only that, she had eyed Tippy's dirty white coat and decided that he, too, needed cleaning. She'd phoned Dr. Valerie Fairchild at the animal hospital and asked her if she had time to groom Tippy today. "He got into some mud last night and he's a mess. Plus, he really needs a haircut."

Valerie had told her to bring him over, so when Linda left the apartment she took Tippy with her. After walking away from her door, she glanced back at it and thought, *If that jerk breaks in and messes up my clean apartment I swear I'll find him myself and brain him.*

It was pure bravado, she knew, for the guy scared her now. He never had before, but then, he hadn't violated her home before, either. Now he had done it twice, and why wouldn't he take a notion to do it a third time?

After dropping off Tippy at the animal hospital, Linda drove to MonMart. Inside the huge department store, while pushing a cart through the grocery aisles, she heard a woman say, "Well, hello, Linda."

Linda turned her head and saw Wanda Cantrell. "Wanda! Hello, how are you?"

"If I said fine, I'd be lying. I loathe grocery shopping."

"I rather enjoy it. Is Guy here with you?"

Wanda scoffed. "Surely you jest. I couldn't get Guy out of his lab with a tow truck. Him and Michael. They're exactly alike, and Max isn't at all thrilled that his son would rather be with his uncle than with him."

Linda didn't want to hear this. She liked Guy and she liked Michael. She had met Max Cantrell but couldn't say she really knew him. But the Cantrell family's problems should not be announced in the aisles of MonMart, and Linda resented Wanda's assumption that she would be interested.

"Well, I have to move along. I've got a lot of shopping to do," she said a bit coolly and pushed her cart away from the woman. In a few minutes she forgot about Wanda Cantrell and enjoyed filling her grocery list. Tomorrow's picnic was going to be sumptuous, with lots of finger foods and things that would please Samantha. Tag, too, of course. Linda smiled at the picture in her mind of the three of them and Tippy sitting on blankets and eating and laughing together.

Her cart was getting full and her shopping nearly finished when she headed for the housewares department looking for some brightly colored tablecloths and napkins. When she spotted some in a red-and-white-checkered pattern, she happily added them to her cart. "That about does it," she said to herself and started down an aisle that would eventually lead her to the checkout. But then some dishes in vivid colors caught her eye, and she stopped to look them over.

Concentrating on colors and prices, she paid little attention to the two women in the next aisle who were talking a mile a minute, and not in undertones, either. But then she heard Tag's name. Her head snapped up and she returned the plate to the shelf.

"Well, of course she likes Tag. Everyone likes Tag, but not everyone should sleep with him just because he's a Kingsley," one female voice said.

Linda froze and listened to the next barrage with bated breath. "He is twenty-six years old, the same age as my Donald. I should know, they went to school together. And she's way past thirty, maybe pushing forty. If you were looking for a man, would you rob the cradle? I sure wouldn't. She should be ashamed of herself, being a teacher and all."

Oh, my God, they're talking about me! Queasiness hit Linda's stomach. *Tag is twenty-six?*

The women were still talking, and Linda heard, "Well, I don't think their affair is at all beneficial to Samantha. It's always the kids who get hurt, isn't it? I really thought Tag had better sense."

Linda pushed her cart down the aisle. She didn't want to hear another word, or see who the gossiping biddies were. Nor did she want them to see her. Trembling and fighting tears, she hurried to one of the checkout stands and waited in line. If the checker had accidentally charged her double price, she would have handed over the money without question.

Once her purchases were in the back of the SUV, she climbed into the driver's seat and put her head on the steering wheel. Tag was only twenty-six, six years younger than she was. Did six years really matter that much?

"It matters," she said in a tortured whisper. But what mattered more was that he hadn't been truthful about his age. No one could possibly hate deception worse than she did, and she had been so impressed with Tag's basic decency, his honesty. What a sap she was. Okay, maybe it hadn't been a bald-faced lie, as it had always been with Paul, but Tag obviously didn't hesitate to stretch the truth when it helped get him what he wanted. He'd wanted her…and he'd gotten her.

"You fool," she mumbled as she forced her head up and started the engine. "You stupid, damn fool." The glowing image of tomorrow's picnic that she'd been carrying around in her mind crumbled and fell apart. The sacks of groceries in the back of the SUV seemed like proof of her stupidity. Her chest hurt, her eyes burned and she couldn't stop thinking of herself as dense beyond belief. Tag had gotten what he wanted just as Paul had. Their tactics weren't identical, but neither were the two men. Paul hadn't worried about her safety for one single second, for instance, and Tag went too far in the opposite direction.

But she really wasn't comparing them, man to man. It was the dishonesty for personal gain that gave them something in common; she hadn't been equipped to abide Paul's behavior and she wasn't even going to try to abide Tag's.

Instead of stopping at the animal hospital for Tippy and then going home, she drove straight to Tag's house. His truck was in the driveway and she parked her SUV right next to it. Climbing out, she heard sounds coming from the shop. She had found him.

Feeding her cold rage with a replay of what she'd overheard at MonMart, she headed for the shop.

"Linda! Linda!" a small voice called.

Linda's breath nearly stopped. She should have realized that Samantha would be here if Tag was. She stopped her intent-to-kill march and bent over to give the little girl the hug she always seemed to want from her.

"Hi, sweetie," Linda said weakly. Her anger could not be discharged in front of this precious and trusting child, even though she felt ready to burst from the force of her explosive fury.

"Wanna play house with me?" Samantha took Linda's hand and urged her to a patch of grass that was littered with toy furniture and a beautiful dollhouse that Tag had probably built for his daughter.

They were a family; *she* was merely a convenient lay.

"I can't today, sweetie," she said with a soft smile for Sammy.

"Daddy said we're going on a picnic someday."

"He said *someday?* He used that word?" Samantha nodded happily, and Linda's spirits fell another notch. She'd been sure he had heard her last night, and she had bought all those groceries. Today had been so good, so fulfilling, until a short time ago. Happiness could fall apart in the blink of an eye, and hers had. Through sheer willpower she maintained an air of normalcy, only because of Samantha, of course. "Sweetie, I need to talk to your daddy about something. Can you be a big girl and stay out here and play with your things while I go to the shop and speak to him?"

Samantha looked a bit reluctant at first, but then she nodded and said, "Okay."

"Thank you, sweetie." Drawing a big breath, Linda made a beeline for the shop. She turned and looked back to make sure Samantha hadn't followed and was relieved to see the little girl on her knees by the dollhouse, intent on placing her miniature furniture and talking to imaginary playmates.

Tag was wearing goggles and using a sander when she stepped inside. He didn't see her and she stood there and watched him working while her heart shattered into a million pieces. He *looked* twenty-six, she thought bitterly, possibly younger. And when she turned forty he would be thirty-four. No, she couldn't pretend the difference in their ages didn't matter, because it did.

What mattered more, though, was his lie. Any lie would have affected her the same way. He acted as if he knew her and he didn't. On top of that he made damn sure that everything went his way. Last night's surprise should have been proof enough of that major flaw in his character, but she had liked his family so much that she had let it slip by without serious repercussions.

This, however, could *not* be ignored. "Tag," she said loudly.

He glanced up, saw her and grinned. Turning off the sander and pushing up the goggles to his forehead, he said, "Hey, nice surprise. What's happening?"

"There's not going to be any picnic *someday,* as you told Samantha, not with me there's not, and I do not ever want to see you again under any circumstances. Did you get all that or should I repeat it?"

Tag's grin vanished. "What brought that on? What the hell are you talking about?"

"Does the word *lie* ring any bells?"

It did, and Tag's face got red. "I never lied. I just let it slide when you talked about age. It doesn't mean anything. Don't ruin what we have because I'm younger than you by a few years."

"Oh, stop! A few years? Six is not a few. And besides, you're not younger, I'm older! My God, I feel like your grandmother!"

"Now, that's ridiculous." Tag pulled off his goggles and laid them on the workbench. "Let's go in the house and talk this out, all right?"

"No, it's not all right. You can't weasel out of a lie, Tag. Once said, it's out there forever."

Tag was getting ticked. She was insisting he'd lied, and he hadn't. This was such garbage, and she was letting it come between them. His lip curled. "Out there? Is it floating in space, or does it hang around town for a while?"

Linda gasped. "You're not a bit funny. Think of that lie as a huge neon sign attached to your forehead, and you'll have some idea of what I see when I look at you now!" Whirling, she strode from the shop and out to her vehicle.

"Bye, Linda," Samantha called.

"Goodbye, sweetie," Linda called back. Her voice wasn't steady and neither was her body. She jerked open the driver's door and stumbled into the seat. While she started the engine, she saw Tag come to the doorway of his shop. He stood there and watched her, and he looked more like a lost boy than a full-grown, self-sufficient adult.

Yeah, right, an adult that lies about his age and God only knows what else!

Giving her head an angry toss, she backed out of the driveway and drove home with tears blurring her vision and making driving hazardous.

But *hazardous* seemed to be a way of life for her these days.

It wasn't fair.

* * *

Linda forgot to pick up Tippy. She remembered him when she started hauling in groceries. It seemed like an awful crime to forget her best buddy, and once all the food had been transported from the SUV to her kitchen, she fell onto the sofa and cried for an hour. Everything had fallen apart so fast, including herself. She knew she had to pull herself together and go pick up Tippy, but she hated facing Rumor and Dr. Fairchild with red, puffy eyes.

She dragged herself to the kitchen to unload all those sacks. It took a while, but finally the freezer compartment of her refrigerator had been crammed full and everything else put away. She stuck dark sunglasses on her face because her eyes were still red, took her purse and keys and headed out.

Her hand was on the knob when the doorbell pealed, and she jumped back in such stupefied surprise that she came close to losing her balance. Regaining her equilibrium, she gingerly approached the peephole in the door, thinking that if that moronic burglar had the bloody gall to ring her bell again he was going to come face-to-face with a hellcat.

But it wasn't Mr. No-Name out there on her stoop, it was Tag! Something joyous zinged through her system. Was he here to talk her into forgiving him?

But how could she forgive a lie?

You're still in love with him. How can you not *forgive him? At least listen to what he has to say.*

Inhaling deeply, she unlocked and opened the door. He wasn't smiling. His face, in fact, had a stony quality that she'd never seen before. Her heart thumped.

"I have the rest of your bookcases on my truck," Tag said flatly. "I also listened to your message on my answering machine. We're on the same track about what that guy's after, and we need to talk about it. I have a plan. Can I come inside?"

Linda bit her lower lip. He wasn't there to beg her

forgiveness, he was there to talk about Mr. No-Name. She might as well face facts; she was going to have to learn to live with a broken heart.

"Sure," she said listlessly. "Come on in." Standing back, she held the door open for him. When he stepped past her she breathed in his unique scent, a combination of wood, the outdoors and some wonderfully masculine aftershave. He was still in his work clothes, and there were remnants of fine sawdust on his collar and caught in the roll of his shirtsleeves that encircled his forearms just below his elbows.

She got weak. Just from looking at him, from smelling him, from remembering the many erotic moments in his arms, the strength in her legs came close to completely deserting her.

Tag waited for her lead.

"Do you want something to drink?" she asked. "I've got… almost everything." It was true. Her refrigerator contained fruit juices, soft drinks and several kinds of flavored water, along with regular bottled water. For tomorrow's picnic that wasn't going to be, of course. She really was a sap. A fool blinded by love, she thought.

"Nothing, thanks."

"Then let's sit in the living room." She went first and took a chair. Tag sank onto the sofa.

He got right to the point. "You've got a book this guy wants. I don't know what kind of book it is or his reason for wanting it, but he's going to keep coming back until he finds it. But it's not in the apartment. It's out there in your storage shed, in one of those cartons."

"I have a lot of books, but I've never collected rare or first editions. I can't begin to guess which book he's after, and believe me, I've given it plenty of thought." Her gaze locked with Tag's then, and all thoughts of books fled her mind. She loved him and always would, regardless of his age, regardless of anything.

She heaved a painful sigh and broke eye contact.

Tag cleared his throat. "Here's my plan. Cliff and Tommy, the deputies that were here last night, will be here again in about—" he checked his watch "—ten minutes. We're going to catch that jerk."

Linda stared. "Tonight? How do you know he'll come back tonight?"

"Because we think he's watching this building…your apartment…very closely, and we're going to put on a little show for him."

"Tag, I was gone for almost two hours. If he was out there watching with such dedication, he would have come in again while I was away."

"You'd think, wouldn't you? Obviously, he's not around *all* the time, which pretty much rules out one possibility I discussed with Tommy and Cliff, that he's living in one of the other apartment buildings on this street. But he *is* watching you, Linda, or maybe I should say, this apartment, and I'm sure he knows your timetable as well as his own by now. He's made friends with Tippy, and so far he's avoided breaking in when you're home. But you have to know that could change at any time. He knows that the law is on to him, as well as the people who live here. The deputies and I are banking on his making another attempt tonight. Don't worry, you will never be put in danger."

Linda frowned. "I can't figure out how you're going to lure him in. What, exactly, is your plan?"

Tag explained it in great detail. When he was finished he asked, "Does it meet with your approval?"

There was only one part that unnerved her: she would be spending the night at Tag's house. He might be there, he might not, but Samantha would be at her aunt Maura's.

"Uh, yes, sure, it…it's a good plan," Linda stammered, and then had to suck in a huge breath because she was suddenly without oxygen. "I…approve," she whispered, wishing with all her might that she really did. Catching Mr. No-Name was crucial to her safety—she finally believed heart and soul that the man was dangerous—but staying at Tag's house could be almost as perilous for her.

Didn't Tag understand that?

Or had he already forgotten how angry she'd been with him today in his shop? After all, she had told him she never wanted to see him again and here he was, seated on her sofa and explaining how he was going to keep her safe.

No, he was nothing at all like Paul, who had never once worried about her being alone so much of the time, spending night after night by herself. She never should have compared the two men, not even in small ways. In truth, Tag was like no one else she'd ever known. If only he'd been truthful about his age. Tears burned the backs of her eyes.

Chapter Seventeen

Tag left and returned thirty minutes later with two men—Deputies Cliff Halpin and Tommy Royce, dressed almost exactly as Tag was, in jeans, boots, T-shirt and an unbuttoned shirt over that with the sleeves rolled up. In fact, the similarities between the trio amazed Linda. They were all young, tall, well-built, dark-haired and clean-shaven. From a distance they looked like family, especially when they put on their dark sunglasses.

"You know what to do," Tag said to her.

"Yes." She knew what he'd asked her to do, and yes, she would give it her best. But her faith in his plan wasn't exactly set in concrete, and she wondered about Cliff's and Tommy's participation. What made any of them think they could draw Mr. No-Name to the scene and even cause him to repeat his crime so they could arrest him?

"Okay," Tag said. "You two all set?" he said to the deputies. They told him they were.

Linda was positive she saw excitement in the three men's body language. Why, they were enjoying this, she thought, and the operation hadn't yet gotten started. They would be flying high if their antics actually worked and they caught Mr. No-Name.

The macho Montanans, as Linda had begun thinking of them, left the apartment and Linda went to the one window with a view of the carport and watched through a tiny slit in the blinds, which were closed, as were the blinds on every window in the place. Per Tag's instructions, of course.

Tag had parked his truck almost dead center of the paved area between the building and the carport. In the bed of the truck were three tall bookcases, protected with strategically placed furniture pads and secured by ropes. While Linda watched, the three men walked around the bed of the truck almost lazily, looking at the tie-downs, ostensibly discussing the bookcases, laughing and gesturing. It was all a big act designed to draw attention to themselves and what they were doing in the parking lot. One of the residents of the building came into Linda's line of vision. He seemed to be headed to his vehicle in the carport, but he obviously was in no hurry because he stopped to talk.

She couldn't hear what was being said, but there seemed to be a lot of kidding around going on out there. A glance at her watch told her it was time for her to make her appearance— also per Tag's instructions. She left the window, picked up her ring of keys and went outside. The fourth guy had gone on to his vehicle and it was just Tag and the deputies by his truck when she reached it.

As instructed, she held up the key ring, jangled the keys and said loudly and distinctly, "I'm going to get started on my books in the storage shed. What's the holdup on getting these bookcases unloaded?" She had earlier moved her SUV; it was now parked in a visitor space, leaving her carport space vacant and with a clear view of the storage shed.

"We're working on it," Tag said, and the deputies killed themselves laughing.

Muttering under her breath—they were really bad

actors—Linda proceeded to the storage shed and unlocked it. Grabbing several books from one of the cartons, she walked back to the truck and waved them around.

"Hey, you guys," she said. "You should really read these. They're great."

Cliff was lounging against the truck with a big grin on his face. "Chick books, no doubt." After a second he added in a falsetto voice, "Oh, you big, tough man. You're so cute and I just love your bow tie."

Tag and Tommy broke up. Linda rolled her eyes and was about to defend her taste in fiction when Tag's laughter died and he said, "A white car just rolled into sight. It's moving slow and the driver is looking this way." From behind their dark glasses they had watched every car going past, and so far none had driven by that at least one of the three men hadn't recognized as belonging to someone in Rumor. This one was different.

No one changed positions. No one turned to look at the street. Linda realized then that while the trio had been walking around the truck and playacting, they had been watching the street and every possible avenue of access to the apartment complex. Maybe their acting wasn't bad at all, she thought with a suddenly quickened heartbeat.

"Can you make out its plate?" Cliff asked.

"Now I can," Tag replied. "It's a California plate."

"It could be him."

"It *could* be a tourist headed for Lake Monet," Linda drawled, still unconvinced about the success of this charade.

"California tourists don't usually arrive in beat-up cars," Tag said. "That one's really been through the mill." In a second he announced, "It's gone, out of sight."

"How long did you say this guy's been bugging you?" Tommy asked Linda.

"Five to six weeks," she said. "Maybe longer. It began

shortly after I moved here. But while I saw him quite a few times, I never saw his car."

"Hey, it's back. Obviously he turned around down the road."

The men gestured and laughed and Linda waved her books and thought to herself that they must look like a pack of idiots. But in spite of her deeply rooted misgivings, she was beginning to think this plan just might work. Putting it mildly, Mr. No-Name was no rocket scientist. Even before today she'd been thinking of him as a pretty dim bulb. If he was going to drive back and forth in front of her apartment house to get a clear idea of what was going on in the parking lot, he had to be even dimmer than she'd previously thought.

"Go inside now," Tag said to her. "Don't lock the shed."

"I should stay out here. I'm the only one who knows what he looks like."

"Linda, I've seen him, too, the day he walked into your apartment. You must remember my first day at your place, painting the kitchen." Tag said.

"Oh. Yes, of course," she murmured as a horde of memories of the two of them bombarded her.

Tag knew he'd struck home with his reminder, he could see it on her face. But he wouldn't press the point in front of Tommy and Cliff, although it had been a terrific opening for some straight talk. She needed to listen to his side of this thing. So he'd stretched the truth, but only once and over something that shouldn't be considered a hanging offense.

He spoke gruffly, keeping his personal emotions strictly in check. "We're all going to stick with the plan."

"He's going to ditch his car somewhere and come back on foot," Cliff said.

Linda swung her gaze from Tag to him. "How do you know that?"

"I don't *know* anything. But we have a good plan and it just might be working."

"It's working only if that car belongs to Mr. No-Name," Linda said, drawing a deep breath. Tag had unnerved her, and she had to stop thinking about him and his bedroom innuendos. Looking at Cliff helped alleviate her discomfort, and she asked him a question that had started to gnaw at her. "Why do you suppose no one in the town's law enforcement ever noticed a car with a California plate before this? If it's his, then it's been around Rumor for well over a month."

"You got a point, Linda, but how about you raising hell over that some other time and stick with our plan for today?" Tag said.

She jerked her head around and looked directly into his eyes. Or tried to. His dark glasses were far too effective for anyone to probe his expression, but even so, for a few seconds she got the strangest sensation of the two of them being all alone in the world. Tommy disappeared, Cliff disappeared, the apartment building and parking lot disappeared; it was just her and Tag in some far off place, loving each other, being honest with each other.

It hadn't happened, it wasn't *going* to happen. She was dreaming again and she had to get over such adolescent non-sense. Sighing, she turned and walked away. She heard Tag say, "She'll be all right."

She also heard Cliff ask, "Is she your girl, Tag?"

Linda hurried into the apartment so she wouldn't hear Tag's answer. She didn't like them talking about her in such a personal way, but considering the fact that everyone in Rumor seemed to discuss everyone else's business whenever they felt like it, she supposed Cliff's curiosity was inevitable. Besides, he must have heard gossip similar to what she'd heard with her own ears in MonMart.

Tears flooded her eyes. Every single time she released the tight grip she'd been holding on her emotions and let that awful incident replay in her mind, she absolutely could not suppress the tears. The worst part of it all, she had come to realize, was what she'd done after leaving MonMart. Yes, she'd had every right to let Tag know how much she despised a lie, and yes, she hated being six years older than him, but she'd said some really nasty things in his shop, and why hadn't she come home first, cooled off and then gone to Tag's?

Linda walked the floor and wished Tippy were there with her. But Tag had said that as long as Tippy was already at Dr. Fairchild's, he would prefer that she leave him there until this was over. "He's friendly with that guy now, Linda, and if he got in the way he could get hurt. He's better off out of this."

She couldn't disagree.

But she still wished he were with her now.

Ten minutes later all three men came in. They stayed inside exactly two minutes and then Tag and Tommy went out again. Two minutes after that Tommy returned to the apartment, stayed for two minutes and left. Cliff and Tommy came in and went out, Tag came in and went out. They came and went so many times Linda lost count. But the final scene of that confusing little charade had Tommy in the apartment and Tag and Cliff out by the truck.

Linda offered the deputy coffee. "Thanks, but not now." He was at the window, peering through the little slit in the blinds. "Did you happen to see the boys on the bikes?" he asked with his back to her.

"No."

"Well, they raced past us like bats out of hell, heading to that open field between this address and Kingsley Avenue, the one with all the jumps that a bunch of kids and their dads built out there. Anyhow, they went through those thick bushes at the back of the lot. We didn't know there was a trail out there, and we think it's been used by our man to get to this property without being seen."

"At first he didn't seem to worry about being seen," Linda said.

"Yes, but that was when he thought it was going to be a

fast job. In and out of town in a day is how Cliff and I see it. Obviously, he was way off base in his calculations, but that book he's after has to be important enough for him to try and try again."

"I wish I could figure out which one he's after. I'd dig it out of those boxes and give it to him."

"I don't think it's that simple. It couldn't possibly be an ordinary book, Linda. Wait, Tag and Cliff are untying some of the ropes. They must have spotted the guy."

Linda's pulse took a suddenly nervous leap. "Really? Oh my God, is this really going to do it? I didn't think it would work."

"I'm going out now so Tag can come in."

Linda didn't have to ask why. Tag had laid out the entire plan for her, from beginning to end, hopefully to a success-ful end. Cliff and Tommy were armed—their weapons were in the small of their backs, concealed by the big shirts worn over their T-shirts—and Tag wasn't. The deputies knew how to deal with criminals, Tag didn't, and they didn't want him injured or worse while they did their job.

Tommy left and Linda waited, with her heart in her throat, for Tag to come in. The final phase of the plan was now in progress, and Linda knew she would be greatly relieved if everything went well and that weird little man was finally in police custody, whatever his story.

But she and Tag were going to be alone in her apartment for only God knew how long.

It made Linda excruciatingly apprehensive, for what in heaven's name would they talk about?

Deep into the line of dense bushes along the far backside of the property, Alfred nervously watched for snakes while keeping an eye on the men and the truck with the bookcases in its bed. Even afraid and anxious, though, he was excited enough to fly. He'd figured it out, the whole damn thing. Paul wasn't nearly as smart as he thought he was. He'd told Alfred that it would be an easy job to find the journal among Linda's books, and Alfred had nearly suffered a nervous breakdown over *not* finding it in that woman's apartment. But how could he have succeeded when the journal had never been in the apartment and instead had always been in that little shed?

When he'd seen Linda carrying books from the shed to the truck it had all come together for him. He'd nearly swooned from the excitement of such brilliant deduction. James Bond could not have done a better job, and Alfred could hardly wait to tell Paul all about it. Maybe he'd boast about his deductive powers and gloat a little. Paul was a jerk. He'd been mean and nasty on the phone, and even if Paul gave him a huge bonus when he delivered the journal, Alfred wasn't sure he could forgive some of the things Paul had said to him.

Every cell in Alfred's scrawny little body suddenly came to full alert. The two men had started unloading one of the bookcases. Alfred's eyes shifted from them to the shed at the back of Linda's parking space in the carport. He'd seen now that each space under the roof of the long carport contained a small shed, obviously for additional storage. The sheds must come with the apartments, and from the new bookcases being delivered to Paul's ex, she must not have had enough shelf space to unpack all her books. It was all so simple. Thank goodness he'd taken a notion to drive past the apartment complex today. It must have been intuition, Alfred thought happily.

Carrying the bookcase, the two men were out of sight in seconds. Alfred's pulse went wild. How long would they be inside? He eyed the shed and the distance between the bushes and the carport. If he ran, would he have enough time to grab the journal and get back to the bushes before those guys came outside again?

The door of the shed was open, he could see that. Maybe it had always been open, or at least not locked. But Alfred didn't like thinking that he could have been back in Los Angeles weeks ago if he'd figured it out before today, so he concentrated on his final task before finally leaving this horrible place. Make a run for that shed, grab the journal and run back. What would it take, two minutes, five?

But what if those guys came back for another bookcase right away? Sweating by then, Alfred wiped his face on his shirtsleeve and decided he'd better stay put for a while longer.

He was glad he had, because in hardly no time at all the two men walked out laughing and talking and began unloading the second bookcase.

Alfred settled back. Obviously they were going to unload all three pieces. That was fine. They'd leave once their job was done and then he could do his thing.

The bookcase had been brought up the stairs and placed in Linda's bedroom. Tommy and Cliff had gone out again.

"Is it where you want it?" Tag asked.

"Yes." She'd been trying not to look at Tag too closely. His dark glasses no longer covered his eyes, and she was afraid of what she might see in them. Surely he was furious with her for lambasting him so cruelly, and what if he said awful things to her, as she'd done to him?

She wasn't comfortable being in her bedroom with Tag. Too much had happened between them in that room, in that bed, in fact. Just thinking of making love with him gave her a horrendous hot flash, and she went to the sliding glass door for some fresh air.

Her hand was on the handle, all set to pull it back, when Tag pulled *her* back. "What are you doing?" she asked nervously.

"You can't open it." His hands were still on her and he would have liked to keep them on her for the rest of his life. "You can't even disturb the drapes. I want that jerk's full concentration on what's going on outside, not on what might be happening in this apartment."

"Nothing's happening," she whispered.

"Like hell it's not," he growled. "Every time I'm near you something's happening, and you know what it is, too."

"Sex," she said after clearing her throat and finding her voice. "That's all you ever think about."

He grinned. "Mighty fine subject to take up a man's time, don't you think?"

"How about thinking about lies once in a while?"

Tag's eyes darkened. "You're not being fair, Linda. You'd think I was a habitual liar from the way you're reacting."

"One lie is as bad as a thousand."

"It is not, and if you let one stupid mistake break us up you're not the woman I thought you were. And I can't let myself think that way. I'm nuts about you."

She bit down on her bottom lip. Tears stung her eyes. "Don't…say things like that."

"I'm not giving up on us, if that's what you see in that imaginative brain of yours. So you might as well get over it right now, and forgive and forget. Why drag it out and make us both miserable when we're going to end up together no matter how many times you screech at me."

Her eyes widened. "I did *not* screech!"

They both heard Tommy and Cliff bringing in another bookcase. Tag quickly planted a kiss on the tip of her nose and said, "Tell me I'm forgiven."

She said nothing. Instead, she wiped her eyes, slipped from his grasp and went to the top of the stairs. "That one comes up here, too, guys," she called down.

After placing the third bookcase, Linda led them all downstairs and offered cold drinks or coffee. They took sodas and stood around the kitchen drinking them, taking their time and giving Mr. No-Name time to figure out his next move.

"Did you actually see him in the bushes?" Linda asked.

"Just a glimpse, but he's there, don't doubt it," Cliff said.

"I can just imagine what Mrs. Raymond is making of this charade," she said. "Three men coming and going, in and out of my apartment for several hours? Oh, yes, I'm sure she's devised quite a story to explain why it took so long to unload three bookcases."

Tag grinned and shrugged. "If it makes her happy, I say more power to her. When we're her age, we might find ourselves doing the same as she does."

"Never," Linda said with a deliberately visible shudder. "I hate gossip almost as much as I hate lies."

Tag's grin faded, and he turned to Cliff. "Do you think we should leave now?"

"I'm not sure you should leave at all, Tag. Here's the deal. When Tommy and I drive away in your truck, we're going to go around the block to Kingsley Avenue, park in the courthouse lot and then hotfoot it back here. We're going to sneak up on Mr. No-Name from behind and, hopefully, arrest him without a big hullabaloo. Tommy and I were talking, and we think it would be best if you were in here keeping an eye on the guy's moves. Not that we want you getting physically involved. I mean, if you see him doing something he shouldn't before we get to him, we don't want you rushing outside and taking any chances. But if he should happen to wander off before we get to him, you'd know in which direction we should start looking. Do you follow me?"

"Sure do, and it's fine with me. But maybe Linda should drive off alone. I could give her the key to my place and she could—"

Linda jumped in. "Just hold on a minute! I'm not going to your place or any other. I've decided that I want to be in on the grand finale. I helped out today and I'd like to be in on the finish."

Cliff frowned and rubbed the back of his neck. "Well, I'd sure hate to put you in any danger, Linda."

"This guy is going to cave when he first sets eyes on you and Tommy and realizes who you are. No one's going to be in any danger, least of all me."

"I don't like saying this to a lady's face, Linda, but you don't know what the hell you're talking about," Cliff said. "The most meek and timid criminals can turn into killers when they realize they're about to be arrested."

Linda's face reddened. "Well, I'm sure you know what you're doing. But I'm still not going to Tag's house." She hadn't liked that part of the plan from the get-go and this was her chance to get out of it. Of course, Tag wouldn't be with her at his place now and, in fact, they would both be here at *her* place. But she just couldn't see herself walking his gorgeous hardwood floors and worrying about what was going on over here. No, she definitely was not going anywhere.

"She's stubborn," Tag said matter-of-factly to Cliff, as though she wasn't standing there listening to his every word. "Don't waste your time trying to change her mind."

She glared at Tag. "Speak for yourself, you…you mule!"

Cliff chuckled and Tommy laughed out loud. "Looks like love to me," Tommy quipped.

Tag grinned. "It does, doesn't it?"

Cheeks burning, Linda spun on her heel and marched from the kitchen. She took up residence on the sofa in the living room, loathing all men and their twisted senses of humor and superior attitudes. She was still steaming when the trio came from the kitchen. Tommy called, "See ya, Linda," Cliff said, "Keep your fingers crossed, Linda," and out the door they went.

Tag stepped into the room, crossed to a chair and sat down. "Are you okay? We were only kidding around, you know."

"Do boys ever really grow up?" she asked dryly.

"Probably not. Some girls, on the other hand, seem to get too serious too young. Sometimes I wonder if they aren't trying to rush old age, maybe so they can gossip with Mrs. Raymond."

"You think you're so funny, and you're not."

"How come you laugh then?"

"Am I laughing?" she demanded, sticking out her chin belligerently.

"Are you gearing up for another fight? I'm not sure we have time for a really good fight, but maybe we could get in a few nasty digs before I have to start watching the bushes."

"Oh, go soak your head. You drive me crazy sometimes."

"You drive me crazy *all* the time. Wanna know why?"

"No, I do not."

"Yes, you do. You drive me crazy because I can't look at you without wanting you naked and hot and whimpering in my arms."

She swallowed hard. "Are you intending to talk like that all night?"

"Hey, babe, if I'm here all night, I intend to do more than talk."

She got to her feet. "In that case, I believe I will go to your house. Give me your key."

"Nope. You missed your chance for a clean getaway, sweetheart." He flashed his astounding grin and waggled his eyebrows. "You're in my clutches for the night, or however long it takes our fearless lawmen to capture the villainous Mr. No-Name."

Linda walked out, saying as she left, "That pitiful little specimen is not nearly as villainous as you are, Taggart Kingsley." Then she stopped to add, "I'm going to make some dinner. Since I practically bought out MonMart's grocery department because of the big picnic we were supposed to go on tomorrow, I think I have enough food on hand to put a respectable meal together. Will Your Highness be eating?"

Tag jumped up. "Damn, Linda, I didn't realize you went

to that much trouble. Honey, you'll have your picnic tomorrow, I swear it. This little caper will be wrapped up tonight, and—"

"Listen, sport, you told Samantha we were going on a picnic *someday.* Don't deny it."

"Linda, I didn't know you meant tomorrow when you mentioned a picnic last night."

"If you heard the word *picnic,* then you heard the rest of what I said." She strode away and disappeared into the kitchen.

"But…I didn't," he said with a frown between his eyes. She hadn't heard his denial, he knew, but would it have mattered if she had? Her mind was made up. He'd committed one more unpardonable sin, apparently.

The path of true love didn't always run smoothly, he'd always heard, but did it have to be quite this bumpy?

Chapter Eighteen

Tag took up his post at the window with a view of the parking lot and carport, and Linda tried hard to ignore his lean, sexy body—which in her tiny kitchen was much too close for her personal comfort, and concentrate on putting together a meal. She was bending over, peering into her loaded refrigerator when Tag suddenly exclaimed, "My God, there he is!"

"What?" Linda gave the refrigerator door a push to close it and ran after Tag, who was already only two steps away from the front door. "What did you say?" she asked with her heart pounding like a wild thing.

"I said that he's out there. We all thought he'd hang in the bushes at least until the sun went down, but he's out there right now! I've got to stop him from finding that book and getting away."

"But Tommy and Cliff are supposed to stop him! Where are they?"

"I'm sure they're on their way." Tag opened the door and gave her a stern look. "You stay inside, Linda. You've been in a lot more danger than you realized, almost from the day you moved to Rumor, and I don't want you getting hurt now when it's almost over." He went through the door and pulled it shut behind him.

Linda felt almost glued to the spot. She stared at the door and felt fear building within her. But it wasn't fear for her own safety, it was for Tag's!

She ran back to the kitchen and the little window. Before she saw Tag, she spotted Mr. No-Name digging through her boxes of books like a madman. Her precious books were flying everywhere, falling on asphalt with pages flipping open and no doubt torn.

"You moronic cretin," she shouted, even though she knew he couldn't hear her. Then Tag came into view. He had circled a bit so he would come up on the jerk from behind. What if Cliff was right and even the most timid of men became snarling animals when threatened?

As the scene unfolded, Linda watched with her heart in her throat. Tag got closer to her space in the carport, looking as though he was trying to approach without noise. But the guy must have had really good hearing because he turned suddenly and spotted Tag sneaking up on him. Linda recognized panic when she saw it, and Mr. No-Name was suddenly crazed from it.

"Tag! Tag! He could be carrying a gun!" she shouted.

He wasn't, but he grabbed the only weapon on hand, a book, and he threw it at Tag with all his might. It was a lucky shot, for a corner of the book struck Tag on the temple and he went down like a sack of potatoes.

Linda screamed, left the window, quickly scanned the kitchen for a weapon of her own and settled for the broom. Running full tilt, she left the apartment and raced to Tag's rescue with broom in hand.

Alfred was back to tossing books this way and that, frantically searching for the journal. He heard something, but he was breathing so hard and working so furiously in an effort to get hold of the journal and get the hell away from that insane place that he ignored the sounds behind him.

He looked up just as the broom came down and whacked him on the head. "Ouch!" he cried and dropped a book to rub his head, but a second whack struck him and then a third, and when he saw that the broom-wielder was a woman, Paul's ex, to be exact, he tried to get to his feet and run.

But the whole world suddenly seemed to close in on him. From the bushes ran two big guys with drawn guns, and from the apartment building came the old lady who looked like his grandmother. She was brandishing a gun, as well.

Alfred dissolved into a limp bundle of sorry humanity. Cliff snapped the cuffs on him and Tommy bent over Tag and asked, "Hey, buddy, how many fingers am I holding up?"

"Four."

"Nope, two. You're seeing double."

"I am not. I just said that to get you going. Move out of the way and let me up."

Linda went over to him and sank to the asphalt next to him. There were tears in her eyes. "He hurt you," she whispered.

"Knocked me plumb off my feet," Tag agreed. "The question is, who knocked *him* off of his feet?"

"Linda did it with her broom," Cliff said, and turned to Mrs. Raymond. "I'll take that weapon, ma'am," he said.

She handed it over. "Oh, pshaw, it isn't loaded. I just thought the sight of it might put the fear of God into him."

Linda looked over to the elderly woman. "You came outside to help Tag. Thank you."

Mrs. Raymond cocked her eyebrow. "There are simpler ways to get rid of a beau than beating him with a broom, young woman."

"He's not my beau. He never was."

"Oh, who cares? If I were your age again I'd have a dozen beaus. Deputy, I'm going inside. There are some phone calls that should be made right away."

Cliff grinned. "Yes, ma'am."

Tag was staring at Linda with an amazed expression. "You beat him with a broom?"

"It was the only thing I had in the kitchen that might work as a weapon."

"You rushed to my rescue." She nodded. "You shouldn't have done that, babe," he said softly. "You could have been hurt, and I would've been to blame."

"I think I have a better understanding now of what it feels like to be driven to protect someone you love," she whispered.

"Maybe we both understand things a little better, huh?" She nodded again. "Here, give me a hand up, sweetheart."

She got to her feet and helped him to his.

Cliff was looking through his prisoner's wallet. "Alfred Wallinski, from Los Angeles, California. Long way from home, aren't you, bud?"

Tears were streaming down Alfred's cheeks. "I hate this place," he mumbled thickly.

"Well, this place isn't overly fond of you, either. Did you find what you were looking for?" Cliff asked.

"No."

"Mind telling us what it is, exactly?"

"It's a book, a journal. It belongs to her husband." Alfred jerked his head toward Linda.

She gasped. "All this time you've been after a journal that belongs to Paul, who incidentally is my *ex*-husband?" She wanted to make her marital status very clear to everyone present, but especially to Tag. "Cliff, may I go through my cartons? If that journal is in one of them, I could find it faster than anyone else could."

"Have at it," Cliff said.

Linda found it in the third carton she looked through. She held it up and said to Alfred, "You simpleton, if you would have asked me for this the first time you came to my door, I probably would have given it to you. Would have saved you a whole lot of trouble, wouldn't it have? God, some people are such idiots." She gave the journal to Cliff, who thumbed through it for a few moments.

"It's some kind of financial record," he said. "Oh, well, someone smarter than me will know what it's all about. Come on, Alfred. Time to haul your sorry butt to jail." He shook Linda's hand. "Thanks for all your help. I would never have recommended you do what you did out here, but you're obviously a dangerous woman when there's a broom within reach. Tag, you'd probably be smart to keep that in mind."

Chuckling, he and Tommy escorted Alfred toward the bushes and to the place where they had parked Tag's truck.

Tag and Linda picked up the strewn books and returned them to the cartons. "You have a bruise from that flying book," Linda said. "I think we should put some ice on it."

"Okay, maybe, but I think we should go in, climb the stairs to your bedroom and make love till the cows come home."

She took his hand and looked into his eyes. "Ice first, love-making second," she said. "And wait a sec while I get my broom."

"Are you planning to use it on me?"

"Of course not, silly."

"Then, fine. Let's take the broom, go inside and call it a day, love of my life."

"You called me that once before," she said with a loving, soft light in her eyes.

"Yeah, but this time I mean it." He saw her startled look and quickly added, "I'm kidding, sweetheart. You've been the love of my life from the day we met." He took her hand. "Come on. There's a face in nearly every window of the building. I think the show is over, don't you?"

Linda looked at the building and saw that he was right. She started laughing and couldn't seem to stop. In fact, she bubbled over with laughter all the way to the door of her apartment, with Tag carrying her broom and leading her by the hand.

When they shut the door behind them, she stopped laughing, as the look on Tag's face wasn't comedic or even lighthearted now. He was seriously in love with her and she with him, and they were both thinking the same thing: To hell with the ice.

Linda couldn't stay asleep. Just before midnight she cautiously slipped out of bed, leaving Tag sound asleep, found her shawl in the dark and, taking pains to move silently, stepped out to her minuscule balcony and settled into a chair.

It was an unusually warm night, she realized, and the sky was crystal clear. The moon was brighter than she'd ever seen it, a glorious sight. She thought of waking Tag so they could share a special moment in the moonlight, but he'd been in a deep sleep and it somehow didn't seem right to interrupt his slumber.

She sighed contentedly. So much had happened in a very short amount of time. Her life had changed dramatically, mostly because of Tag, and she understood things about her past now that had always been murky at best.

One thing she had done this evening that felt so right was to make a phone call to her parents. Their response had truly taken her by surprise. They had sounded thrilled and happy to hear from her, and then they'd bombarded her with questions about her job, the town and the state of Montana. She had, of course, invited them to come and see everything for themselves and they had actually said they would.

So everything was wonderful, she thought dreamily while looking up at that astounding moon. Was it even possible for anyone to be happier than she was?

Tag loaded the huge picnic lunch into the back of his SUV, buckled in Samantha, laughed as Tippy hopped in with hardly a hint that he was invited to join them and gave Linda a quick kiss as he climbed in himself. Finally they were off.

"So where are you taking us this fine Sunday morning?" Linda asked.

"It's a surprise," Tag said with a devilish grin.

Linda groaned in a melodramatic fashion. "I'm not sure you should use that word so carelessly," she said pertly.

"You like some of my surprises," he retorted.

She looked at him, then checked the backseat to make sure Samantha wasn't listening—the little girl was completely engrossed in playing with Tippy—then whispered, "I *love* some of your surprises, and we both know which ones I'm talking about."

"The ones between the sheets?"

She slapped him on the arm. "You're bad, really bad."

"And you love it when I'm bad."

She laughed and turned her head to watch the countryside. "We're climbing, aren't we?" she asked after a few moments. "We're going to picnic in the mountains."

"You'll see," Tag said.

"Fine, keep our destination to yourself. I've figured it out anyhow, so there's no surprise in my future, big boy."

They laughed together then, and since the console between the seats prevented close bodily contact, Linda settled for laying her hand on his thigh.

"I just needed to touch you," she said softly.

Tag sent her a beautiful smile.

They rode for nearly two hours. The scenery had become more astounding by the mile, and when Tag finally parked and turned off the engine they were high in the mountains and very close to a pretty little lake.

Everyone scrambled out. Tag led the group to the water's edge. "I own this lake, Linda," he said quietly.

She jerked her head around to look at him. "You *own* it?"

"It's no big deal. Actually, I own three hundred acres of this mountain and this twenty-acre lake just happens to be in the middle of my land. Other folks from town own property up here. Dr. Fairchild, I know, bought about sixty acres with a small cabin on it a mile or so from my property line on the other side of the lake."

He named a few other individuals who had invested in pieces of that beautiful mountain, then said, "There's trout in the lake. People come here to fish."

"And you let them come?"

"Oh, sure. As long as no one abuses the place, why would I put up No Trespassing signs?"

"You're one heck of a guy," she said and nestled her hand in his.

They spread blankets in a grassy, shaded spot and ate. Samantha and Tippy were still full of life and they chased each other, with Tippy barking and Sammy giggling.

Linda stretched out and put her head on Tag's lap. Smiling, she watched child and dog playing for a long while. Then she glanced up at Tag's face and said, "I love her, you know."

"And she loves you, Linda." Tag didn't often speak in such a serious vein, but to him there was nothing remotely amusing about this topic. "She fell very hard for you right away. Just as fast as I did, in fact. And I worried that you and I might not work out for some reason and then she would be hurt. I don't want her hurt ever again."

"She wishes she had a mother," Linda said quietly.

"All the time." He caressed Linda's cheek and looked into her eyes. "Maybe she has one now."

"I would be so honored," Linda said huskily.

"I want us to be together every day and every night, but we can't live together without marriage, Linda. I can't do that to Samantha. She deserves better from me."

"I understand. Oh, darling, I understand." She saw tears

in Tag's eyes. "I love you so much," she whispered. "And I'll marry you whenever you say."

"I say soon."

"Yes, soon."

"Big wedding or small?"

"Small. Similar to Russell and Susannah's."

"Perfect," he said. "Mom will want some sort of reception afterward."

"Anything is fine with me. I rather enjoyed the butler's service at your parents' table."

"Oh, he's gone. When I was picking up Sammy at Maura's this morning she told me that Harrison and Mabel decided Montana wasn't wild enough for them. Apparently they were expecting the Old West, as depicted in movies and TV shows. Anyhow, they went off to Alaska."

"Well, for heaven's sake," Linda exclaimed.

They fell silent for several minutes, then Tag asked, "Sweetheart, why were you reluctant to meet my family?"

Linda had known he would ask that question sometime. She strove for a honest answer. "It was silly and I'm not sure I can even explain it. But it was their wealth and my parents' wealth and worrying that you might decide to give up carpentry and turn into someone else, someone with too much money, and the art world and how I grew up and—" She stopped for a breath.

"You don't feel that way now, do you? Linda, I love carpentry and I will never become a playboy."

"Now you're teasing me."

"I can't be deathly serious about something that's never going to happen, darlin'. I'll always be a carpenter."

Linda glanced at the lake. "And you bought a lake with your earnings, right?"

"I bought this land with a down payment and monthly installments."

"Oh."

"I don't take money from my folks, Linda. I could, they've offered it plenty of times, and I suppose I would in an emergency. But I like my independence, babe, even more than I like yours."

"I am sort of independent, aren't I?" she said thoughtfully. "I think I always was without really realizing it. Maybe if I had reached out to others just a little, people would have reciprocated and I wouldn't have felt so alone all my life." She paused, then added, "I was happy, though, once I moved to Rumor. I think it was because I had finally taken hold of my life."

Again they fell silent, and again Tag spoke first. "Didn't you bring the Sunday paper along?"

Linda sat up. "Yes. I didn't have time to read it this morning. I've been neglecting the paper for days and days, so I tucked it into the pocket on the passenger door. I'll get it."

"Stay put. You worked hard on that terrific lunch and you deserve to be waited on. I'll get it."

Tag rose and went to his SUV. Linda drank in the sight of Samantha sitting on the ground a short distance away and holding Tippy like a baby. The little girl absolutely adored Tippy, and he apparently had gotten over his fear of small people, for he let Samantha do anything to him that took her fancy. The whole scene said *family,* which was exactly how Linda felt about the joy in her soul. She was truly part of a family now.

Tag returned, chuckling. "What's so funny?" she said, looking up at him.

He dropped the newspaper in her lap. "You're front-page news, sweetheart."

"What?" Linda read the headline: Teacher Nabs Book Bandit with Broom. "Oh, no," she moaned. "How did they find out about this incident so fast? It only happened last night."

"Late afternoon, sweetheart, and do you really have to ask about the speed with which news travels in Rumor?"

"I'll be a laughingstock at school tomorrow."

"Hey, you're a hero. Nobody's going to laugh." But he couldn't keep a straight face when he said that, and he began laughing so hard that he collapsed on the blankets.

She refused to laugh with him, but she could only hold the urge in check for so long. In a few minutes they were both laughing and rolling around on the blankets. It went on until Samantha came over and asked, "Daddy, what's so funny?"

He wiped his eyes and sat up. "I'm laughing 'cause I'm happy, sweetheart. Com'ere and give me a hug."

Tippy decided to join in the fun, and they all laughed and rolled around on the blankets.

All in all it was a marvelous picnic.

Sheriff Holt Tanner called Linda on Sunday night. She was fresh from the shower and alone. Tag had brought her and Tippy home, unloaded the remnants of their picnic lunch and then taken Samantha to their home. He had kissed Linda and said, "Soon, my love, very soon," and she had smiled wistfully, hating to be separated from him even for a minute but knowing in her heart that they would be married soon and living together for the rest of their lives.

"Yes, this is Linda Fioretti," she said after the sheriff identified himself.

"I wanted to thank you personally for your cooperation with law enforcement, Linda. Also, I figured you had a right to know what the whole mess was all about."

"That's very thoughtful. Thank you."

"The journal is a record of underground, illegal gambling and bookmaking in southern California. It and Alfred Wallinski are already in Los Angeles, and it took an expert about ten minutes to figure out the meaning of the journal's entries. Paul Fioretti, who I understand is your ex-husband, has been arrested, as well as a dozen others. Apparently, the Los Angeles vice squad has been after that crowd for several years, and I find it amazing that their case was resolved right here in Rumor by a woman with a broom."

Linda laughed self-consciously. "I'll never live that down, will I?"

"Don't even try. You should be proud of yourself. We certainly are."

"Well, not everyone is as kind as you are, Sheriff. I still find it hard to believe that I packed that journal with my books and didn't spot it."

"Thank you again, Linda. Good night."

The last day of the school year finally arrived. The atmosphere at the high school wasn't the least bit scholastic, and there were no serious lessons in any of the classrooms. When the noon bell rang, the students scurried about, gathering belongings from lockers, shouting to friends, and one by one happily deserting the building for the summer.

As silence descended and even a quiet footfall echoed in the empty corridors, Linda went to the lunchroom for a little goodbye get-together with the teachers. At least that's what Shelby had told her it was about. When she walked in and saw the brand-new broom with a huge red bow on it, however, she knew she was in for some good-natured ribbing.

The teachers applauded her entrance, and she joined in the fun by bowing to the group. "Speech! Speech!" everyone called.

Linda went to the head of the room, accepted the beribboned broom from a grinning Shelby and said, "Thank you so much. Since I wore my old one out, I really needed this."

"We are all dying to hear your version of the incident," Shelby said, and prompted everyone in the room to clap and whistle.

Linda smiled. "But if you read the newspaper, you already know what happened."

"But not in your words," Shelby insisted.

"All right. I saw that awful little man throwing my books around in my carport parking space and I grabbed the broom, ran outside and knocked him senseless with it." She went on to explain the background details, omitting only one thing, that Alfred Wallinski had been sent to Montana by her ex-husband. That fact hadn't been in the *Rumor Mill,* and she saw no good reason to publicize it now.

After coffee and cake, the party broke up and everyone said goodbye to each other. Linda got into her SUV, wiped a sentimental tear from the corner of her eye and drove directly to Tag's house. Samantha was at Rugrats and he had asked her to come by when she left school.

He came out of the house the second she pulled into his driveway, and he gave her a big hug before they went inside. To her surprise he began walking her through his house and asking questions. "Do you like this room? Will you be happy living here? You can change anything you don't like about the place, you know. Or would you rather have a new house?"

"Tag, Tag." She stopped walking and cupped his face with her hands. "I love your house."

"But it's not very well decorated."

"I might want to make a few changes someday, but not now. I only want one thing now...no, make that two. I want to be your wife and Samantha's mother."

He embraced her almost fiercely, holding her close to his heart for a very long time. "It's what I want, too, my love, it's exactly what I want."

The science fair opened at 10:00 a.m. the following day. Linda was amazed at the number of people who came to see what the area's young people had devised or invented, all on their own, to enter in the fair.

Linda looked for Guy Cantrell in the crowd and couldn't find him. She walked over to Michael's display. He stood behind it with a grin a yard wide.

"Do you know where your uncle Guy is?" she asked while scanning his project.

"Haven't seen him," Michael said, watching Ms. Fioretti's face closely as she realized what she was looking at. "What d'ya think?" he asked. "Pretty cool, huh?"

"It's remarkable. Very unusual," Linda managed to squeak out. Michael had drawings, graphs, photographs and hardboards pinned with what looked like bits and pieces of earthworms. She cleared her throat. "Those tiny pieces are...?"

"Their organs, or what passes for organs. These terrestrial annelid worms live, eat, procreate—they're hermaphroditic, you know—and die in a short span of time, but they're almost solid protein and if ingested in a high enough quantity could keep a human alive for years. Got to have drinking water, too, of course."

"Are you actually eating a worm in that photo?" Linda felt her stomach turning over.

"Yeah, and it's grossed out about thirty kids already. I've been having a blast. Hey, the judges are coming back. I think they like my presentation."

Linda swallowed hard. "I can certainly see why. Talk to you later, Michael. I'm going to look for Guy."

She worked her way through the display tables and the milling crowd, hardly able to believe that Guy wasn't there. The fair was his idea, his pet project. Only something huge would prevent his being there.

Uneasy and instinctively worried, Linda went to the door and looked out at the parking lot. Guy's vehicle wasn't there. He was missing the fair!

She was just outside the door, standing on the sidewalk with her arms crossed over her chest and a concerned frown furrowing her forehead, when she heard a voice from inside. "After much deliberation, we have decided that this year's first prize for the most imaginative entry in the science fair belongs to Michael Cantrell. Michael, would you please come to the podium and accept your prize?"

In almost the next heartbeat she heard someone screaming in the parking lot. "Fire! Fire! There's a fire on Logan's Hill!"

Obviously, she wasn't the only person who had heard the alarm, for people began pouring from the gym, looking at the smoke with worried expressions then rushing to their vehicles. Linda recognized Reed Kingsley racing past her, and she watched as he climbed into the bed of someone's pickup and shouted, "This could be bad, folks. It's already got a good start and the forest is tinder-dry. I think we're going to need more than just the regular volunteers for this one. Everyone willing to fight that fire should go home for shovels, picks, axes, power saws and protective clothing. We'll meet up at the foot of the hill at the end of Lost Lane. Don't anyone take any chances and don't go off by yourself. Let's keep this organized." He jumped to the ground.

Cars and trucks began roaring away. Linda's hand was pressed to her chest over her own fluttering heartbeat. That smoke looked terribly ominous. The fire was moving fast. This was serious business, she realized, *very* serious indeed.

* * * * *

USA TODAY *bestselling author B.J. Daniels*
takes you on a trip to Whitehorse, Montana,
and the Chisholm Cattle Company.

RUSTLED

Available July 2011 from Harlequin Intrigue.

As the dust settled, Dawson got his first good look at the rustler. A pair of big Montana sky-blue eyes glared up at him from a face framed by blond curls.

A woman rustler?

"You have to let me go," she hollered as the roar of the stampeding cattle died off in the distance.

"So you can finish stealing my cattle? I don't think so." Dawson jerked the woman to her feet.

She reached for the gun strapped to her hip hidden under her long barn jacket.

He grabbed the weapon before she could, his eyes narrowing as he assessed her. "How many others are there?" he demanded, grabbing a fistful of her jacket. "I think you'd better start talking before I tear into you."

She tried to fight him off, but he was on to her tricks and pinned her to the ground. He was suddenly aware of the soft curves beneath the jean jacket she wore under her coat.

"You have to listen to me." She ground out the words from between her gritted teeth. "You have to let me go. If you don't they will come back for me and they will kill you. There are too many of them for you to fight off alone. You won't stand a chance and I don't want your blood on my hands."

"I'm touched by your concern for me. Especially after you just tried to pull a gun on me."

"I wasn't going to shoot you."

Dawson hauled her to her feet and walked her the rest of the way to his horse. Reaching into his saddlebag, he pulled out a length of rope.

"You can't tie me up."

He pulled her hands behind her back and began to tie her wrists together.

"If you let me go, I can keep them from coming back," she said. "You have my word." She let out an unladylike curse. "I'm just trying to save your sorry neck."

"And I'm just going after my cattle."

"Don't you mean your boss's cattle?"

"Those cattle are mine."

"*You're* a Chisholm?"

"Dawson Chisholm. And you are…?"

"Everyone calls me Jinx."

He chuckled. "I can see why."

Bronco busting, falling in love…it's all in a day's work.
Look for the rest of their story in

RUSTLED

Available July 2011 from Harlequin Intrigue
wherever books are sold.